T...   ...o...

Fiona Ga...   ...e state's
attorney's office, a tough, bare-knuckles
prosecutor who fought crime just as ferociously
as she battled her inner demons. In the past
six years she'd won every major case, including
a high-profile murder trial that had put her on the
radar of Chicago politics. She was *the* prosecutor
who wasn't afraid to take on anyone, including the
rich, powerful and politically connected, and she
had been dubbed the Iron Maiden by the local
press.

But not even a Gallagher would receive immunity
to go after an officer of the law. *No one* had that
kind of clout....

GALLAGHER JUSTICE

Amanda Stevens

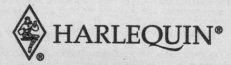

HARLEQUIN®

TORONTO • NEW YORK • LONDON
AMSTERDAM • PARIS • SYDNEY • HAMBURG
STOCKHOLM • ATHENS • TOKYO • MILAN • MADRID
PRAGUE • WARSAW • BUDAPEST • AUCKLAND

ISBN 0-373-83506-X

GALLAGHER JUSTICE

Copyright © 2003 by Marilyn Medlock Amann

This edition published by arrangement with Harlequin Books S.A.

® and TM are trademarks of the publisher. Trademarks indicated with ® are registered in the United States Patent and Trademark Office, the Canadian Trade Marks Office and in other countries.

Visit us at www.eHarlequin.com

Printed in U.S.A.

ABOUT THE AUTHOR

Born and raised in a small Southern town, Amanda Stevens frequently draws on memories of her birthplace to create atmospheric settings and casts of eccentric characters. She is the author of over twenty-five novels, the recipient of a Career Achievement award for Romantic/ Mystery, and a 1999 RITA® Award finalist in the Gothic/Romantic Suspense category. She now resides in Texas with her husband, teenage twins and her cat, Jesse, who also makes frequent appearances in her books.

Books by Amanda Stevens

Many thanks to my editor, Denise O'Sullivan,
whose patience and support
made this book possible.

CHAPTER ONE

IT WASN'T A NOISE THAT awakened Fiona Gallagher, but a scent. A sultry, provocative fragrance that carried a subtle note of sandalwood.

She tried to rouse herself to investigate, but the dream kept pulling her back under.

"You always smell so good."

He tangled his hands in her hair. "How good?"

She looked up with a smile and then showed him.

Heart pounding, Fiona bolted upright in bed, her frantic gaze searching the far recesses of the room. It was dark, but enough light filtered in from the street that she could make out all the corners, all the nooks and crannies.

Nothing stirred, not so much as a ghost. She was alone, safe and sound in her second-floor apartment protected from intruders by a series of locks and dead bolts her brother, Tony, had helped her install when she'd first moved in six years ago. No one could get in. She was fine.

Except…she wasn't fine. She'd been dreaming about David again, dreaming she was still in love with him. That only happened these days when she was under a lot of stress.

The DeMarco case had brought back the nightmares, she thought wearily. As a prosecutor for the Cook County State's Attorney's office, Fiona had come face-to-face with evil before, more times than she cared to remember.

But there was something about Vince DeMarco's eyes... the way he looked at her...that sly smile...

There was something about him that reminded her of David.

Falling back against the pillows, she wiped a hand across her brow. Seven years since that night and David Mackenzie still had a hold on her, one so powerful that sometimes, during moments of weakness, she imagined his scent in her apartment. Heard his voice over her telephone. Saw his smile on every defendant.

Even fully awake now, she could *still* smell his cologne, but she knew it wasn't real. It couldn't be real. She and her therapist had hashed out her hallucinations a long time ago. *"The scent is symbolic, Fiona. Not of David, but of your guilt."*

Her guilt smelled like sandalwood. Good to know.

Realizing she would never fall back asleep now, Fiona got up and went into the bathroom to splash cold water on her face. Pressing the towel against her skin, she studied her reflection in the mirror. Outwardly she looked the same as she always had, but deep inside, where all her dark secrets lay hidden, she'd undergone a drastic metamorphosis.

You can't go through what you did and expect to walk away unchanged, Dr. Westfield had warned her.

She couldn't expect to ever have a normal relationship again, either, but then, relationships were overrated in Fiona's opinion. She had her cat, she had her career, she had HBO. What more did a girl need really?

Flipping off the light, she returned to her bedroom long enough to pull on a robe over her pajamas, then she padded on bare feet down the hallway to the living room. Her apartment was small, cramped and drafty, with lots of creaking floorboards and noisy water pipes, but Fiona didn't mind. The quiet, once-elegant neighborhood on the Near North Side of Chicago with its well-kept lawns and shady streets more than made up for the inconveniences.

And it was a long way from Bridgeport, she reminded herself ruefully as she glanced out the window at the fog-shrouded street below her. Maybe not in miles, but in culture and attitude.

Her parents had grown up in the same blue-collar neighborhood on the South Side where they still lived in the same house they'd bought when they first married. They had the same neighbors, the same circle of acquaintances, the same values and expectations. They'd raised four kids in that neighborhood, and two of Fiona's brothers had moved only a few blocks away from the family home.

By contrast, the ambitious, thirtysomething professionals who flocked to the renovated brownstones in Fiona's neighborhood guarded their privacy like rabid rottweilers. She had a nodding acquaintance with only a handful, knew even fewer by name. Like her, most of them came home late—briefcase in one hand, cell phone clutched in the other—to close themselves off from the rest of the world until it was time again to rush off to work the next morning.

There were hardly any families in the neighborhood, no children playing on the stoops. The streets were sometimes almost unnaturally quiet, and if this deepened Fiona's sense of isolation and the occasional bout of loneliness, well, there was also no one there who knew about David. No one to look out their front window when she drove home each night to shake their heads and wonder how such a nice girl like Fiona Gallagher, someone with her brains and education, the daughter of a *cop,* no less, could have fallen in love with a killer.

In their own way, though, they were still proud of Fiona

in the old neighborhood. She was a rising star in the State's Attorney's office, a tough, bare-knuckles prosecutor who fought crime just as ferociously as she battled her inner demons. In the past six years, she'd won every major case, including a high-profile murder trial that had put her on the radar of Chicago politics.

Fiona had been so ruthless in her cross-examination of the defendant, a well-known businessman, that a reporter from one of the local papers had dubbed her the Iron Maiden, the prosecutor who wasn't afraid to take on anyone, including the rich, powerful and politically connected.

"No one is above the law," she'd been quoted in the papers, and if she and her brother, Tony, were the only ones who could fully appreciate the irony of her motto, that was just the way it had to be, Fiona had long ago decided.

Turning from the window, she walked over to the small dining table she used as a desk and surveyed the usual mess: an empty Diet Coke can, a greasy paper plate with a half-eaten slice of pizza, stacks of files, police reports and a yellow legal pad with a blank sheet of paper staring up at her.

She'd been working on the closing argument for the DeMarco case when she'd staggered off to bed just after midnight. Staring at the blank page now, Fiona frowned. She hadn't made much progress earlier, and she knew why. She was nervous about this case. Nervous in a way she hadn't been in years.

It was a rape case, for one thing, and, aside from the fact that she'd worked almost exclusively on homicides for the last four years, rape cases were notoriously unpredictable. In this instance, there wasn't even DNA evidence to corroborate the woman's testimony. Vincent DeMarco had used a condom. He was also a cop, a veteran detective who worked under Frank Quinlan's command.

Quinlan was one of those clout-heavy cops who was virtually untouchable. Fiona had found out just how well connected he was when she'd cooperated with an Internal Affairs investigation into Quinlan's interrogation methods.

A man she'd successfully prosecuted for murder, who was currently serving a life sentence at Stateville, had brought a lawsuit against the police department alleging that Quinlan and some of the detectives under his command, including DeMarco, had forced his confession by using physical and verbal intimidation, i.e. torture.

Fiona had been outraged. She always set out to win in the courtroom, but the last thing she wanted was to send an innocent man to prison or have a legitimate conviction overturned because of sloppy investigative work or police misconduct. It reflected badly on her and on the office of the state's attorney, and she took the allegations personally.

Eventually the lawsuit was dropped, and Quinlan was exonerated by a police review board. But to this day, he carried a fierce grudge against Fiona. He'd refused to cooperate with her in the DeMarco investigation, partly out of loyalty to one of his own cops, but mostly, Fiona suspected, because he wanted to see her fall flat on her face.

A possibility that seemed more likely with each passing day. The case wasn't going well and Fiona knew it.

She stared at the blank page for another moment, then jotted down the first statistic that came to her mind. *One out of every three women in this country will be sexually assaulted in her lifetime. One out of every three…*

When the phone rang, she continued to write as she automatically reached behind her for the cordless unit on the counter. Then her hand froze as she realized the time. It was after two o'clock in the morning. No good news came after two o'clock in the morning.

"Hello?"

"Fiona? It's Guy Hardison."

At the sound of her boss's voice, Fiona frowned. "Do you have any idea what time it is? What's going on?"

"I just heard from Clare Fox," he said referring to the police department's deputy chief of detectives for the North Side. "We've got a problem. Could be a big one." The smooth, polished timbre of his voice always took Fiona by surprise. Like her, he'd been raised in Bridgeport, but any trace of the stockyards had long since been stripped from his speech.

He was Fiona's immediate supervisor in the Homicide/ Sex Crimes Unit and over the years, the two of them had managed to hammer out a fairly congenial working relationship in spite of their sometimes huge philosophical differences. Guy was a shrewd, ambitious prosecutor who'd long ago mastered the art of political expediency and compromise. Fiona had not. Her passion for justice was only equaled by her temper and by her natural inclination to leap before she looked, a tendency that almost always landed her in hot water.

"A woman's body was found in an alley at the corner of Bleaker and Radney tonight," Guy continued. "Looks like a professional hit, and if it is, the press will have a field day. It's just the kind of thing some ambitious reporter would love to sink his teeth into, particularly considering the latest headlines."

He was alluding to a recent Justice Department report that showed Chicago moving ahead of New York in the number of murders per year. The crime statistics had made the front page of all the local papers, and the mayor, facing reelection in a few months, was livid.

"The police department is taking a lot of heat from both the mayor and the press." Guy's voice sounded tense, as if he might be catching some of the flak himself. "Clare wants to make sure this one is handled strictly by the book. No mistakes. No one walks on a technicality. She's asked for an ASA on the scene to advise."

He paused. "I'm assigning you as lead prosecutor, Fiona. You've got credibility with the press right now, and they like you. Plus, another capital murder conviction under your belt could make certain people sit up and take notice."

Fiona wondered if he was throwing her a bone after the DeMarco case debacle, or if he had an ulterior motive up his sleeve. "You said Radney and Bleaker, right? That's Area Three." Frank Quinlan's territory.

"You're not afraid of Frank Quinlan, are you, Fiona?" His voice held the merest hint of a challenge, one he knew she wouldn't be able to resist.

She scowled. "Hardly." She'd proved that, hadn't she?

"Then get over there and make sure his detectives don't screw up the investigation before they even make an arrest. Take Milo with you."

Milo Cherry was Fiona's second chair. He was a young, eager prosecutor with a quirky sense of humor and a nearly photographic memory.

After several tries, Fiona finally managed to reach him on his cell phone. She could hear music and laughter in the background, and assumed he was at a late-night party or nightclub, which surprised her, considering they were due in court at nine that morning. But as long as he did his job, came through in a crunch, his social life was none of Fiona's concern. And he certainly didn't seem to mind

being summoned at such an ungodly hour. He readily
agreed to pick her up in ten minutes.

Fiona hurried to get dressed, and in the flurry of activity, she completely forgot about the nightmare that had
awakened her earlier. But on her way out, the dream came
back to her suddenly and she paused at the door, the uneasy notion that David Mackenzie's ghost might be lurking on the other side niggling at her confidence.

For one brief moment, she couldn't bring herself to turn
the dead bolt, to step into the dimly lit hallway, to go
downstairs and wait for Milo by the front door. She
couldn't seem to move at all.

This was crazy, she told herself firmly. David Mackenzie was dead. It wasn't his cologne she smelled in her
apartment. He wasn't the killer who had dumped that poor
woman's body in an alley. David was dead and buried,
and he wasn't coming back.

But as Fiona mustered her resolve and stepped out into
the hallway, something made the hair on the back of her
neck stand on end.

For one split second, she could have sworn she felt an
invisible presence in that hallway. A ghost from her past
that had risen from the grave to demand justice.

CHAPTER TWO

THE MURDER OF RAY DOGGETT'S first wife had haunted him for twenty years, but it had been on his mind more than ever lately. *She'd* been on his mind. He didn't know why, but he'd been remembering little things about Ruby that he hadn't thought of in years. Things she'd said. The way she dressed. Her smile. He'd been dreaming about her, too, and obsessing about the murder.

That was why Frank Quinlan's call earlier had hit him so hard. *"...a body found in the north alley of Bleaker and Radney. Young, female Caucasian. Get your ass over there, Doggett. Sounds like a bad one."*

In all the years Doggett had been with the Chicago PD, he'd seen his share of homicides. He'd seen some he knew he would never forget. But it wasn't another young woman's death that was eating at him tonight so much as the fact that her body had been found in an alley. That brought back memories.

Ruby's body had been left in an alley, too. She'd been missing for three days when they found her.

The call had come in from dispatch just after midnight, Doggett remembered. He and his partner, Joe Murphy, had the third watch that night and they responded to the call immediately. But by the time they arrived, another squad car was already on the scene. Murphy got out and headed down the alley, but instead of following him, Doggett walked slowly toward the street. He'd spotted something beneath one of the streetlights.

He recognized the shoe at once. A red high heel trimmed with ruby rhinestones. The kind of shoe an unsophisticated farm girl from Indiana might think was glamorous.

"Look, Ray! Aren't they beautiful? Don't you just love them? They're my ruby slippers. Get it? Ruby's slippers…"

Doggett turned and started running toward the alley. Murphy met him halfway down, grabbed his arm, threw him up against the wall when Doggett fought him.

"Take it easy, kid."

"Let go of me, Murphy. Let go of me, damn you. It's Ruby."

"I know."

Doggett closed his eyes. He'd been praying he was wrong, but Murphy's words confirmed his darkest fear. "I have to see her. I have to see for myself—"

"No, you don't. You don't need to see her like that."

"Let go of me, damn it!"

When Doggett tried to fight his way free, Murphy strong-armed him again. "You can't go down there. You hear me? It's bad, kid. Blood all over the place. You don't want to look. That's not the way you want to remember her."

But that was exactly the way Doggett had remembered her for months after her death. He couldn't seem to remember her any other way. He hadn't viewed the body at the crime scene, or even later at the morgue, but he'd witnessed enough crime scenes to imagine the blood-splattered clothing, the vacant, staring eyes.

Twenty years later, that image was still with him, at every crime scene, in every investigation. The knowledge that her killer was out there, unpunished and unrepentant, still kept him awake at night.

Maybe he was getting old, Doggett reflected. Dwelling on the past because his life hadn't turned out the way he wanted. But to hell with it, because now he had another murder to worry about, another killer to find. That was one thing about being a cop. Always plenty of bad guys out there to occupy his mind.

He pulled to the curb and parked behind one of the squad cars. The dense fog softened the flashing lights, and at such an early hour, the scene was still relatively quiet. No spectators to be kept at bay. No news cameras, yet. It was an almost surreal calm, as if he were still caught in one of his dreams, Doggett thought. But when he got out of his car, the scratchy transmission of a squad unit radio grounded him firmly back in reality.

He followed voices down the alley, showing his identification to the young patrolman manning the perimeter. Then he stepped under the crime scene tape and glanced around.

The buildings that rose on either side of the alley were several stories high, stark and graffiti-tagged, with only a few windows that overlooked the alley. Several blocks over on Rush Street, bars and clubs would still be rocking with the young and the hip who were looking to have a good time or score a few drugs, but the immediate crime scene vicinity was a no-man's-land, an area trapped between the affluence and glamour of the Gold Coast and the misery and desperation of the projects.

Most of the buildings housed small offices and mom-and-pop businesses that had closed up shop hours ago. Even the cleaning crews had long since gone home. The potential for witnesses was pretty much nil. Doggett wondered if the killer was familiar enough with the area to have planned it that way, or if he'd just gotten lucky.

A few feet from where he stood, a crime scene tech photographed the body from several different angles while another narrated as he videotaped. Deeper inside the alley, flashlight beams bobbed up and down as officers searched the ground for evidence.

The victim laying in front of a trash bin, but in the semicircle of officers and detectives that had formed around the dead woman, Doggett could see nothing but a spill of blond hair. He felt his gut tighten as he mentally braced himself for what else he might see.

Meredith Sweeney, a petite, dark-haired assistant medical examiner, glanced up as he approached, and when she nodded, two detectives from Doggett's unit, Jay Krychek and Skip Vreeland, glanced over their shoulders. Krychek immediately turned back to the body, but Skip nodded and spoke. He was a tall, thin man with a grim expression and stooped, narrow shoulders that made his rumpled suit jackets constantly ride up in the back.

Krychek was partial to the gangster look—dark shirts, light ties, and in the daytime, he was never seen without his badass cop sunglasses.

"Yo, Doggett, how's it going?" Skip greeted him.

"Not too bad."

Krychek turned back around to Doggett. "Took your sweet time getting here."

Doggett shrugged. "Fog's a bitch out there."

"Tell me about it. Playing hell with Forensics. They won't be able to find shit out here." Krychek stepped back, making room for Doggett. "Take a look."

"It's bad, kid. Blood all over the place. You don't want to look."

The woman was lying on her back, eyes closed, her

expression almost peaceful. To Doggett's surprise, there really wasn't much blood. On first glance, she appeared to be sleeping, but someone who looked like her wouldn't be snoozing in an alley. She was beautiful, a real knock-out. Blond. Young. No more than twenty, if that.

Damn shame, Doggett thought.

There was a dark stain on the pavement beneath her head, and her hair was matted with dried blood. She wore a light dusting of makeup—eye shadow, mascara, pale pink lip gloss—that didn't detract from her natural beauty. The black dress she wore was short and slinky, her shoes spiked and sexy. Expensive and seductive clothing designed to attract the attention of the opposite sex.

By contrast her jewelry was simple and unpretentious—tiny diamond studs in her earlobes and a pearl ring on the third finger of her right hand. The presence of the jewelry seemed to rule out robbery as a motive.

"She was shot in the back of the head," Krychek told him.

"Do we know who she is?" Doggett asked.

Krychek shook his head. "Not yet. CSU found an evening bag in the Dumpster that we think belonged to her. The wallet was missing, but they found a phone number scribbled on a piece of paper inside a gold compact. We're checking the cross directory now to see if we can come up with a name."

Doggett's gaze was still on the body. "Who found her?"

"Wino by the name of Teddy Scranton. Says this alley is on his regular beat. He hangs around Restaurant Row until midnight or so, then heads over here where it's quieter. When he spotted her, he walked down to the corner store and had the night clerk call 911. We've got him in one of the squads right now, trying to sober him up with coffee and food, but I don't think he's going to be much help. Claims he didn't see anything.''

"Could he have been the one who stole her wallet?" Meredith asked. "Somebody turned her over. Maybe he was looking for her purse."

"Don't think so." Krychek ran his hand down his tie. "If he lifted the wallet, why hang around and call 911? He would have hightailed it out of here ASAP. He got what he wanted for his good deed—a free meal and a little attention."

A cynical observation, but Doggett figured Krychek was probably right on the money.

Doggett stood with his hands behind his back, a habit he'd picked up at the academy so as not to inadvertently contaminate the crime scene. When the tech gave him the go ahead, he donned surgical gloves and squatted beside the body, still careful not to touch anything as he examined the wound in her head.

"Looks like a .45," he murmured.

"She was kneeling when he plugged her," Meredith said.

"Any other injuries?"

"Ligature marks around her wrists. He had her tied up at some point."

"What about the exit wound?"

Meredith shook her head. "The bullet's still lodged somewhere in the body cavity. I'll find it when I open her up."

"Any idea about time of death?"

"Liver temp would be more accurate, but judging from the thermal scan, I'd say two hours, tops. But that's just an educated guess."

It always was. Even with modern forensics, the most reliable way of pinpointing time of death was still to find the last person who'd seen the victim alive, other than the killer, of course, but that wasn't always possible. Doggett glanced at his watch. If Meredith's guess was accurate, that would put time of death around midnight.

He bent over a tiny mark on the woman's left shoulder. "You see this?"

Meredith nodded. "Looks like one of those fake tattoos. I thought it was the real thing at first, but if you look closely you can see where the edges are blurred into the pores."

"You used to work in Gang Crimes, Doggett." Krychek's tone held an edge of resentment. "You recognize that symbol?"

"It's a trident," Doggett said. "The Gangster Disciples use it, but they mostly operate on the South Side. This is a long way from their home turf. Besides, I don't think this is a gang hit."

"I agree," Skip Vreeland put in. "Look at the hoochie-mama threads she's wearing. That girl was out for a good time."

"Hoochie-mama threads with a Michigan Avenue price tag," Krychek, the fashion expert, muttered.

"We need to get a picture over to Rush Street and start canvassing as many of the nightclubs as we can hit." Doggett stood and walked back over to the other two detectives. "If she was there tonight, someone's bound to remember a girl like that."

Krychek stuck his hands in his pockets, jingling his change. "So what's the deal here, Doggett?"

Doggett frowned. "What do you mean, what's the deal?"

Krychek shrugged. "Skip and I were the first detectives on the scene so that makes this our case."

"Quinlan called me at home and told me to get over

here ASAP," Doggett said. "It's my understanding this is *my* case."

Krychek gave a nervous laugh. "No way."

"Then looks like we've got a problem."

The two men eyed each other warily until Meredith muttered behind them, "Oh, great. A pissing contest between two cops. How unusual."

Skip said gruffly, "Hell with this shit. Let's just get on with what needs to be done and let the boss figure out whose case it is later. Right now, somebody needs to go check on that phone number." He started to walk away, then turned back to his partner. "You coming?"

Krychek held his ground for a moment longer, his gaze faintly menacing, before he stalked off behind Vreeland.

Doggett moved back to the body. He was glad they were gone. He needed a moment alone here, needed time to think. He frowned as he studied the dead woman. He was missing something.

Carefully he cataloged her features, trying to commit every detail of her person and the crime scene to memory. He'd go over it in his mind a dozen more times before this night was out.

He rubbed his chin. Something was bothering him about that mark on her left shoulder. Doggett had the niggling feeling that he'd seen that symbol before, that it should mean something to him, but he didn't know what.

He was troubled by her appearance, too. The dress and shoes screamed for attention, but everything else, her makeup and jewelry, were understated. His gaze rested on her fingernails. They were neatly trimmed and squared off, but unpolished, as if this were a detail she'd forgotten because she wasn't used to getting all dressed up. Or as if she'd been in a hurry to go out.

You know what I think? I think you were pretending to

be something you're not. You were trying to fool someone, weren't you? But who? And why?

And suddenly, in asking those questions, Doggett found what had been missing for him, the connection he needed with the victim.

I'm going to find out all about you, he silently told her. *And then I'm going to find out who did this to you. You have my word on that.*

CHAPTER THREE

"SO THIS IS WHERE YOU LIVE," Milo Cherry commented as Fiona climbed into his car, a vintage '69 Corvette Stingray beautifully restored. "Nice neighborhood."

"Thanks." She sank comfortably into the bucket seat and glanced around. "Is this new? I've never seen you drive it before."

"I've been working on it in my spare time for a couple of years now. Cars are kind of a hobby of mine."

She ran her hand over the leather. "I'm impressed, Milo. I had no idea you were so mechanically inclined."

He gave her an enigmatic smile. "There's a lot about me you don't know."

"It would seem so."

Fiona was certainly witnessing a whole new side of him tonight, and it wasn't just the car. She was used to seeing Milo in his conservative, slightly geeky, lawyer persona— dark suits, sedate ties, brown hair neatly combed. Tonight his hair was gelled and he wore slim black pants and a black shirt opened at the collar.

But the change went deeper than just the surface. Milo was usually one of the most laid-back people Fiona knew, but tonight he seemed restless, almost wired. His fingers tapped a nervous tattoo on the steering wheel as he waited for her to settle in.

"I don't mean to alarm you," she told him as he pulled

away from the curb. "But I think something may be burning in here."

"It's just incense. I put it out earlier, but the smell is still kind of strong. Sorry."

"No, it's okay. But would you mind if I rolled down the window a little?"

"You can't." He shrugged another apology. "The power windows don't work. Some kind of glitch with the wiring I haven't been able to figure out."

Fiona smothered a sneeze. "You've got the address of the crime scene, right?"

"You said the corner of Bleaker and Radney. That's a few blocks west of Rush Street. Speaking of which." His fingers continued to drum on the steering wheel as they headed down her street. "I had no idea you lived so close to the party zone. Do you go there much?"

"To Rush Street?" Fiona shook her head. "Rarely."

"There's a nightclub on Division Street called Blondie's. Have you ever heard of it?"

"No, but I don't get out much," she said dryly. "And besides, I'm not really the nightclub type."

He shot her a glance. "I think you might like this place."

"Is that where you were tonight when I called?" she asked curiously.

He studied the road. "What makes you think I wasn't home?"

"Oh, I don't know." She stared at his clothes. "Maybe because you don't look as if you just woke up."

"I never said I was asleep." An intriguing little smile played at the corners of his mouth, and it occurred to Fiona that he had the look of a man with a secret he was just dying to tell. She wondered if, like a lot of males she'd known, he was preening over a recent conquest and couldn't wait to brag about it in the locker room. He glanced at her again. "You want to go sometime?"

"Go where?" Her mind had drifted, and she'd forgotten what they were talking about.

"To Blondie's."

"Are you sure a redhead can get in?" she teased.

"As long as you're with me, you'll be okay." His tone was dead serious. "What do you say?"

Fiona hesitated. "You don't mean like a date or anything, do you?" She winced the moment she said it. *Gee, Fiona. Could you be any more insulting.*

His smile disappeared. "Not a *date* date. Of course not. I thought we could drop by after work and have a drink sometime. Listen to some music. Maybe even dance if the mood strikes us. You know, do that whole Ally McBeal thing."

Fiona feigned shock. "Don't tell me you actually watched that show?"

He gave her a warning look. "If you repeat that to anyone, I'll deny it. Plus, I may have to kill you."

"Not funny, considering where we're going," she grumbled.

"Sorry." He downshifted as he rounded another corner. "So is that a yes or a no to Blondie's?"

"It's a maybe. Let me think about it."

He slanted her a glance. "Just out of curiosity…if I *had* asked you for a date, what would your answer have been?"

"No. But it's nothing personal," she was quick to assure him. "I don't date people I work with."

"Does that include big shots like, say, Guy Hardison?"

Fiona turned in genuine shock. "What?"

"Nothing. Forget I said that."

"I don't want to forget it," she said sharply. "You've

implied something I don't think I much care for, and now you owe me an explanation.''

"Look, it's nothing." He lifted a hand off the steering wheel. "Just talk around the office, that's all.''

"What kind of talk?" Fiona folded her arms as she glared at him. She knew what he was getting at, but she wanted to hear him say it.

"Nothing really. Just some grumbling about all the hot cases you've been getting lately.''

"If by hot you mean high profile," she snapped, "Maybe it's because I win them." It annoyed Fiona that she felt she had to defend herself. She was a damn good prosecutor. No one had given her anything.

"Don't take it personally." Milo gave her a cool smile. "Like I said, it's just gossip.''

Fuming, Fiona turned to stare out the window. She hated gossip. It had taken her a long time to live down all the talk after the scandal with David broke. She didn't need people speculating about her love life now and re-membering what had happened to her in the past.

She certainly didn't need her own colleagues spreading rumors about her.

The silence grew so awkward that Fiona was relieved when they turned down Radney a few minutes later, and she saw the police cars and the crime scene unit pulled to the curb in front of the alley. Milo parked behind them, and Fiona started to get out, but the door wouldn't open. "Another glitch," he said.

"Good way to hold your dates captive," she muttered.

He turned back and stared at her. "What?"

She shrugged. "Nothing.''

She waited for him to come around and open the door, and then, still angry, she climbed out of the car and headed toward the alley without a word. Milo hurried after her and caught her arm. She spun, stared at his hand for a split second, then lifted her gaze to his.

He got the message loud and clear and removed his hand from her arm. "Sorry. And I'm sorry about earlier, too. I was out of line."

"Yes, you were." She held his gaze for a moment longer, then relented. "But let's just forget it. We've got work to do."

He shifted nervously from one foot to the other. "I'd like to forget it, but I can't. Look, Fiona, I've got to say this. There's a reason why people are talking."

"What reason?" she asked coldly.

"It's Hardison. The way he looks at you. He has a thing for you. It's obvious to everyone but you."

"That's ridiculous! He's a happily married man, for God's sake."

"Is he? How long has it been since you saw the two of them together?"

That gave Fiona a moment's pause. She'd always thought Guy and Sherry Hardison had the perfect marriage. They seemed so close. "Their marriage is none of my business. If they're having difficulties, it has nothing to do with me." She started to turn away, but Milo stopped her again.

"Just…be careful around Hardison, okay? There's a lot more to that guy than he lets on."

"Like what?"

"Take my word for it. Guy Hardison is not the picture of propriety he wants everyone to believe he is."

"You know what I think?" Fiona challenged him. "I think you've been listening to too much office gossip."

"And you know what I think? I think you have no idea the effect you have on men."

A shiver ran up Fiona's spine at the strange note in

Milo's voice. She could barely make out his features in the darkness, but she could feel his eyes on her. She could sense his intensity, and the chill inside her deepened. She was suddenly aware of how alone they were on the street. There were cops at the scene, but their voices sounded a long way off. She felt a prickle of alarm as he continued to stare down at her.

Then he laughed softly, and his mood seemed to change instantly, as if the whole thing had been a huge joke. He jammed his hands into his pockets, looking like the Milo she saw every day at work. "Lucky for me," he said with a disarming grin, "I'm immune to tall, gorgeous redheads. Blondes have always been my downfall."

THEY SHOWED THEIR credentials to the police officer guarding the perimeter, and then Milo went off to find the medical examiner.

"Who's in charge of the investigation?" Fiona asked the uniformed officer.

"Talk to Doggett." He nodded toward a man who stood a few feet away, busily scribbling something in his notebook.

"Thanks." Fiona knew most of the detectives who worked out of the Area Three Detective Division, but she didn't recognize this man. "Are you Detective Doggett?" she asked as she approached him.

He didn't look up. "Who wants to know?"

His voice caught Fiona off guard. It was deep and husky. Might even be considered sexy in certain situations.

But the man himself was nothing to write home about. He was around forty or so, with close-cropped brown hair, high, rugged cheekbones and lips that were well-shaped but humorless. Fiona had the immediate impression he wouldn't be an especially pleasant man to be around, but that could be said for about ninety percent of the cops she'd met in her lifetime. And she'd met plenty.

"I'm Fiona Gallagher. I'm with the state's attorney's office."

"Gallagher?" He finally looked up, and she was immediately struck by his eyes. They were a light, eerie blue. Piercing one might say.

And that stare. That stare could freeze meat, Fiona thought with a shiver.

"You related to Tony Gallagher?" he asked her.

"He's my brother. Do you know him?"

"Yeah, I know him."

And judging by his scowl, the experience hadn't been all that pleasant. Fiona wondered what the source of friction had been between Doggett and her brother. Tony could be a bit…unpredictable at times. She suspected the same was probably true of Doggett.

"Are you the lead detective on this case?" she asked briskly.

"Let's assume that I am."

She wasn't sure what he meant by that, but the last thing Fiona wanted was to become embroiled in a turf war between two homicide detectives. "What can you tell me about the investigation?"

He gave her a mild once-over, but that laser beam stare didn't tell her a damn thing about what he was thinking. "The victim was shot in the back of the head with what looks to be a .45 caliber slug."

"Have you identified her yet?"

"We're running her prints now."

"Any witnesses?"

"Not that we've found so far. The buildings in this area

are mostly office space, and everything's closed at this hour.''

"What about security cameras? Maybe something was caught on tape.''

Doggett nodded. "We're working on that.''

Someone called out his name, and he turned as another detective hurried toward him. When the man saw Fiona, he stopped abruptly.

"This is Fiona Gallagher. She's an ASA,'' Doggett said. "This is Detective Vreeland.''

Vreeland nodded. "We've met.'' His tone inferred it had been a pleasure he'd just as soon not repeat.

Vreeland and his partner, Jay Krychek, along with Vincent DeMarco, had been part of the Internal Affairs investigation into the allegations of misconduct by some of the detectives under Frank Quinlan's command. Unlike DeMarco and Krychek, Vreeland had struck Fiona as a by-the-book cop. A basically honorable man doing a sometimes impossible job. If anything unethical and illegal had gone on during Quinlan's watch, she doubted Vreeland had been a party to it. But, like any good cop, he wasn't about to testify against one of his own.

He turned back to Doggett. "We checked the cross directory. The number isn't in there, which means it's either unlisted or a cell phone.''

"You try calling it?'' Doggett asked.

Vreeland shook his head. "We didn't want to tip our hand unless we had to.''

"What phone number?'' Fiona asked.

"The crime scene techs found a purse in the Dumpster they think belonged to the victim. A phone number was stashed inside a compact, and we're trying to track down a name to go with it.'' Doggett took out his cell phone, and turned back to Vreeland. "Let's give it a shot. Maybe we'll get lucky and get a name off an answering machine.''

Doggett punched in the number, then lifted the unit to his ear and listened. A second later, the phone in Fiona's purse started to ring.

CHAPTER FOUR

"THAT HAS TO BE A coincidence," Fiona said as she fished in her purse for her cell phone. "The timing's too perfect to be anything else."

"One way to find out," Doggett said.

She pressed the talk button and lifted the phone to her ear. "Hello?"

"Coincidence, huh?"

Fiona was looking at Doggett, saw his lips move, but it took her brain a split second to register his voice in her ear. Then her gaze met his, and simultaneously they hung up their phones.

"I guess you'd better have a look at the body," he said grimly.

She would have anyway, but now Fiona's stomach churned in apprehension. If her phone number had been in the victim's possession, then she was undoubtedly someone Fiona knew. Maybe a client, maybe just an acquaintance, but someone who had crossed her path. Fiona prayed it was nothing more personal than that.

The body was already being prepped for transport to the morgue, but Doggett waved the attendants aside. As they stepped back, one of them momentarily blocked the light so that Fiona could barely make out the victim's features. She didn't recognize her at first, but then the man moved away, and the light hit the dead woman's face full on.

Fiona gasped. She took an involuntary step back, straight into Doggett. Rather than moving away to give her some room, he put his hands on her arms to steady her. "Easy."

He was strong in spite of his lean physique. Beneath the dark suit he wore, his body was hard and muscular. More than capable of holding Fiona up if she needed him to.

But she didn't need him to. Or want him to. She was still in shock, but she could stand on her own two feet just fine. She'd seen corpses before, only usually, thank God, they weren't someone she knew.

She stared down at the victim's beautiful face. That beautiful, pale, lifeless face, and Fiona's legs began to tremble in spite of her resolve.

Doggett's hands tightened on her arms. "You're not going to faint or anything, are you?"

"No, I'm okay," she insisted.

"Do you know her?" His deep voice rumbled in her ear and Fiona shivered.

"Her name is Alicia Mercer. Her mother is a friend of mine."

"Then I assume you know how we can get in touch with her next of kin?"

Fiona nodded. Doggett's hands were still on her arms, but for some reason, she didn't seem to mind. She hardly even noticed until he took them away. "Her parents—her mother and stepfather—live in Houston. Lori and Paul Guest. They're both attorneys. I have their phone number and address at home. Alicia and her twin sister, Lexi, are students at Hillsboro University. They share an apartment off campus. Or at least…they did."

Doggett jotted down the information in his notebook,

then glanced up. "You say the victim is a twin? You're positive about her identity?"

"Yes, I'm positive. It's Alicia. She and Lexi look a great deal alike, but they're not identical. You can check her fingerprints, but I know it's her..." Fiona trailed off as she gazed down at the body. "She does look different, though."

"Different how?" Doggett said sharply.

"I never saw her dressed this way. And she's changed her hair. I didn't know the girls all that well, but I had the impression Alicia was the conservative one."

"What about the mark on her shoulder?" Doggett asked. "You ever see it before, on either sister?"

Fiona shook her head. "No. Alicia certainly didn't seem the type who would go in for tattoos. She was so levelheaded—" She stopped abruptly as something occurred to her. She turned, putting an unconscious hand on Doggett's sleeve. "Oh, my God."

"What?" Something flickered in his eyes, a curious little flame that made Fiona suddenly aware of how close they were standing.

Most of the time she tried very hard to keep herself aloof—from situations and from the people around her. Body contact, even a touch as slight as her hand on a man's arm, was never something she instigated. Ever. It didn't bode well, she decided, that she'd done so now quite automatically. She dropped her hand. "Alicia called me last week. She left a message on my voice mail. I'd forgotten about it until now."

If he noticed her reaction, he didn't let on. "Did she say what she wanted?"

"No."

"Did you call her back?"

Fiona swallowed. "No."

One brow lifted slightly. "So how well *did* you know her?"

"As I said, I didn't know either of the girls very well. Their mother moved to Houston several years ago after she remarried. Alicia and Lexi were maybe fourteen at the time. I didn't see them again until last year when the girls started the fall semester at Hillsboro. Lori called and asked if she could give them my phone number."

"Why?"

"She said she'd feel a lot better if they had someone nearby they could call if they...got into trouble." The irony was devastating. Fiona had to work to keep a tremor from her voice. The guilt, for a moment, was almost overwhelming.

"When was the last time you saw Alicia?" Doggett asked.

"Last winter. She, Lexi, and I had dinner just before they left to go home for the holidays."

"Did she mention any problems she might have been having? Trouble with a boyfriend? A professor? Anything like that?"

Fiona shook her head. "We didn't talk about anything personal. I don't think either of them would have felt comfortable confiding in me about their private lives. I'm sure the only reason they agreed to see me at all was to appease their mother."

"Did you have dinner with them often?"

"Only a couple of times."

"Did you have the impression that Alicia got along with her parents?"

Fiona glanced at him in surprise. "As far as I know. I never saw her with her stepfather, but Lori and Alicia were very close."

"What about the sisters?"

"They were inseparable."

"But you did say that you didn't know the girls all that well, right? And you hadn't seen much of the mother in recent years?"

Fiona hesitated. "It was my impression they were all very devoted."

"Still," he said, "Families have problems. It would be pretty unusual if they didn't tick each other off at least once in awhile."

"All I can tell you is that I never saw it," Fiona said a trifle impatiently.

He didn't press the point further. "So you haven't seen or talked to Alicia since before Christmas."

"No."

"Tell me about the message you got from her last week."

Fiona closed her eyes briefly. "I was in court when she called, and by the time I got her message, I was swamped with meetings and interviews. I completely forgot about it."

"She called on your cell phone?"

Fiona nodded. "I gave them my cell phone number because I'm hardly ever at home."

"What was the message?"

Fiona frowned, trying to recall Alicia's exact words. "She identified herself and then she asked me to call her back. She said she needed to talk to me."

"Did she sound frightened? Anxious?"

"I don't remember noticing anything out of the ordinary about her tone or the message. I assumed she wanted to set up another dinner before she and Lexi went home for the summer break. I intended to call her back in a day or two when my schedule lightened up."

"But you never did."

"No."

Behind her, Fiona heard the rasp of the zipper closing on the body bag, but she didn't turn. She didn't want to look. Didn't want to see that face, so rigid and silent but still so beautiful in death.

"I have to call Lori," she murmured. But it was a call Fiona dreaded making more than anything in the world.

"Don't make that call just yet," Doggett said.

Fiona glanced at him. "She has a right to know what's happened to her daughter."

"The mother may be a personal friend of yours, but this is still a homicide investigation," he said gruffly. "And you know as well as I do that first impressions on hearing this kind of news are important. I'd appreciate you letting me get in touch with the parents when I feel the time is right."

Fiona frowned. "And when will that time be, detective?"

"You let me worry about that."

"What about Lexi? Someone has to tell her, and I don't think she should hear something like this from a complete stranger."

But Doggett was no longer listening to her. He was staring over her shoulder, scowling deeply. Fiona turned to see what had drawn his attention.

She sucked in a sharp breath. Frank Quinlan had just arrived with a couple of uniformed minions in tow. He stepped under the crime scene tape and bulldozed his way through the alley. Those not in his immediate orbit scurried for cover.

Quinlan was a stockily built man with close-set eyes and a hawkish nose that gave him a mean, predatory look he'd perfected to his advantage over the years. He was intimidating, arrogant, and had so many connections in the department, knew so much dirt on city officials, that even his superiors were afraid of him.

Fiona consciously straightened her posture because she knew that in a one-on-one confrontation with Quinlan, her height was *her* advantage. Men like Quinlan couldn't stand tall women.

He strode past her to Doggett and stabbed a finger in her direction. "What the hell is *she* doing here?"

That was like him, not to speak to her directly, Fiona thought. *Jerk.* She pitied the women under his command.

"Commander, this is Fiona Gallagher. She's an ASA—"

Quinlan cut off Doggett's introduction with an obscenity. "I know who she is, Doggett. I asked what she's doing here."

"Deputy Chief Fox asked for an ASA on the scene to advise." Fiona was pleased that her voice sounded smooth and professional, as if his little tirade didn't bother her at all.

He whirled. "Let me give *you* a piece of advice, Gallagher. Stay the hell out of our way. You interfere with this investigation, you'll have me to answer to."

"And if you screw up my case, you'll have me to answer to," she shot back. "I expect to be notified the moment you have a suspect in custody. I want to be present for the interrogation."

Her insinuation was crystal clear, and if there had been sufficient light where they stood, Fiona was certain she would have witnessed Quinlan's face turn a dark, livid purple. As it was, his rage rendered him incapable of speech for a moment before he sputtered another obscenity, then turned on his heel and stalked off.

Milo materialized beside Fiona. She hadn't even known he was around, but he must have heard the sordid little showdown, because he muttered, "Asshole," in a low voice, then said anxiously, "Are you okay?"

She shrugged. "Sure. Why wouldn't I be?"

Doggett said behind her, "What the hell was that all about?"

She turned. "Let's just say, I'm not one of Commander Quinlan's favorite people."

"Yeah, I got that," he said dryly. "You want to clue me in on what's going on?"

Before Fiona could answer, Milo said, "You ever hear of the Fullerton Five, detective?"

"You mean those guys who killed that little girl a few years back?" Doggett's expression subtly altered. "Wait a minute." He glanced at Fiona. "Gallagher. That's why I know you. You're the prosecutor who went after Quinlan when one of those guys brought a lawsuit against the department. No wonder he's pissed at you."

"I didn't go after him," Fiona argued. "Allegations were brought against him and some of the detectives under his command that I believed to be credible. I cooperated with the IAD investigation because I wanted to get at the truth."

"He was cleared by Internal Affairs and by the Office of Professional Standards," Doggett said. "You still believe he coerced those confessions?"

Fiona shrugged. "I know I can't prove it. But I learned a long time ago that this is a town built on clout and cronyism. I've had to accept that justice is sometimes hard to come by."

"Yeah," Doggett said with a frown. "I guess that's a lesson we've all had to learn." He glanced back down at the body bag, then turned on his heel and disappeared into the darkness.

FIONA STARED OUT THE CAR window as Milo drove her home a little while later. They were just coming back from Lexi and Alicia's apartment on the north side of the city, near the university. Doggett had agreed to let Fiona be present when he broke the news to Alicia's sister, but when they arrived at her apartment, no one was home.

Which was very odd and troubling to Fiona. Where could an eighteen-year-old girl be at four o'clock on a Tuesday morning? Any number of places, of course, but with her sister lying dead in an alley—

She's okay, Fiona told herself. Wherever Lexi was, she was fine. They couldn't both be gone. Fate wouldn't be that cruel to Lori, but Fiona knew all too well that it could be. She'd seen enough heartbreaking cases in her years as first a defense attorney and now as an ASA to know that fate had nothing to do with fairness.

"Fiona? Did you hear what I said?"

Milo's voice drew her out of her deep reverie. She turned from the window. "Sorry. What?"

"I was asking you about the other twin. Is she—" He broke off, looking sheepish. "I don't want to sound insensitive here."

"But you want to know if Alicia's twin is as beautiful as she was." Fiona sighed. "Even more so, if you can believe it."

Milo shot her an incredulous glance. "You're kidding, right?"

"I'm not kidding. You should see her. Lexi is…" Fiona trailed off. "I don't know how to explain it exactly. She has this quality about her. Men are…drawn to her."

"Like she's always in heat," Milo said under his breath.

"What?"

He shrugged. "Nothing. I was just projecting, I guess."

"But you nailed it perfectly," Fiona said with a frown. "That's exactly how men look at Lexi."

Milo was silent for a moment. "Were they models or something? I'll have to take your word about Lexi, but let's face it. Alicia was drop-dead gorgeous."

Fiona winced at the description. "They had offers to model, but their mother tried to shield them from all that."

"Shield them how?"

By asking me to look out for them, Fiona thought. But for crying out loud, who was she to supervise teenagers? She'd fallen in love with a killer. Hardly a role model most mothers would welcome, but Fiona and Lori went way back.

She could still remember that day after school when Lori had confided in her that she was pregnant. Fiona had been stunned. She wasn't even allowed to date, and her best friend was *pregnant!*

Tearfully Lori had explained how she'd met this guy at the mall. He was older, more experienced, and claimed he was in love with her. Fiona could believe that. Even so young, Lori was a blond, blue-eyed stunner, the kind of girl that men couldn't take their eyes off.

The two of them had started meeting after school and on weekends. Not for real dates, of course. Lori wasn't allowed to date, either. She'd tell her mother she was going to Fiona's house, and then she'd meet up with this guy. They'd have a soda together. Go to the movies. All very innocent at first, then things got out of hand.

He dumped her when he found out she was pregnant. Lori was devastated.

"You have to tell your parents, Lori. What else can you do?" Although secretly Fiona thought that the last thing she would ever do was tell her parents something like that. She'd rather die first because her father would kill her anyway, and her brothers.... She shuddered. She didn't even want to think about what her brothers would do.

But somehow Lori had managed to work up the courage to go home and tell her parents everything. She certainly wasn't the first girl in their neighborhood to find herself in that predicament, and this was the enlightened eighties after all. But her father had still been so angry that he'd sent her to Detroit to live with his sister while arrangements were made to put both babies up for adoption.

When they were born, however, Lori couldn't go through with it. She kept the babies and stayed with her aunt until her father finally relented and came for her.

The moment Wayne Mercer laid eyes on the twins, it was love at first sight. He and Lori's mother doted on the girls, and did everything in their power to help Lori get her life back on track. She graduated with honors from both high school and college, and, like Fiona, was near the top of her class in law school. The two of them had even been associates at the same law firm in the Loop, but then Lori had met Paul Guest, a Houston attorney, and was swept off her feet. They were married two months later, and he took Lori and the twins back to Texas with him.

For a couple of years after the move, Lori and Fiona kept in touch with phone calls and letters, but the calls eventually stopped, and gradually, the correspondence dwindled to only Christmas cards.

Then last summer, Lori called Fiona out of the blue. "I need to ask a big favor of you," she said, after the two had spent a few minutes catching up. "The twins will be starting college in the fall."

"That's impossible," Fiona insisted. "They were in kindergarten just last week."

"They were already out of kindergarten by the time we started law school, Fiona."

She groaned. "Stop. You're making me feel ancient."

"Now you know how I feel every day." Lori laughed, but there was some tension in her voice. "Oh, Fiona, you should see them. They're all grown up and so smart. And so beautiful! I know every mother thinks that about her children, but Alicia and Lexi *are* special. You wouldn't believe all the modeling offers they've had. But Paul and I have tried to shelter them from all the attention because we don't want them to get caught up in something they can't handle."

Fiona wondered if Lori was thinking about her own trouble as a teenager.

"We always planned on the girls going to school here in Houston," she continued. "Paul wanted them to go to Rice. It's a wonderful school, and his father is one of the trustees. And, of course, the best part is that they would be close enough for us to keep an eye on them."

"I take it the girls have other ideas," Fiona murmured. She could sympathize with Alicia and Lexi. Growing up with a father and three brothers who were all cops, Fiona had felt pretty smothered herself at times.

Lori sighed. "Evidently they talked to a recruiter from Hillsboro University, and now that's where they want to go. They're bound and determined, especially Lexi. Alicia, I think, would still like to go to Rice, but she'd never let her sister go off to Chicago alone. They have that twin thing, Fiona. Where one goes, the other goes. When one is upset, the other is upset. If one gets hurt, well, you get the idea. They're so attuned to one another, it's almost scary."

Fiona frowned, still uncertain where she fit into the equation. "Hillsboro is an excellent school, Lori. My sister-in-law is head of the forensics anthropology lab there."

"I know it's a great school, but it's so far away. And now that my parents are dead, I don't have any family left in Chicago. No one to look after the girls." Lori paused and took a deep breath. "That's why I'm calling you, Fiona. Would it be a terrible imposition if I gave them your phone number? It would make me feel so much better to know there's someone in the city they could call if they needed to."

"I don't mind at all," Fiona said impulsively. "In fact, I insist. Tell you what, when are you coming up to help them settle in?"

"Next week."

"Let's all have dinner together so the girls can meet me. Maybe then they'll feel less awkward about calling."

"I'd love that. Oh, Fiona. I can't tell you what this means to me." Lori sounded so relieved that Fiona felt a little guilty. She'd readily agreed to the arrangement because it was an easy thing to do. She didn't think, for one second, that two gorgeous teenage girls, on their own for the first time, would really feel the need to call on a complete stranger.

She didn't say as much to Lori, however, and the following week, they met for dinner at a restaurant on Michigan Avenue. Lori and Fiona had arranged to arrive early so they could have a chance to chat before the girls joined them. They were exchanging stories about some of their more interesting cases when Lori suddenly touched Fiona's hand. "There's Alicia. She just came in."

Lori's whole face was suddenly aglow. For one split second, Fiona almost resented the adulation that radiated from her friend's eyes. Motherhood couldn't be that grand, could it? Fiona wasn't missing out on something that spectacular, was she?

Then she turned. And for several long seconds, she could do nothing but stare at the girl making her way through the crowded tables toward them.

She was, without a doubt, one of the most beautiful young women Fiona had ever laid eyes on. "Oh, my God," she blurted. "No wonder you didn't want to let them out of your sight."

Lori's smile turned wistful. "She is lovely, isn't she?"

Lovely was an understatement. In spite of the sedate way she dressed, Alicia Mercer turned heads as she walked through the crowded restaurant. But when she sat down at the table, she seemed oblivious to the stares and admiration. Fiona was instantly charmed. The girl was as modest and unassuming as she was gorgeous. She was almost too good to be true.

And then her sister walked in.

Lexi Mercer was tall like Alicia, with the same pale blond hair and blue eyes, but there was nothing understated about her appearance. She had on low-rider jeans and a cropped shirt that showed off a very flat, tanned stomach and a belly button ring that sparkled in the lighting.

If admiring eyes had noticed Alicia, men literally drooled over Lexi. It was more than just her physical beauty. She had a kind of magnetism that would make even the most principled man have some very dark thoughts.

Fiona tore her gaze away long enough to glance at Alicia. She was staring at her sister, too, and there was something in her eyes. Not jealousy. Not envy. Not even resentment, but...something.

It made Fiona wonder instantly what it must have been like, growing up in Lexi's shadow. In any other family, Alicia would have been the golden child, and even now, she would still be the most desirable woman in any room—until her sister arrived.

And Lori? What had it been like raising such a child? Lori was still a young, beautiful woman in her own right, but in her daughter's presence—

Let's face it, Fiona thought grimly. *With Lexi Mercer around, we all look like hags.*

But in spite of any latent rivalry, it was obvious the three women were close and had such a wonderful relationship that Fiona again felt twinges of jealousy. It was at that moment that she suddenly became aware of the ominous ticking of her own biological clock.

After that day, Fiona didn't see the girls again until just before Christmas, when Alicia called to set up a dinner. Fiona had been so pleasantly surprised at how much she enjoyed the girls' company that she'd honestly meant to keep in touch. But work became extremely hectic. Cases piled up. Every once in a while, if she thought about the Mercer twins, Fiona would promise herself she'd call them when she had a spare moment, just to say hello.

But that spare moment never came. Not even to return Alicia's call last week.

And now it was too late.

Soon, it would be Lori who received a phone call, one that would turn her perfect little world into a nightmare.

CHAPTER FIVE

"WOULD YOU LIKE ME TO WALK up with you?" Milo asked as he pulled to the curb in front of Fiona's building. In spite of the earlier tension between them, he'd been very solicitous since they'd left Lexi's apartment, and Fiona appreciated his effort to return their relationship to normal. The last thing either of them needed was a strained working environment.

She gave him a tired smile. "No, thanks. I still need to do some work on the DeMarco case. We're due in court in...exactly..." She glanced at her watch and groaned. "Four and a half hours. What about you? Are you ready?"

"I will be." He frowned suddenly. "Tell me the truth, Fiona. Do you think we have even an outside shot at a conviction?"

"I don't know. It's always hard to predict what a jury will do in a he said-she said case like this. With no forensic evidence, it'll be a hard sale to the jury."

"How could there not be one single piece of evidence against that bastard?" Milo muttered. "I get that he wore a condom, but no hair, no fibers, no DNA beneath her fingernails? What the hell did he do, scrub her down afterward?"

"You know what happened," Fiona said. "Same thing that happens in too many of these cases. She went home and showered." Although in Kimbra's case, she'd gone to a runaway shelter. She'd gotten rid of her clothes, too, because she'd never planned to report the rape at all. But Rachel Torres, a woman who ran the runaway shelter, saw the bruises and forced the truth from Kimbra. She was the one who took her to the emergency room, but by then a rape kit was almost useless. Whatever evidence there might have been to help put DeMarco away had been washed down the drain.

"I watched the jury yesterday when DeMarco took the stand," Fiona said. "He scored some serious points." And nothing she'd been able to do during cross-examination had rattled him. If she didn't know better, she would have sworn the man was on something. How could anyone remain that calm when she'd gone straight for the jugular?

Milo nodded morosely. "I thought so, too. And Kimbra's testimony was shaky, at best."

That was another thing that made this case so difficult. The accused wasn't just any cop. DeMarco was a decorated veteran of the Chicago Police Department and a war hero from Desert Storm. Good-looking, well-educated, the kind of defendant that was easy to root for because people wanted to believe he was exactly what he seemed to be—one of the good guys.

Kimbra, on the other hand, was a troubled young girl who'd lived on the streets for years. Moody, defiant, and tough as nails, she'd been a difficult and reluctant witness from the start, the kind that sometimes made Fiona wonder if the aggravation was worth it.

She sighed wearily. "Since we didn't get any help from Kimbra, it's imperative we make up ground in the closing argument. We'll both have to be at the top of our game, Milo."

"Oh, no pressure there," he grumbled as he got out of

the car and came around to open her door. When she stepped out, he said awkwardly, "Look, Fiona, that business about Guy—"

She cut him off. "Let's just forget it, okay? I don't want to talk about it anymore."

"I understand." He ran a hand through his hair, messing his gel job. "Maybe I shouldn't have said anything. About the gossip, I mean. I don't want you to feel uncomfortable at the office."

She shrugged. "I hate gossip, but maybe it's best that you did bring it to my attention. It's always a good idea to know what people are saying about you behind your back. But just for the record? I'm not involved with Guy Hardison. On any level. I want you to know that. I want you to believe that."

"Maybe you're not involved, but—"

"Milo." Her tone held a warning note. "There is nothing going on between Guy Hardison and me. Period."

He nodded. "Okay. I get the message. Case closed. I'll see you in a few hours."

They said their good-nights, and then Fiona ran up the front steps and inserted her key into the lock. She couldn't wait to be inside her own apartment, to lock the door behind her and close herself off from the rest of the world, if only for the next few hours.

Resolving herself to the work she'd left earlier, she went into her tiny kitchen to brew a fresh pot of coffee. But instead, she climbed up on the counter and reached into the far corner of a top cabinet to retrieve the bottle of scotch she'd stashed several months ago when she'd quit drinking.

She stared at the bottle for a moment, then got out a glass and poured herself a drink. Her grandmother's voice seemed to echo through the silent apartment. *"You drink alone, you're apt to die alone, Fiona Colleen."*

"Sorry, Gran," she muttered. But dying alone was pretty much a foregone conclusion for her anyway.

Fiona downed the whiskey sitting on the edge of the counter, then poured herself another. The liquor seared a comforting path all the way to her stomach, and she closed her eyes, letting the familiar numbness take hold.

Hopping off the counter, she carried the bottle and the glass into the other room and dropped into a chair at the dining table. Sipping her drink, she read over the notes she'd made earlier.

One out of three women in this country will be sexually assaulted in her lifetime. One out of every three.

She finished her drink, then began to write.

It could happen to me, it could happen to you, it could happen to anyone at any time.

She stared at the words and frowned. Had Alicia been sexually assaulted? Was that the reason she'd been murdered?

They would have to wait for the autopsy to find out, and even then the results, except in the more brutal cases, could be ambiguous.

However, the way she'd been murdered, one shot to the back of the head, suggested—as Guy had said earlier—an execution-style hit. Very deliberate, premeditated, someone wanting to shut her up. But why? What could an eighteen-year-old girl who'd lived a very sheltered and protected existence know that would make someone want to kill her? What might she have seen? *Who* might she have seen?

And where the hell was Lexi?

The questions swirled inside Fiona's brain, and she rubbed her temples, trying to shut them out so that she could concentrate on her work. She poured herself another drink and scribbled:

Think of three women in your own life. Your mother, your daughter, your sister...

As she stared at what she'd written, Lori Guest's words suddenly came back to her.

"They have that twin thing, Fiona. Where one goes, the other goes. When one is upset, the other is upset. If one gets hurt, well, you get the idea. They're so attuned to one another, it's almost scary."

Had Lexi sensed that Alicia was in trouble? Had she felt her sister's terror?

Did she know the exact moment when the bullet had pierced her sister's skull?

Or was Lexi...beyond knowing?

"Why did you call me, Alicia?" Fiona wondered aloud. "And why in God's name didn't I call you back?"

Don't dwell on it. Nothing could be done about it now. Recriminations could come later, but for now, the only productive thing Fiona could do was concentrate on her work.

She glanced back down at her notes, tried to pull her thoughts together once again, but her mind kept rambling and the words on the page blurred. Her eyes suddenly burned with exhaustion, and Fiona thought that if she could just rest them for a moment, she'd be good to go.

But the moment she closed her eyes, she drifted off and the image of Alicia's pale, still features materialized in her dream. Mist swirled around the body as Fiona stared down at her, and somewhere in the darkness behind her, a tape played over and over. *"Fiona? This is Alicia Mercer. Please call me when you get this message. I really need to talk to you."*

And then suddenly the tape stopped. The fog faded, and

Fiona was standing on a lonely road in the harsh glare of headlights as she stared down at David Mackenzie's lifeless body. Someone said in horror, "He's dead, Fiona. My God, you killed him."

She came awake with a start, the ringing of the telephone as jarring in the early morning hours as a scream. Glancing around, Fiona tried to orient herself, and when the sound persisted, she finally got up to answer it. Finding herself not quite steady on her feet, she put a hand on the table for balance.

Carefully she walked across the room to the sofa where she'd tossed the cordless phone earlier. Halfway there, she realized it wasn't the phone ringing, but the doorbell.

She adjusted course and moved very deliberately to the door to glance through the peephole. Detective Doggett stood on the other side. She undid the dead bolts and drew back the door to let him in.

He walked inside and glanced back at all the locks. "How many of those things you got on there?"

Not enough. Fiona pulled fingers through her messy hair as she closed the door, then turning, she caught her breath when she found him standing right behind her. His eyes…those laser blue eyes…were staring at her intently. And he was frowning. Fiona had the vague notion that he was scowling at her in disapproval.

Not a comfortable revelation for any woman.

"Sorry to drop by like this," he said. "But I told you I'd be in touch as soon as I heard something."

Fiona had made sure he had her home phone number before they left the crime scene, expecting that he would simply call when he had news. But here he was, alive and in person, and she realized that he must have looked up her address in the cross directory. She wondered if she should be annoyed at his presumption. Maybe when she was thinking a little more clearly she would be.

She felt dizzy, all of a sudden, and put a hand to her forehead.

"Hey, you okay?" Doggett asked her.

"I'm fine." But her words sounded slurred even to her.

"Maybe we'd better sit down. You don't look too steady on your feet."

"No, I told you I'm fine—" But Fiona was horrified to feel herself sway. She put out a hand to stop the room from spinning, but there was nothing to grab hold of. "I think I'm going to—"

The next thing she knew, she was lying on the sofa, staring up at the ceiling. Doggett was standing over her. Still scowling. Still disapproving.

"I'm all right," she muttered. "I just felt a little woozy." So woozy, in fact, she couldn't quite remember having gotten from the door to the sofa.

"You fainted," Doggett said. "Or maybe I should say, you passed out."

Disgust in his voice. Not a good sign. Fiona gritted her teeth and sat up. "I couldn't have. I didn't have that much to drink."

"You had enough to knock you on your butt. Is that the norm for you? You come home from a crime scene at four o'clock in the morning and start drinking?" His expression was so grim that Fiona thought if he'd had a rolled up newspaper, he probably would have bopped her on the nose with it. She had the sudden urge to tuck her tail between her legs and slink off to the nearest corner.

"I didn't get home until four-thirty," she said coolly as if that made any kind of difference whatsoever. Humiliation always made her irreverent...irrelevant...shit.

"And if I want to have a drink in the privacy of my own home, I don't see how that's your business."

"I'll tell you how it's my business. You're the prosecutor assigned to my case. I don't want a bad guy slipping through the cracks because you weren't up to the job."

"You don't have to worry about me," Fiona assured him, wishing she didn't feel as if she might throw up at any moment. Barfing on Doggett's shoes would definitely undermine her credibility. "I know how to do my job. You just make sure the bad guy doesn't slip through the cracks because you or some other detective in your division decides to ride roughshod over his rights."

"So we're back to that again, are we? Let's get one thing straight. I'm not Frank Quinlan."

Well, on *that,* they were in perfect agreement.

As Doggett turned on his heel and headed for the kitchen, Fiona leaned forward slightly, watching him exit the room. He had a nice butt, and the fact that she noticed told her that she must, indeed, be just a tiny bit hammered. After a moment, she heard him fiddle with the coffeemaker as he tried to figure out the controls.

"Make yourself at home," she grumbled, wondering if she had enough strength to make it to the bathroom, wash her face, and then crawl back before Doggett ever missed her. She decided she didn't, and let her head fall back against the sofa instead.

When Doggett returned, he set a steaming cup of coffee on the table in front of her. "Drink it. Let's get you sobered up so we can talk."

"I'm not drunk. And, for God's sake, do you have to hover over me like that? You're not my mother."

His lips thinned in displeasure. "No. But you're reminding me a little too much of mine just now."

Oh, God, she really was going to be sick. "What's that supposed to mean?"

He glared down at her, then shrugged. "Just drink the coffee."

"When you stop hovering."

He walked over and sank down in a chair opposite the sofa. "Better?"

She picked up the cup and sipped. The coffee was hot, bitter and strong. Just the way she liked it. The caffeine went straight to her head, and Fiona sat back against the sofa, cradling the cup between her hands.

After a moment, she glanced at Doggett. "Okay. Tell me why you're here. Did you find Lexi?"

Something flickered in his eyes, a shadow that sent a shiver of dread up Fiona's spine. "No, not yet." He leaned forward, resting his forearms on his knees. "But I did manage to track down their roommate through a neighbor. Her name is Kelly Everhardt. She drove up to Wheeler on Sunday morning to visit her parents for a couple of days. She's coming back sometime this morning."

"Does *she* know where Lexi is?"

Doggett paused. "She hasn't seen Lexi for nearly a week."

A chill shot through Fiona's heart. "Where's she been?"

"No one seems to know. The roommate says she didn't come home last Thursday night, and she hasn't been seen since."

"Has a missing person's report been filed?"

He shook his head. "The roommate said Alicia didn't want to get the police involved."

"Why not?"

"Because she didn't want their parents to find out. According to the roommate, Lexi has a habit of disappearing. Seems she got involved with a married man last semester, and the two of them used to sneak off for days at a time without telling anyone because he insisted they keep the affair a secret. The roommate says Lexi broke off the relationship before Christmas, but when she didn't come home this time, Alicia was afraid she'd gone off with him again. The roommate said Alicia thought she could find her on her own, talk some sense into her, and the parents would never have to know.''

Fiona leaned forward and carefully placed the cup on the table. The sudden infusion of caffeine had given her a bad case of the shakes. ''Did their roommate say who this married man was?''

''She didn't know. She said Alicia didn't know for sure, either, but she told the roommate she had her suspicions.''

''Do you think this guy could have had something to do with Alicia's death? Maybe he was afraid she knew about him and Lexi.''

Doggett shrugged. ''It's possible. Right now it's the only lead we've got. Hopefully we'll know more after the autopsy.''

''Did you call Lori?'' Fiona asked anxiously.

''I spoke with her a little while ago.''

''How did she take it? Is she…okay?'' A stupid question. Lori Guest had just learned that one daughter had been murdered and the other one was missing. Of course, she wasn't okay. She'd probably never be okay again.

Oh, God…

''She's flying into O'Hare sometime later this morning,'' Doggett said.

''Did you talk to her husband?''

''No, just Mrs. Guest.''

Fiona rubbed her forehead with her fingertips. ''I've

been asking myself over and over why Alicia called me last week, and now I think I know. She wanted me to help her find Lexi. When I didn't call her back, she went searching for her sister on her own. And now she's dead."

"You're not blaming yourself for that, are you?" Doggett's blue eyes pierced through Fiona's armor with hardly any resistance, and she found herself wondering, unaccountably and inappropriately, if there was a woman in his life.

"I know Alicia's death wasn't my fault," she said with a frown. "But I'll always wonder what might have happened if I had called her back. Maybe I could have helped her, and maybe she'd still be alive."

"And maybe," Doggett said in that deep, rumbling voice of his. "You'd be lying in the morgue with her right now."

CHAPTER SIX

MEREDITH SWEENEY, the assistant ME, had Alicia Mercer's X-rays waiting for Doggett a few hours later when he arrived at the Chicago Technical Park where the morgue was located.

He studied the skull X-rays. "Was I right about the bullet hole? A .45 caliber slug, right?"

Meredith shook her dark head. "No, but that's what I thought, too, at first, so don't feel bad. When I calibrated the hole, though, I found it somewhat smaller than .5 inches. The wound is more consistent with a .40 caliber or 10 mm bullet."

Doggett glanced at her. "You sure about that?"

She shrugged. "You can measure it for yourself if you want."

"I'll take your word for it." The information didn't necessarily mean anything, but on the other hand, Doggett found it interesting. In recent years, .40 caliber weapons had come into wide use by law enforcement agencies all over the country, including the Chicago PD. Doggett's own service weapon was a Glock 27, a piece favored by a lot of undercover cops.

"I wouldn't get my hopes up for any kind of ballistics match," Meredith told him. She pointed to the left side of the victim's skull, in the area behind the eye socket where metallic density showed as white flecks on the X-ray.

"A lead snowstorm," Doggett muttered.

"Exactly. You can actually see where the bullet disintegrated as it traveled through the body, which means it must have been partially jacketed." She moved to another X-ray and indicated an anomalous object in the pelvis area. "I suspect this is where we'll find the bullet, what's left of it."

Doggett nodded. "What about the bruises around her wrists?"

"Looks like he used a nylon cord, the kind you can buy in any hardware store."

"And the mark on her shoulder?"

"We've sent a sample of the ink to the lab, but you can get stamp pads in any discount or office supply store, and those temporary tattoos are sold out of vending machines."

"It's the symbol that's bugging me," Doggett said. "Why a trident?"

"At least it's not a swastika," Meredith said dryly. "Or a pentagram. God knows we see our share of those." She gave Doggett a moment longer to study the X-rays. "Are you staying for the autopsy?"

"Yeah." It wasn't just a matter of duty, but a matter of conscience. His way of paying respect to the victim. Doggett never walked out on an autopsy, no matter how gruesome.

Meredith nodded briskly. "Let's get started then, shall we?"

Doggett followed her into the autopsy room where Alicia Mercer's nude body waited for them on a cold, stainless-steel table.

THE AIR-CONDITIONING in the courtroom was operating in hyperdrive, and Fiona shivered as she glanced around the packed benches, picking out faces in the crowd that she recognized. She was seated at the prosecution table with Milo, who was busy going over his notes. Fiona knew that she should do the same, but her gaze kept straying back to the visitors' block where a dozen or more cops from Area Three, both in uniforms and plainclothes, had turned out in a show of support for Vince DeMarco.

Fiona came from a long line of cops. The Gallaghers were almost legendary in the police department. Her grandfather, her father, her three brothers…all Chicago PD. So she knew cops. She knew how they walked, how they talked, how they thought. But the one thing she'd never been able to understand about them, no matter their rank, was the blind loyalty to the brotherhood.

Most of the police officers she knew were good, decent, hardworking guys who would never, in a million years, condone rape. They recognized the crime for what it was—an act of violence. In most cops' estimation, a rapist ranked just slightly above a child molester, and yet here a dozen or so of Chicago's finest—those good, decent, hardworking men—sat lending moral support to a creep like DeMarco. And all because he was a fellow police officer.

But that view was simplistic and more than a little unfair, Fiona knew. Most of the officers in the courtroom had undoubtedly managed to convince themselves, with Quinlan's help, that DeMarco was the victim. He was a good cop being railroaded by a vindictive junkie and by an out-of-control prosecutor who had started to believe her own press. Fiona Gallagher, the Iron Maiden, was building herself quite the reputation by going after cops—first Quinlan and now DeMarco.

As for Fiona, she had no doubt whatsoever of De-Marco's guilt. She didn't care what his fellow cops thought. She didn't care what Frank Quinlan had force-fed them into believing. All she had to do was look into DeMarco's eyes, those cold, dark, soulless eyes, to know the truth.

"You raped that poor girl, didn't you, Detective DeMarco? You saw her on the street that night, you accosted her, and you're not the type to take no for an answer. When she wouldn't go with you willingly, you forced her into that alley, tried to beat her into submission, and then, when that *didn't work, you put your gun to her head and threatened to blow her brains out if she screamed. Isn't that what happened? Admit it, Detective. You raped that girl, didn't you?* Didn't *you?"*

"No! I didn't touch her! I swear! I wouldn't do something like that. I'm a cop, for God's sake. I took an oath to protect people like Kimbra Williams. I would never hurt anyone."

So earnest, so sincere. The jury had hung on his every word.

But his eyes had told Fiona something very different. His eyes had taunted her, conveyed to her secretly that, yeah, he'd done it. He'd do it again, too, if the mood struck him, and there wasn't a damn thing she could do about it.

Maybe you'd like to be next, Counselor.

He hadn't said it aloud, but the message was so clear in his eyes that for a moment, Fiona was the one who had been rattled by the cross-examination. And it hadn't helped her poise to know that Frank Quinlan was sitting on the front row, his beady eyes tracking her every move as she walked back to the prosecution table.

He was there again today. Fiona had seen him when she first entered the courtroom. He'd been sitting front and center, in full-dress uniform, brass stars shimmering in the fluorescent lighting as he'd clapped a supportive hand on DeMarco's shoulder.

Milo muttered something under his breath, then leaned toward Fiona. "Did you see all the brass from police headquarters walk in? What the hell are they doing here?"

"Are you kidding? Didn't you see the TV cameras out front?" Fiona glanced over her shoulder, her gaze once again sweeping the crowded courtroom. Milo was right. The big guns were out in full force, including Deputy Chief of Detectives Clare Fox. She wore her dress uniform, too, and her stars seemed to shine just a little more brilliantly than Quinlan's.

Milo tugged at his tie. "Hell, with all this attention, you'd think we had O.J. in here."

"A cop accused of rape is pretty good copy," Fiona said. "Especially a hero like DeMarco. But at least the reporting so far has been fair."

"Fair?" Milo grinned. "Ever since you cooperated with that IAD investigation, you own the guy at the *Trib*."

"Which I'm sure endears me even more to Frank Quinlan," she said dryly.

Milo's grin disappeared. "Quinlan's got some heavy-duty connections, Fiona. Don't underestimate him."

She turned in surprise. "Gee, if I didn't know better, I'd swear you were starting to get paranoid on me, Milo. What's with all these warnings? First Guy and now Quinlan?"

He frowned. "Those two have more in common than you might think."

She lifted a brow. "Such as?"

Milo turned away, but not before she'd seen something dark flicker in his eyes. That secret again. "They can both be major-league assholes," he muttered, but Fiona didn't think that was what he'd meant to say at all.

More and more, she was starting to think that there was something on Milo's mind, something he wanted to confide in her, but for some reason, felt he couldn't. The vague warnings were starting to make her uneasy around him.

But at least his appearance was somewhat reassuring. He was dressed today like the Milo she was accustomed to—gray suit, neatly combed hair, dark-rimmed glasses that made him look boyish and earnest. A persona that might or might not be an asset if the jurors compared it to the dark, smoldering sex appeal of Vince DeMarco.

"Only one person missing from this circus," he said, turning to scan the courtroom. "Where in the hell is Kimbra? Have you heard from her this morning?"

"I haven't talked to her since court yesterday, but she promised me she'd be here."

Milo's lips thinned. "And if she doesn't show?"

"Then we could be in some deep you-know-what here. But she still has a few more minutes. I'm not giving up on her just yet."

But it wouldn't be that much of a surprise if Kimbra didn't show, even though Fiona had stressed over and over how important it was for the jury to see her in the courtroom today. But that was Kimbra's MO. When the going got tough, she ran.

Not that Fiona could blame her. It couldn't be easy sitting in court day in and day out with her attacker only a few feet away, his smoldering gaze mocking her at every turn. The jury saw only one side of Vincent DeMarco, the good-looking, sexy cop who wouldn't need to resort to rape when he could have any woman he wanted, even one as young and exotically attractive as Kimbra.

But rape wasn't about sex. It was about power. It was about domination and humiliation.

And humiliation was something Fiona could relate to.

You didn't fall in love with a man who'd killed three women and not want to curl up and die at your own gullibility—at your own blind stupidity for not having seen through such evil, for not having been able to stop it.

Which was why Fiona *had* to stop it now.

Almost against her will, she glanced at the table across the aisle. Vincent DeMarco met her gaze and smiled, as if he knew exactly what she was thinking.

Then a commotion at the back of the courtroom drew his attention, and Fiona saw anger flash across his face. He turned and said something to Quinlan, and the older cop nodded in grim agreement.

Fiona shifted her gaze to see what had caused their agitation, and relief swept through her. Kimbra and Rachel Torres, the woman who ran the runaway shelter where Kimbra sometimes stayed, had just come into the courtroom. They paused at the back, and then Kimbra started forward with a little stumble, as if Rachel had had to nudge her to get her to move. The girl's expression was frozen. She glanced neither to the right nor to the left as she stepped up to the prosecution table and took her seat.

Fiona turned and put her hand over Kimbra's. "Thanks for coming."

Kimbra shrugged. "I said I would, didn't I?"

Fiona squeezed her fingers. "I know this isn't easy for you, but you've done great so far. Just hang in there a little longer, okay? It'll all be over soon."

"Then he's goin' to prison, right?" Kimbra turned eyes that looked as old as time on Fiona. "Cuz if he don't do no time for this, I'm a dead woman."

A shiver crawled up Fiona's spine at the certainty in the girl's voice. "If he threatens you in any way—"

"What y'all gonna do 'bout it, Miss Lawyer? Huh?

That man's Five-O. They do what they want," she said bitterly. "Who's gonna stop 'em?"

"I'll stop him. If he comes near you, we'll get a restraining order—"

Kimbra all but laughed in her face. "You still don't get it, do you? If he wants me dead, I'll just disappear one day. Won't nobody ever know what happened to me. That's how he'll do it."

She paused for a moment, her gaze sliding past Fiona as a look of pure terror crept into her eyes. Then she blinked it away and the defiant mask slipped back into place. "Y'all keep messin' with the wrong people, Miss Lawyer, they might just disappear you, too."

FIONA WALKED OVER TO THE jury box and planted her hands on the railing. Milo had done a fantastic job summarizing the evidence and recounting witness testimony in his closing remarks, but the defense attorney, Dylan O'Roarke, had been masterful.

He'd wasted no time in getting to the heart of the case. "In spite of the prosecution's attempts to muddy the waters at every turn, the case is a simple one, ladies and gentlemen. It boils down to one single question. Who do you believe? A troubled runaway with a long history of drug abuse and a willful disobedience of the law? One who openly bragged about her hatred of the police? One who, as you heard more than one witness testify, swore to get her revenge on Detective DeMarco for an old arrest?

"Or do you believe Vincent DeMarco, a decorated police officer, an ex-Army Ranger who distinguished himself on a desert battlefield as well as on the mean streets of Chicago?"

Dylan had gone on and on, hammering home the same

point until Fiona had seen at least one juror nod very slightly in agreement.

And now it was her turn to offer a rebuttal. She surveyed the twelve members of the panel, noting their expressions as they stared up at her expectantly, and then she said, very quietly, "One out of every three women in this country will be sexually assaulted in her lifetime. One out of every three."

She emphasized the last five words as her gaze slid to a well-dressed, middle-aged woman in the second row who had sat rigidly throughout the whole trial. Her expression rarely showed anything more than an intense concentration, as if she were determined to perform her civic duty to the best of her ability, but beyond that the trial couldn't touch her. Rape couldn't touch her.

Fiona stared at her for a long moment until the woman was forced to meet her gaze. "It could happen to any woman in this courtroom. It could happen to me. It could happen to you."

Something flashed briefly in the woman's eyes. Denial, Fiona thought. She often found the toughest jurors to sway in a rape case were upper-middle-class white women who had a hard time identifying with a victim like Kimbra.

"Think of three women in your own life. Your mother. Your sister." Fiona paused, letting her gaze move to a male juror seated directly in front of her in the first row. "Your daughter."

He flinched.

"One out of every three women in this country will be sexually assaulted in her lifetime."

Fiona straightened and paced slowly back and forth in front of the jury box. "The defense would have you believe that a man like Vincent DeMarco, a decorated police officer, a war hero from Desert Storm, a man of impeachable honor and character, could not have perpetrated such a terrible crime. A man like Vincent DeMarco could not be guilty of rape. And yet…''

Fiona turned to Kimbra. "Someone did rape Kimbra Williams on the night of April 17. Someone forced her into that alley and beat her until she could barely move. And when she still fought back, her attacker held a gun to her head and threatened to blow her brains out if she screamed.''

Fiona paused again, letting the mental picture seep in. "You heard testimony from the doctor who examined Kimbra on that same night. You saw photographs of the severe bruises and swelling left by the beating. Kimbra Williams was brutally attacked and raped. Of that, there is no doubt.

"But the defense has also implied that Kimbra's fear may have impaired her ability to correctly identify her assailant. After all, it was a dark, moonless night, and she was terrified beyond reason. How could she—how could anyone—be so certain, under the circumstances, of her assailant's identity?''

Fiona's expression hardened. "I'll tell you how. Vincent DeMarco's face was only inches from Kimbra's as he held that gun to her head. It didn't happen instantly. It took minutes. For Kimbra, it took an eternity. Not only was she able to correctly identify her attacker, but I can pretty much guarantee you that his is a face she will never forget.''

Fiona allowed a shudder to ripple through her.

"The crux of the defense's case, though, rests on Kimbra's alleged hatred of the police. Her loathing for authority, they want you to believe, is the real reason for the charges against Detective DeMarco. She held a grudge against him for hassling her on the street so what better way to get back at him than to accuse him of a brutal crime? It's been known to happen, they warned you.''

Fiona let contempt creep into her voice. "Only one thing wrong with that theory, ladies and gentlemen. Kimbra Williams was raped and beaten on the night of April 17. She didn't lie about those bruises. You saw the pictures.

"For all we know, she was left for dead in that alley, but even if her attacker never meant to kill her, you can be certain that a man like Vincent DeMarco would not expect her to press charges against him. After all, as a police officer, he would know that fifty percent of all rapes go unreported every year because the victim is either worried she won't be believed or is afraid of retaliation by her assailant.

"Retaliation is what the defense wants you to believe motivated Kimbra Williams. But let's examine that for a moment. A girl in Kimbra's position, a runaway who spends most of her life on the street, falsely accuses a police officer, of all people, of rape. How easy would it be for *him* to retaliate against her? She's vulnerable. She's alone. No friends or family to come to her rescue. Do you really think she'd take that chance?''

Fiona walked back to the jury box and once again placed her hands on the rail, leaning forward. "Vincent DeMarco's fate is in your hands today, ladies and gentlemen, but regardless of what you decide, Kimbra Williams's life is never going to be the same. Thirty-one percent of all rape victims develop Rape-Related Posttraumatic Stress Disorder, and they are nine times more likely to attempt suicide. A pretty grim statistic, isn't it?

"But the most frightening statistic of all isn't about the victim. It's about the assailant. Studies have shown that the recidivism rate among rate among rapists can be as high as 50 percent. That means if Vincent DeMarco is allowed to walk out of this courtroom a free man, there is an extremely high probability he will rape again.

"Who will his next victim be, I wonder? That one woman out of three who will be sexually assaulted in her lifetime?"

Fiona gazed at them for a moment longer, then turned and strode back to the prosecution table to await the judge's final instructions to the jury.

CHAPTER SEVEN

HANDSOME AND CHARMING, with a confidence that Fiona found exceedingly annoying, Dylan O'Roarke had become her number one nemesis in the courtroom since she'd moved to the Criminal Prosecutions Bureau five years ago. Which was only fitting, she supposed, seeing as how their families had been mortal enemies for decades, Chicago's own version of the Hatfields and the McCoys.

The feud had spanned three generations, beginning in the Prohibition Era when Fiona's grandfather, William Gallagher, had played Eliot Ness to James O'Roarke's Al Capone. Once close friends, the two Irish immigrants had become bitter rivals, not only because they'd chosen different sides of the law, but also because they'd fallen in love with the same woman, Fiona's grandmother, Colleen.

Two recent marriages between the clans, including Dylan's union with Fiona's cousin, Kaitlin, had brought an uneasy truce between the families, but as far as Fiona was concerned, the peace accord didn't extend into the courtroom.

So when he approached the prosecution table after court was adjourned, she glanced up with a fair amount of suspicion.

"Have you got a minute?" he asked her.

She snapped closed the latches on her briefcase and stood. "That depends." Her gaze slid past him to where

Vince DeMarco stood talking and laughing as if he didn't have a care in the world. "Is your client ready to accept my offer?"

Dylan gave a sharp laugh. "Are you kidding? That wasn't an offer, it was an insult. Second degree sexual assault and seven years at Stateville? No way my client's doing any time. He's walking and you know it."

She gave him an angry glare. "He's guilty, and *you* know it. Kimbra Williams is only seventeen years old, Dylan. How do you sleep at night?"

Dylan's mouth tightened as he returned her glare. "I sleep just fine. How about you, Fiona? Ever have nightmares about Jessie Carver?"

An arrow straight through the heart.

Jessie Carver was one of the Fullerton Five who'd maintained his innocence from the first. He claimed that one of the other suspects in the case had implicated him in order to cut a deal with the prosecution, and then, after forty-eight straight hours of verbal intimidation, beatings and sleep deprivation, he'd signed a confession out of sheer desperation.

In one of those ironic twists, Dylan had represented Jessie Carver three years ago, and now he was defending one of the cops Jessie claimed had coerced his confession, proving that Chicago politics wasn't the only profession that made for strange bedfellows.

"I believed Jessie Carver was guilty three years ago, and my feelings haven't changed," Fiona told him. "The investigation into the Area Three Detective Division was never about Jessie's innocence. At least not for me."

Dylan started to say something else, perhaps to argue the finer points of her logic, but then he shrugged. "Believe it or not, I didn't come over here to start an argument with you."

"Yeah, well, that's sort of a fait accompli when you put a Gallagher and an O'Roarke in the same room." She picked up her briefcase and started walking toward the exit. "So what did you want to talk to me about?"

Dylan fell into step beside her. "Kaitlin wanted me to remind you about her father's retirement party."

Fiona rolled her eyes. "Honestly, how many times do she and my mother think they have to nag me about that?" Between the two of them, they must have called her half a dozen times in the past two weeks. It wasn't like she was senile, for Christ's sake.

"She's worried because evidently you forgot Erin's baby shower last month, and before that, it was Nikki's birthday party," Dylan helpfully pointed out.

"I explained all that."

"You were busy. Yeah, we all know how hectic your social life is, Fiona."

Screw you, she thought angrily.

"Look, I know you have quite the progressive attitude regarding family these days, but this retirement party is a big deal to Kaitlin. She sees it as a way to cement her reconciliation with her father, and she wants the whole family together. And in her condition, I'd rather not have her upset."

"I know it's a big deal," Fiona said impatiently. "I said I'd be there, and I will be. It's next week, right?"

"Fiona, it's tomorrow night."

She stopped dead in her tracks. "Tomorrow night? That's impossible." Where had the days gone?

"So I guess you did need another reminder after all."

Honest to God, if he smirked one more time—

"Oh, like you'd even be there yourself if it wasn't for Kaitlin," Fiona grumbled. Dylan and his father-in-law were hardly bosom buddies. Liam Gallagher had dis-

owned his daughter when he'd found out about her elope-
ment to Dylan, and had ordered her out of his house,
never to return until she came to her senses and divorced
that lowlife, scum-sucking O'Roarke.

Liam had only recently reconciled with the couple because Kaitlin was pregnant and he didn't want to be cut
off from his only grandchild.

Kaitlin was pregnant.

Could another baby shower be far off?

Fiona winced inwardly at the thought. The Gallaghers
were suddenly procreating like bunnies. Her brother, John,
and his wife, Thea, had had two sons in the space of six
years, in addition to Thea's daughter from a previous marriage. Her brother, Nick, and his wife, Erin—also an
O'Roarke—were expecting their first child any day now.
Fiona was happy for her brothers, she truly was, but seeing them with their families, all that love…

Even Tony and Eve, who still remained childless but
who couldn't keep their hands off each other, seemed
blissfully content. Who would have thought it? The conservative Eve Barrett paired with Tony Gallagher, the
hell-raiser. Fiona supposed that only went to prove that
there was someone out there for everyone.

Except her.

She was destined to be alone. Fated to remain childless,
husbandless, loveless. Her own fault, really. That was
what happened when you fell in love with a psychopath.
They didn't stick around for the long haul. Thank God.

She and Dylan walked out into the corridor, and Fiona
groaned when she saw the crowd gathered in front of the
elevators. "I'm taking the stairs," she muttered.

"Okay," Dylan said. "But if you don't show up for
the party and Kaitlin calls, you'd better tell her I delivered

the message. She's not exactly the easiest person to live with these days.''

Oh, cry me a river, why don't you? Kaitlin's the one who's pregnant. Fiona smiled sweetly. "I certainly wouldn't want to make your life any more difficult, Dylan. You tell my cousin I'll be there. With bells on.''

She left him in front of the elevators and headed for the stairwell. Judge Hartner's courtroom was on the seventh floor, and Fiona's three-inch heels were hardly made for walking, but what the hell? She'd lived dangerously before, why stop now?

Pushing open the door, she entered the stairwell and headed down the first flight of steps. Her heels clicked an even staccato on the concrete surface as she set herself a fairly brisk pace.

As she neared the bottom of the second flight, she heard the door above her open and then close with a soft thud. Footsteps tapped on the stairs overhead. Someone else hadn't wanted to wait for the elevators, either. Fiona thought it might even be Dylan, but she didn't wait for him. They'd said all that needed to be said, and she didn't want to get into another argument about Vince DeMarco or Jessie Carver or which local baseball team had the most loyal fan base, for that matter. She and Dylan could remain civil for just so long, and besides, everyone knew White Sox fans were almost rabid in their devotion. And Fiona should know, because she came from a long line of Sox fans. When she'd moved from Bridgeport to the Near North Side—Cubby territory—you would have thought she'd committed treason.

On the next landing, Fiona paused to adjust the strap on one of her sling backs. The stairwell went completely silent.

Odd, she thought, glancing up and over her shoulder.

She'd heard footsteps only moments earlier, but now she heard nothing, and she couldn't see anyone on the stairs above her. Maybe the person behind her had exited on the previous floor and she hadn't heard the door.

She continued down the stairs and almost immediately heard the unmistakable clap of shoes on concrete. Someone was still behind her, a man by the sound of his shoes, and he was keeping pace with her. Slowing when she slowed. Speeding up when she sped up. Stopping when she stopped.

Fiona halted abruptly on the next landing. The footsteps behind her paused.

A shiver ran up her spine. What the hell was going on?

She was more than a little uneasy by now. Stranded on the landing between floors, she had no choice but to either go up, where he was, or continue down to the next level and exit.

That was the thing to do. Get out of the stairwell ASAP. The guy was probably harmless, but Fiona couldn't help being spooked.

As she hesitated a moment longer, something moved above her, a shadow on the wall, and Fiona panicked. It was obvious to her now she was being followed.

She whirled and rushed headlong down the stairs. One of her heels caught on a step, almost tripping her, but as soon as she had her balance, she plunged toward the landing and the exit.

She grabbed the handle and pulled, but the door wouldn't budge.

Now why the hell would a stairwell door in a public building be locked in the middle of the day? Surely it was just stuck, Fiona thought desperately.

But as she gave the door another tug, the footsteps behind her sounded louder. He was getting closer...

Okay, this is stupid. Just open the damn door!

If it was stuck, a good strong yank should release it. If it was locked, she could pound until someone on the other side heard her.

All that would take at least a couple of minutes, however, and Fiona wasn't about to wait. She wasn't about to try and stay calm, either. What would be the point of that?

Abandoning the exit, she hurried down the next flight of steps. Every door on every level couldn't be locked or stuck, she told herself, but if she stopped to check, *he* would get closer. She couldn't take that chance, either. Besides, it was only another two flights to the lobby where there would be lots of people around, not to mention armed guards and cops waiting to testify in various courtrooms.

One more flight.

The footfalls behind her had sped up, trying to catch her, or was that her imagination? Was he still keeping pace with her?

Halfway there.

A few more steps.

At the bottom, Fiona jerked on the door with such force that it flew back and almost knocked her down. She righted herself and stumbled into the corridor.

The lobby was to her left, and she hurried toward it, turning to glance over her shoulder. The exit remained closed. No one had followed her out.

But she continued to watch the door until her shoulder collided with a helpless bystander. Fiona whipped around, gushing her apology. "I'm sorry. It was my fault. I wasn't watching where I was going—"

She stopped abruptly when she recognized the electric-blue eyes regarding her so intently.

"Are you okay?" Doggett asked her.

His hands were on her arms, and Fiona became aware of a warm, tingly sensation along her spine. Why did she suddenly feel a little too much like he'd just rescued her?

She frowned and stepped back from him. "I'm fine. Are you?"

His gaze flickered. "No harm done."

"What are you doing here?" she asked, for lack of a better question. She was still shaking off the last of her panic, and his sudden appearance had completely thrown her. She felt...tongue-tied. Unusual for her. Very unusual. "Are you testifying this afternoon? Or..." Her tone changed suddenly. She had an unpleasant thought. "Were you coming to lend your support to Vince DeMarco? If so, you're too late. Court's adjourned."

"I came here to see you. Your office said you were in court all morning." He glanced around. "Could we go somewhere and talk?"

"Have you found Lexi?" she asked anxiously.

He shook his head. "No, it's not about her. Someone else is handling the missing persons investigation. I'm here to talk to you about Alicia. I just came from the autopsy."

A cold chill shot through Fiona. "Let's go outside then. I could use some fresh air."

Actually, what she could really use was a drink, but given Doggett's reaction to her condition that morning, Fiona decided she'd just keep that little craving to herself.

THEY WALKED ALONG California toward Twenty-sixth Street, a busy avenue lined with billboards in both English and Spanish, advertising everything from lawyers and bail bondsmen to Empire Carpet and Mancow, a local radio personality.

Behind them, the fourteen-story administration building

and adjoining courthouse, along with the barbed-wire enclosed jail compound, loomed over the old Hispanic
neighborhood's crumbling brownstones and corner gro-
ceries. The area was impoverished and neglected, a haven
for the drug dealers and pimps who negotiated openly on
street corners.

Fiona, hiding behind dark glasses, seemed oblivious to
any danger. They strolled along in silence for a moment,
and Doggett covertly studied her from the corner of his
eye. She sure seemed different from the woman he'd
found half-smashed in her apartment this morning. Somehow, in the space of a few hours, she'd transformed herself into the cool, aloof prosecutor he'd read so much
about.

She was dressed in a gray suit with a light blue top
underneath, and her hair, a mess of wiry red curls earlier,
was now tamed with a silver clip at her nape. She was a
tall woman, but she wore heels, three-inchers at least,
which put her dead even with Doggett. But that was fine.
At six feet, he didn't have height issues. And he liked
high heels on women. He always had.

He caught a whiff of Fiona's perfume, and something
tried to stir to life inside him—desire, maybe—but he beat
it back with a cold dose of truth. Fiona Gallagher was
about as far out of his league as a woman could get. She
wasn't from a wealthy family, he knew that, but it wasn't
her background that put her out of his reach. It was the
woman. It was him.

"You were going to tell me about the autopsy," she
said quietly.

"Yeah." He tore his gaze away from her profile and
glanced at the street. "Other than the gunshot wound to
the head, which killed her, and the ligature marks around

her wrists, she didn't have any other injuries. And there was no sign of sexual assault.''

Fiona let out a breath. ''I'm glad about that. She's still dead, but somehow that would have been worse.''

''We're still waiting for the toxicology screen,'' Doggett said. ''That may tell us more.''

''What about time of death?''

''Somewhere between 10:00 p.m. and 1:00 a.m.''

''She was found just after two,'' Fiona mused. ''That was cutting it close. Are you sure the homeless guy who discovered the body didn't see something else? A car speeding away from the scene? *Anything?*''

''I've interviewed him a couple of times. His story hasn't changed.'' Doggett paused. ''One other thing you should know about. The murder weapon was a .40 caliber. The ME recovered the bullet from the body, but it's pretty mangled. I don't know how much the lab will be able to do with it.''

Fiona frowned. ''A .40 caliber semiautomatic is CPD's standard issue weapon. I remember when they changed from a .38. My brothers had a big discussion about it.''

Doggett gave her a sidelong glance. ''A lot of people own .40 caliber weapons. Doesn't mean a cop shot her.''

Fiona stopped and turned in surprise. ''I never said anything about a cop shooting her.''

''You weren't getting at that?''

Her mouth tightened. ''Seems to me you were the one who jumped to that conclusion. Which leads me to believe the possibility might already have crossed your mind, Detective Doggett.''

''Ray.''

''What?''

''My name's Ray.'' He shrugged. ''What the hell, we're going to be working together, right?''

She glanced away, as if she didn't much like the idea. "Okay, *Ray.* Let's get one thing straight." Her eyes were very blue in the sunlight. A darker, deeper blue than his. Irish blue. "Regardless of what you've read in the paper or heard from Frank Quinlan, I'm not trying to build a career or prove how tough I am by going after cops. The DeMarco case was dumped in my lap by my boss because he didn't have the guts to prosecute it himself. He hasn't made the announcement yet, but I know he plans to run for state's attorney when the current one steps down. Therefore, he couldn't afford to tick off the police department. He needs their support.

"Plus, I suspect he might not like some of the media attention I've been getting lately. The DeMarco case was his way of keeping me in my place in the event I decide to get a little too ambitious and challenge him in the primary.

"As for Quinlan, I didn't bring that lawsuit against him, nor was I responsible for the IAD investigation. All I did was cooperate. And do you know why I cooperated…? Not because I think those men are innocent. I don't. But if they could have proved Quinlan compelled their confessions, they would have walked. And if Quinlan did that to them, he could have done it to others. He could still be doing it. I didn't want murderers and rapists being put back out on the street because Quinlan wants to prove what a badass detective he is."

She paused and drew a breath. "I'm not the Iron Maiden. I'm not a crusader against police corruption. I don't hate cops. I'm just a prosecutor trying to do my job to the best of my ability."

Doggett stared at her for a moment, then turned his gaze to the street. "You hungry?"

"What?" Her tone was incredulous.

"Have you had lunch?"

She shook her head, as if trying to figure out where she'd missed something. Glancing at her watch, she said, "Yeah, I guess I'm hungry."

"There's a hot-dog stand a couple blocks up. Not exactly gourmet, but it's quick."

"I know the one you mean," she said. "I eat there all the time."

Now it was Doggett's turn to be incredulous. A tall, good-looking redhead who liked hot dogs was too good to be true. Now, if she was into baseball...

"You ever get nervous walking around out here like this?" he asked as they started up the street.

She gave him a look. "I'm with a cop. Why should I be nervous?"

"You aren't with a cop all the time," he said. "This is a pretty rough area."

She glanced around. "I don't even think about it anymore. I used to get spooked after dark, though, when I was assigned to the Night Narcotics Courts. The judges didn't start hearing cases until four o'clock in the afternoon and sometimes they went until after midnight. It was a pretty dicey situation for everyone involved. There wasn't any security personnel outside the courtrooms, and each judge was assigned only one deputy, who also had to retrieve prisoners from the lockup which meant there was no security at all in the courtrooms for a good portion of the time."

"Why'd you leave Narcotics?"

She shrugged. "Because trying homicide cases was the reason I joined the state's attorney's office in the first place. I started out as a defense attorney, but I wasn't cut out for that. Don't get me wrong, I believe in our criminal justice system. I believe everybody is entitled to the best defense possible, but…I couldn't do it. I couldn't give my all for a client I believed, deep down, was guilty.''

She was wrong, Doggett thought, listening to her. There *was* a bit of the crusader in her. Maybe she just didn't know it.

They walked up to the hot-dog stand and Fiona spoke to the attendant. "Hey, Manny. I'll have my usual.''

"Coming up. And you?''

Doggett placed his order and then when he and Fiona had their food and drinks, they found a nearby bench and sat down.

He watched as she peeled back the foil from her hot dog. "Everything but the kitchen sink,'' he said dryly. "It figures.''

She glared at him. "And what's that suppose to mean? You think you can glean some insight into my psyche because I like everything on my hot dog?'' She waited while he tore back his wrapper and then said, "Plain. Not even ketchup or mustard. What do you suppose that says about *you?*''

"That I'm a simple guy with simple tastes?''

Fiona's gaze held his. "Somehow I don't think you're quite as simple as you'd like me to believe.''

"I'm not all that complicated, Counselor.''

"Fiona.''

"What?''

"You can call me Fiona.'' She took a healthy bite of her hot dog and glanced away.

Fiona.

Doggett tested the name in his head. It suited her, with that red hair and those blue eyes. That pale, Irish complexion. Sitting this close to her in the sunshine, he could see freckles across her nose peeking through whatever she'd used to conceal them. He wondered, suddenly, what she would look like without any makeup…without any clothes. Her red hair loose and flowing over her shoulders—

Not going to happen. Not in this lifetime.

"Well," she finally said, oblivious to his fantasies. "I'd better get back."

"Look, before you go—" He turned and threw away his trash. "There was another reason I wanted to see you."

Something flickered in her eyes, something that might have been dread.

She's afraid I'm going to hit on her, Doggett thought. And if he'd ever been of the mind to do so, the notion died a premature and relatively painless death. The look in her eyes told him exactly what he needed to know. She was out of his league. Nothing surprising about that.

"What is it?" she asked cautiously.

"The Mercer girls' parents are in town. They flew in this morning, and I'm on my way over to the Coronet Hotel to interview them. I thought it might make it easier for them if you came along."

"It might," she agreed, but her expression was suddenly anguished as she turned to face him. "But what am I going to say to Lori? How am I going to tell her that Alicia called me last week, that she might still be alive if I'd called her back, but I just didn't have the time?"

"I figured you were still beating yourself up over that," he said quietly.

"It's something I'll always wonder about," she said with a hopeless shrug. "How can I not?"

CHAPTER EIGHT

THE PENTHOUSE ELEVATOR at the Coronet Hotel on State Street was about the size of Fiona's bathroom in her apartment, and a whole lot more glamorous. Everything about the hotel screamed money, the old kind.

It was small by chain hotel standards, with only fourteen stories, all elegantly decorated in rich shades of lapis, garnet and gold. The walls of the elevator were mirrored, and the floor was some exotic wood inlaid in the center with a coronet. That same coronet was gilded on the marble floor in the lobby, embossed in the heavy satin drapery at the windows, even stamped in the sand in every smoking receptacle.

The elevator glided to a stop on the penthouse floor, and Fiona and Doggett got out. Their steps were silenced by the plush carpeting, but their approach to the Guests' suite was closely monitored by a man in a dark suit who stood guard in the hallway. They showed him their identification, and he radioed their names to someone inside. In a matter of seconds, a man in an identical dark suit let them into the suite. He ushered them into a small, ornate sitting room, told them Mr. and Mrs. Guest would be out shortly, then disappeared.

After he was out of earshot, Fiona turned to Doggett. "Who are those guys? Not cops."

He glanced over his shoulder. "Private security. Paul

Guest is a big-shot attorney with a lot of connections, I hear. And he's loaded.''

Fiona remembered that Guest came from a wealthy family—shipping or oil tankers or something. She couldn't quite recall the specifics.

She looked around the lush suite and thought briefly that for a girl from Bridgeport who'd gotten knocked up at fifteen, Lori had done all right for herself. And then Fiona remembered that one of Lori's beloved twin daughters was dead and the other missing, and a fresh wave of guilt stole over her.

A door opened, and she turned as Lori drifted through, followed by her husband. Fiona barely glanced at Paul Guest. She couldn't take her eyes off Lori. She hadn't seen her since their lunch last fall, and Fiona remembered thinking at the time that the years had barely touched Lori. She was a slim, blond woman with the kind of smooth, dewy complexion and classic features that would still be just as fresh-looking and gorgeous when she turned sixty.

Today, however, she looked...ashen. That was the only way Fiona knew to describe her. She wore a gray dress for one thing, but it was her skin tone that was so appalling. She looked like a walking corpse, Fiona thought in shock.

Lori crossed the room and gave Fiona a perfunctory hug, but she almost immediately pulled away, as if she couldn't bear any kind of physical contact with another human being.

"I'm so sorry," Fiona whispered. "Lori...I'm so sorry."

Her blue eyes looked hard and brittle, as if they might shatter at any moment. "Just tell me you've found Lexi. Tell me that's why you're here."

Fiona shook her head. "I'm sorry."

Paul Guest came up to Lori and put an arm around her shoulders. He wore his black hair smoothed back from his forehead, highlighting thick, winged eyebrows. There was a touch of gray at his temples, lines around his mouth and eyes, but he was still an elegant, handsome man. He was tall, too, with muscles that seemed to bulge against the expensive fabric of his jacket.

"Come and sit down," he said to Lori, and he led her over to a silk settee upholstered in a delicate green and gold stripe. He kept his arm around her, but the gesture seemed wooden somehow, as if he were merely going through the expected motions. He'd raised Lexi and Alicia since they were fourteen, and Fiona supposed that he was as shell-shocked as their mother, or nearly so.

Doggett made the introductions. "I'm Detective Doggett. And you know Ms. Gallagher. She's the assistant state's attorney assigned to the case."

Paul Guest's gaze swept over her. "Yes, how are you, Fiona? Nice to see you again."

Did he really remember her? Fiona wondered. They'd only met a few times as she recalled. One time in particular stuck out in her mind, she thought with a sudden frown.

"I'm sorry to bother you at a time like this," Doggett was saying. "But we need to ask you some questions."

"Of course." Guest dropped his arm from his wife's shoulders. She didn't seem to notice. She sat staring at her hands.

"Mrs. Guest, when was the last time you spoke to your daughter?"

Lori glanced up. "Which one? I have two daughters, Detective Doggett."

"I'm asking about Alicia," he said gently. "Another detective is handling the missing persons investigation."

Guest's head snapped up. "Surely you don't expect us to go through this ordeal *twice*."

"I'm sorry," Doggett said. "But right now, we're treating the disappearance and the homicide as two separate investigations."

"You don't believe they're linked?" Guest queried.

"We don't know that yet. But I assure you, the investigations will be closely coordinated. If there is a link, we'll find it." Doggett trained his gaze on Lori. "When was the last time you spoke to Alicia?"

"Last week," she said in a flat, colorless voice. "I guess it must have been on Friday. I called early so that I could catch her and Lexi before they left for class. She said Lexi had already gone. Of course, I know now that Lexi didn't come home the night before, but Alicia didn't say a word to me."

"How did she sound?" Doggett asked. "Was she upset? Angry? Worried?"

"She didn't seem to be. I thought she was a little distracted," Lori said, "But I knew she was in a hurry to get to class. She never liked to be late. She was a very conscientious student." She glanced at Fiona. "She wanted to be a doctor. Did I tell you that?"

Fiona shook her head, and Lori looked away.

"Mrs. Guest, did Alicia ever mention any problems she might be having at school? Maybe a professor or another student that was giving her a hard time?"

"No. She seemed to enjoy all her classes."

"Do you know if she was seeing anyone? Did she have a boyfriend?"

Lori shook her head. "She's never been that interested in dating. She's always been extremely dedicated to her schoolwork."

"How well do you know your daughters' roommate?"

Lori looked surprised by the question. "Kelly? I've met her a few times when I've come up to see the girls. She seems nice enough. Why do you ask?"

"She indicated to me that Alicia and Lexi might have had some problems over a relationship that Lexi was involved in last semester."

Paul Guest made a jerky motion with his hand as he seemed to come alive all of a sudden. "What does that have to do with Alicia's murder? I thought you said you're treating the two…incidents as separate investigations."

"We are," Doggett said. "But as I mentioned, I'm not ruling out the possibility that the two cases are somehow linked. According to the roommate, Lexi's boyfriend insisted they keep their relationship a secret. She and Alicia had words about it."

"No, I don't believe that," Lori said almost angrily. "My girls never argued. They were always so close—" Her voice cracked and she buried her face in her hands.

Guest absently reached out and patted her shoulder, but he was looking at Fiona. She could have sworn she saw his gaze drop, very briefly, to her legs, and the notion made her stomach churn. She remembered now, with vivid clarity, why she'd never liked Paul Guest.

"Do you have any idea who this man might be?" Doggett asked them. "Did either of the girls ever mention anyone, even in passing, that might give us a hint who Lexi was seeing?"

"Are you implying this mysterious suitor of Lexi's could have had something to do with Alicia's death?" Guest asked. "How?"

"We won't know that until we find him." Doggett's gaze never wavered from Paul Guest's. If the high-powered attorney was used to intimidating the police of-

ficers he came into contact with in Houston, Doggett must
have been an unpleasant surprise to him.

"Why didn't Kelly say anything to me about this
man?" Lori asked suddenly, her features composed once
more. "I spoke to her this morning. I asked her point-
blank if she knew who might have done this terrible thing,
but she said she didn't have a clue. She didn't say anything about a man Lexi was involved with—" Her husband had turned to stare at her, and Lori broke off when
she saw his face. She looked almost stricken, as if she
might have said something she shouldn't have, but then
defiance flashed across her face. She said very softly, "I
called Kelly from the plane and again from the limo. I
needed to know if there'd been any word on Lexi, and I
couldn't reach you," she said accusingly.

"Wait a minute," Doggett said. "The two of you didn't
fly up together?"

Lori stared at her husband a moment longer before she
turned back to Doggett. "No. Paul was already in
Chicago."

It was like a bomb had exploded inside the hotel room.
In the aftershock, everything went dead silent. Then Paul
Guest said a little too smoothly, "I flew up on Monday
morning. Didn't I say that? My firm has an office here."

"So you must come to Chicago often," Doggett said.

Fiona could almost hear the wheels turning inside his
head.

Guest shrugged. "A few days every month or so."

"Did you see your stepdaughters whenever you came
to town?"

"Sometimes, but not always. They were college fresh-
men, Detective. They didn't have a lot of time for me,
but we'd occasionally have dinner. And I always called
when I was here."

"Did you see either of the girls during this trip?"

He shook his head. "I flew up yesterday morning, and I was in meetings all day. I didn't get back here until nearly ten o'clock, and I was exhausted. I fell asleep almost instantly. I didn't have a clue anything was wrong until Lori's call woke me up early this morning."

Their voices drifted away for a moment as Fiona glanced around the suite. She could see signs now that someone had been there longer than a few hours. Dirty glasses on the bar. Papers spread across a table near a window. An open briefcase.

She returned her gaze to Lori. What was it she'd said earlier? *I called her from the plane and again from the limo. I needed to know if there'd been any word on Lexi, and I couldn't reach you.*

She'd just found out hours before that one daughter was dead and the other was missing, and her husband, already in Chicago on business, hadn't seen fit to meet her plane.

Fiona's disgust for Paul Guest was suddenly so strong that it took all her self-control to keep her facial expression neutral. How could anyone be so insensitive? And where the hell had he been that Lori couldn't reach him when she needed him so badly?

"Just a couple more questions," Doggett said, removing a photo from his pocket. He handed it to Paul Guest. "Do you recognize this symbol?"

Fiona couldn't see the picture, but she knew it was a close-up shot of the trident on Alicia's left shoulder. She and Doggett had discussed the possible significance of it on their way to the hotel.

Guest glanced up with a frown. "What is this?"

"It was on your daughter's left shoulder when she was found. Do either of you know if that symbol has any special significance? Maybe to a sorority or something like that?''

Lori all but snatched the photo from her husband's fingers. She stared down at the symbol, one hand going to her mouth before she looked up. "Oh, my God. Don't you see what this means?''

"What does it mean?" Doggett asked quietly.

A fiercely stubborn hope appeared in Lori's eyes. "Alicia wasn't the type of girl who would ever get a tattoo. This has to mean there's been some kind of mistake. This isn't Alicia. It can't be.''

Oh, God, Fiona thought. Oh, dear God, this was a million times worse that she'd thought it would be.

Doggett said beside her, "Maybe I didn't make myself clear. If this is a tattoo, it's a temporary one. It washes off with soap and water.''

"But—"

"I'm sorry," he said. "But there's no mistake. Alicia's fingerprints were on file with the university.''

Fiona had never seen anything as horrible as having to watch the hope die in her friend's eyes. Lori's face became rigid again, as if even the tiniest fracture in her shaky poise would cause her to break into a million pieces.

"Mrs. Guest, I know how difficult this must be for you, and I'm sorry to have to put you through this. But I have to ask these questions.''

She nodded, but her bottom lip trembled violently.

Doggett paused. "Did Alicia ever try to impersonate her sister?''

"You mean, dress like her?" Paul Guest asked.

"Did she ever try to pass herself off as Lexi? Did people ever mistake her for her sister?''

"Oh, God. Oh, my God.'' If possible, Lori's face went

even whiter. Her expression crumpled, and she jumped to her feet. "I can't do this anymore. I'm sorry—"

She turned and rushed from the room, and Paul Guest got to his feet as well. "As you can see, my wife is very distraught. I'm sorry, but we'll have to continue this later."

"I just have a couple more questions for you," Doggett said.

Guest looked as if he wanted to refuse, but Fiona rose before he could object. "I'd like to speak to Lori alone if I may." She didn't wait for his permission, but brushed quickly by him. At the bedroom door, she knocked, then opened it a little. "Lori? May I come in?"

No answer. No sound of any kind. Fiona thought for a moment that Lori might have gone straight through to another room, but then she saw her curled in the fetal position on the bed, and Fiona put a hand to her mouth. Did she really want to do this?

Before she lost her nerve, she walked across the room and sat down on the edge of the bed. "God, Lori. I don't even know what to say to you."

She wasn't crying. In the dim light of the bedroom, Fiona could see that her friend's eyes were dry, her expression frozen. She seemed to be staring at nothing.

"If there's anything I can do…" Fiona said helplessly

Lori sat up so suddenly, Fiona almost jumped. She gripped Fiona's arms almost violently. "There's nothing you can do. There's nothing anyone can do. Don't you understand? Doesn't anyone understand? My daughter is dead, and it's all my fault."

Fiona winced in pain. "It's not your fault, Lori. You can't blame yourself for this."

Lori seemed to collect herself then, and she dropped

her hands to her sides. "If I'd never allowed them to come to Chicago, none of this would have happened."

"You couldn't protect them forever. This is not your fault."

She shook her head, obviously still in shock. "They're gone, Fiona. Lexi, too. I know it. I can feel it."

"Listen to me, Lori. There is a very good chance that Lexi is okay. We won't give up until we find her. Maybe she just went away for a few days. The news about Alicia hasn't broken yet so she'd have no way of knowing."

Something flickered in Lori's eyes, but Fiona wasn't sure it was hope. "Do you really believe that?"

Fiona nodded. "I think it's very possible. Kelly Everhardt said that Lexi has a history of going off without letting anyone know where she was. She sometimes went away with her boyfriend for days at a time. Maybe that's where she is now."

"Her...boyfriend." Lori said the word as if she didn't quite comprehend it. "I never knew," she said numbly. "I never suspected a thing."

"Girls don't always confide in their mothers," Fiona said. "Maybe Lexi didn't want to worry you."

"It doesn't matter now. Nothing matters now." Lori turned to stare out the window. But what she was seeing, Fiona had no idea. "They're both lost to me forever."

"There's still hope."

"You're wrong, Fiona. There's no hope. Not for me."

"HOW WELL DO YOU KNOW Paul Guest?" Doggett asked Fiona in the car as they were headed back to the courthouse.

Fiona turned from the window she'd been staring out. "Not well at all. I met him a few times before he and Lori were married, and a couple of times since."

"What kind of relationship do they have? Any idea?"

"No, not really. I know it was a pretty whirlwind court-ship. They'd only known each other a few weeks when they got engaged. Lori was head over heels in love with him. She didn't have any reservations about marrying him and moving to Houston."

"What about you?"

"What about me?"

"I sense you had reservations for her."

Fiona sighed. "Like I said, I only met him a few times before they married, but there was this one time... actually, it was before he and I were formally introduced. Lori had asked me to meet them at a restaurant near where we worked. I got there early and decided to wait in the bar."

Doggett flashed her a look, but Fiona ignored it. "A guy approached me. He was pretty aggressive, but he didn't really say anything out of line. I wasn't even sure he was coming on to me, but he made me very uncom-fortable just the same. And then in walks Lori, puts her arms around him, and says something about the two of us meeting before she had a chance to introduce us. It was pretty awkward, at least for me, but Paul just shrugged and said something like, 'Yeah, well, you told me to look for a tall redhead.'"

Doggett glanced at her. "So you think he knew who you were all along and was just yanking your chain?"

"I don't know. I never knew. But it left a bad taste in my mouth."

"You didn't say anything to Lori about it?"

Fiona shook her head. "No. I mean, how could I? I knew he would have said what you just did. He was just kidding around, and Lori was so crazy about him, she would have believed him. And besides, maybe I imagined that he was coming on to me. I didn't want to say anything to Lori because she was so happy and because..." Fiona frowned. "Okay, this is going to sound a little shallow, but Lori and her parents had struggled financially for years, and Paul Guest was loaded. He wasn't just a successful attorney, he came from a wealthy family. I thought a little security might be nice for Lori and the girls."

Doggett shot her another glance. "Even if the guy was a real asshole?"

"It sounds bad when you put it like that," Fiona admitted.

She had a feeling she wasn't looking too good in Doggett's eyes at that moment, and she wasn't sure why it bothered her so much.

Okay, maybe she did know. She hadn't been able to forget the look of disgust on his face when he'd found her drinking, and now this. Fiona couldn't help wondering if she was the kind of woman a man like him couldn't stand. A woman too caught up in her own problems and her own life to worry too much about anyone else.

That might have been true at one time, but Fiona liked to think that she'd changed, outgrown the self-absorption she'd plunged into after the debacle with David Mackenzie. Wasn't that why she'd become a prosecutor? To look beyond herself?

Yeah, yeah, we all know how noble you are, Fiona, a little voice taunted her.

So long as being noble didn't put her out any.

CHAPTER NINE

"LADIES AND GENTLEMEN of the jury, have you reached a verdict?"

At the sound of the judge's voice the next morning, excitement shot through Fiona's bloodstream. She was always on pins and needles at this stage of a trial. She tried to swallow away her nerves as she stared at the foreman, trying to divine the jury's decision.

They'd deliberated for nearly seven hours the day before, and at six o'clock when they still appeared hopelessly deadlocked, Judge Hartner had sent them home for the night with a stern warning not to discuss the case with anybody.

Their deliberations had continued for another three hours this morning, and Fiona had begun to worry about the possibility of a hung jury. But just before noon, Milo had stuck his head inside the conference room where she'd sequestered herself to prepare for her next trial, and announced that the jury was in.

Kimbra sat stiffly beside her, her shoulders tensed, her eyes staring straight ahead and not at the jury foreman who rose to answer the judge's question.

"We have, your honor."

Fiona's stomach knotted.

"Will the defendant please rise?"

Vince DeMarco and his attorney stood as one and faced the jury. Fiona's heart started to pound. Win or lose, the whole proceeding never failed to inspire her. She'd spoken the truth yesterday when she'd told Doggett that she believed passionately in the criminal justice system. For all its flaws, it was still the best in the world.

She held her breath as the jury foreman spoke. "We, the jury, find the defendant, Vincent Mario DeMarco, not guilty."

Not unexpected, but the lengthy deliberations had given Fiona a small glimmer of hope. Hearing the actual words read into the silent courtroom was like a well-placed fist to her solar plexus. The air seemed to rush from her lungs.

Kimbra turned to Fiona, her doe eyes wide with shock. "He got off."

Across the aisle, DeMarco and Dylan O'Roarke shook hands before DeMarco turned to his comrades who were eagerly waiting to congratulate him. Out of the corner of her eye, Fiona saw Frank Quinlan pump his fist in the air.

On the other side of Kimbra, Milo swore viciously.

"He got off," Kimbra repeated. When Fiona still didn't respond, Kimbra waved a hand in front of Fiona's face. "Y'all deaf or what? Didn't you hear? He got off."

Fiona tried to rouse herself from her stupor. "Kimbra, I'm sorry. But I told you from the first, there were no guarantees. No one can predict what a jury will do—"

"He's gonna kill me, and that's all you can say? Ain't no guarantees? I already *knew* that. I didn't have to go through all this bullshit to learn that, Miss Lawyer."

She was starting to sound a little hysterical, and Fiona didn't know how to calm her. Before she could even try, Kimbra jumped up and rushed from the courtroom.

Milo gave Fiona a sympathetic shrug. "Hey, we gave it our best shot."

"Did we?"

"Damn right we did. This was a tough case from the

beginning. Without forensic evidence, it was Kimbra's word against DeMarco's and she didn't exactly help the cause with her attitude, so don't let her lay a guilt trip on you now."

Easy for him to say. Fiona had been educated by the nuns at St. Anne's. Guilt was her middle name.

She stuffed her notes into her briefcase, trying to ignore DeMarco as he and his cohorts carried on at the back of the courtroom. Instead she watched the jurors file out of the courtroom, each of them careful not to make eye contact with her. Which was fine by her. She didn't really want to look at them, either.

"He's gonna kill me, and that's all you can say?"

"So," Milo said as he ran a hand through his hair. "Do you want to go back to the office and do a little Monday morning quarterbacking?"

"I don't think I have the stomach for it right now," she said with a grimace. "I think I'll go for a walk, try to clear my head."

He nodded and smiled. "Hey, don't beat yourself up over this, okay? You did everything you could."

Maybe, maybe not, Fiona thought as she stared at the now empty jury box. At some point, she and Milo would have to go over the details of the case, analyze their strategy, figure out where they might have gone wrong. Guy Hardison would want a full accounting as well.

But for now, Fiona needed a little time and distance before she could become objective, before she could turn philosophical. She could feel the anger starting to churn away inside her, and the last thing she wanted to do was take her frustration out on the wrong person.

So she'd stay away from the office for now. She'd go for a walk. Have a hot dog. Give herself a little time to calm down.

Actually, what she really wanted to do, she realized, was talk to Kimbra. To somehow make the girl understand that bad things happened to good people, and in a perfect world, the criminal justice system would make things right.

But this wasn't a perfect world, and just because the verdict hadn't gone their way didn't mean what they'd done in the courtroom wasn't important. Kimbra had taken a stand, and she should feel proud.

"He's gonna kill me, and that's all you can say?"

KELLY EVERHARDT LOOKED PALE when she answered her door that morning. She was dressed in jeans and a blue T-shirt with the name of a local restaurant embroidered across the left breast pocket. Her dark hair was neatly pulled back into a ponytail, and her face was devoid of makeup except for a touch of lipstick.

"I'm Detective Doggett." He showed her his ID. "I spoke with you yesterday morning."

"Yes, I remember you." She rubbed her hand up her arm, as if she were suddenly chilly. "What can I do for you?"

"I need to ask you a few more questions."

A frown flitted across her brow. "I was just on my way out. I have to get to work."

"I'll try not to take too much of your time."

She stepped back with a weary sigh and motioned him inside. "I don't know what else I can tell you."

"You'd be surprised what you sometimes remember after the initial shock wears off." Doggett motioned to a small dining table that was placed in front of a sliding glass door. "Okay if we sit?"

She shrugged and led the way. Once they were seated,

he took out his notebook. "I understand you've met Alicia and Lexi's parents."

"A few times."

"Their stepfather, Paul Guest, has an office here in Chicago. He says he comes to town every month or so on business."

She shrugged. "I don't know much about his business. He's an attorney, I think."

"Did he ever come by the apartment when he was in town?"

"Once or twice. Most of the time he just met Lexi at a restaurant."

"Just Lexi? Not Alicia?"

She shook her head. "I don't think they got along."

"What makes you think that?"

"When he called, Alicia always made some excuse why she couldn't see him. She'd say she was busy or had to study or something. I got the impression she didn't like him, but it was no big deal. Lots of people don't like their stepfathers."

Doggett had a feeling she might be speaking from personal experience.

He watched her carefully. She was an interesting girl. Attractive, but not drop-dead gorgeous like the Mercer twins. She wasn't overweight, but by today's standards, he supposed she would be considered a little plump. Her face was round and full, and her eyes were amazingly dark, almost black.

She glanced at her watch. "I'm sorry, but I really do have to get to work. I'm not rich. I can't afford to get fired. I really need this job."

Was that resentment in her voice? "Just a few more questions. How did you meet Alicia and Lexi?"

"My two previous roommates both graduated last

year," she said impatiently. "I do some reporting for the college paper so I was able to run an ad for free. Alicia and Lexi answered it."

"You didn't have reservations about rooming with sisters?"

Her dark gaze met his, and for a moment, Doggett wondered if she knew what he was really getting at. *You didn't have a problem rooming with two women as beautiful as they were? And as rich?*

"I didn't mind it at first. It solved all my problems. I couldn't afford a place like this on my own, and they were glad to find it. Housing this near the university is almost impossible to come by."

"Did they get along?"

"With each other? Yeah, I guess." She paused. "It was actually kind of weird. At first, they went everywhere together. You never saw one without the other. And then Lexi started making some friends, pulling away. That's when the trouble started."

"What kind of trouble?"

Kelly lifted her ponytail off her neck. "Alicia wasn't exactly the social type, if you know what I mean. She relied a lot on Lexi. When Lexi wanted to do something with her friends, Alicia got pissed."

"Did they argue about it?"

"Not about that. Not until Lexi hooked up with some guy. That's when Alicia really turned mental."

"Mental?"

"She'd get mad," Kelly clarified.

"And you said this guy's name was never mentioned?" When Kelly shook her head, Doggett persisted. "What about where he worked? Did you ever see a number on the Caller ID? Ever get a look at his car?"

"No, they were always pretty careful about that sort of

thing. He never picked her up here. She always met him somewhere else, and he only called her on her cell phone.''

''So Lexi and Alicia fought about this guy?''

She grimaced. ''Yeah. It got really heavy when Lexi started going away with him. It was just a weekend here and there at first, but then sometimes she'd stay away for days at a time, skipping classes. Alicia tried to cover for her, but she'd really be mad when Lexi got home. And she'd bug Lexi constantly about where she'd been and who'd she'd been with. I mean, she was *relentless*. She just never let up. I don't think Lexi ever meant to tell her anything, but they were having a major blowup one day when she let it slip that the guy was married. I thought Alicia would go ballistic.''

Not exactly the serene picture of sisterly love their mother had tried to paint, Doggett observed. ''Did they ever get violent with each other?''

''Not that I know of, except…well, there was this one time.'' Kelly paused, her gaze darkening. ''I came home from work late one night, and I guess Lexi had just gotten back from being with this guy. She and Alicia were in her bedroom, really going at it. I heard something break, like maybe stuff was being thrown. Then everything got real quiet, and Alicia said something like, 'If Mother ever finds out, it'll kill her. How could you do this, Lexi?' And then Lexi started crying. It was a pretty bad scene. I just left and drove around for a while, and when I came home, everything seemed okay.''

''You mean they'd made up?''

She shrugged. ''I guess. They acted as if nothing had ever happened. They were good at that. They were both good at hiding things, too. Alicia told me later that Lexi had agreed to break up with her boyfriend, and Alicia was pretty happy about that. Everything went back to normal for a while, but when they came back from Christmas break, something was definitely wrong. I don't know what happened, but Lexi avoided Alicia whenever she could. She started hanging out with me. She seemed really interested in my journalism courses, so I took her with me to the paper one day. She got an assignment right on the spot.''

Kelly paused again, her gaze slipping away from Doggett's. ''A freshman being assigned a major story is pretty unusual. I had to work for two years as nothing but a glorified—'' She broke off, her gaze meeting Doggett's once more. ''But that's life, right? You look like Lexi Mercer, you get to cut through the bullshit.''

''What kind of story was she working on?''

''I don't know. It was some kind of hush-hush project she and Nick cooked up.''

''Nick?''

''Nick Grable. He's the editor-in-chief.''

The tone of her voice changed very subtly, and Doggett thought, *There's something here. Something she doesn't want me to know about.*

''Anyway, after she got the assignment, she started staying out late again. Sometimes she wouldn't come home until the next morning. She said she was working on an important story for the paper, but Alicia didn't believe her. She thought Lexi was into her married boyfriend again, and when Lexi didn't come home last Thursday night, Alicia was furious. She went out looking for them.''

''Where did she go?''

Kelly shrugged. ''I don't know. I think she'd already figured out who the guy was, but she wouldn't tell me. She just said she was going to put a stop to the relationship one way or another. But I guess someone stopped her first.''

"What about Lexi's clothes? Anything missing from her room?''

"I wouldn't know. She and Alicia both have so much stuff, it'd be impossible to tell if anything's missing. But Lexi's the impulsive type. If she got a wild urge, she wouldn't bother packing. She'd just take off.''

"One last question.'' Doggett shoved a photo across the table toward Kelly. "Have you ever seen this symbol?''

She stared down at the picture and started to shake her head, then paused. "Maybe. Yeah, I think so.''

"Do you remember where?''

She picked up the picture and gave it a closer scrutiny. "Hold on a second.'' She left the room for a few minutes, and when she returned, she handed Doggett a manila envelope.

The pictures inside were violent and graphic. The victim was a young, female Caucasian, and for a moment, Doggett thought that Kelly had somehow gotten her hands on Alicia Mercer's autopsy photographs. But then he realized the victim was a woman he'd never seen before. She had the same general coloring, the same basic look as Alicia Mercer, but the date stamped on the photo was over a year old.

He rifled through the shots until he found the one he knew Kelly had meant for him to see. It was a close-up of a trident tattoo on the woman's left shoulder.

He glanced up. "Where did you get these?''

Kelly looked suddenly worried, as if she'd done something impulsive that she was already regretting. "They're Lexi's.'' She moistened her lips.

"Where did she get them?'' When the girl refused to

answer, Doggett said in a low, hard voice, "Withholding information from a homicide investigation is a serious offense. You know that, right?"

Kelly closed her eyes briefly. "Nick gave the photos to Lexi, okay? They have something to do with the story the two of them were working on, but that's all I know. He called me on Sunday morning before I drove up to my parents' house and asked me to look for them in Lexi's room. I was supposed to drop them by the paper yesterday as soon as I got back in town. But after I found out about Alicia, I forgot all about them."

"Where were they when the police searched the apartment?"

"In my car."

"Do you know who this girl is?"

She shook her head. "I've never seen her before."

Doggett stared down at the photos. Whoever she was, the victim was very blond, very beautiful and very dead.

Just like Alicia Mercer.

DeMarco and his buddies had taken their celebration into the hallway. Fiona saw them as she exited the courtroom, and heard their laughter follow her down the hallway. Someone fell into step beside her, and she knew it was DeMarco.

When she glanced at him, he smiled that sly, cruel smile that always reminded her of a child who'd whiled away a pleasant afternoon torturing small animals.

He was tall and lanky, deceivingly guileless with a lock of dark hair spilling over his forehead. But there was something menacing about the way he carried himself, something sinister lurking in his cold, dark eyes. Why hadn't the jury been able to see that?

He stuck out his hand. "Just wanted to say no hard feelings."

Fiona would rather die than touch him. "Get away from me," she said through clenched teeth. "And stay the hell away from my client."

"Who, Kimbra?" He cocked his head. "Don't worry. I'm not holding a grudge against her, either. Maybe I should go look her up and let her know."

His words sounded innocent enough, but Fiona heard the insinuation in his tone, the underlying threat. An uncontrollable rage swept over. She turned suddenly and lunged toward him.

The move caught him off guard and he stumbled back, a stunned look on his face. Someone grabbed Fiona's arm and pulled her back. "Are you crazy?" Dylan whispered furiously in her ear. "Get a grip, for God's sake."

Embarrassed to have been caught off guard, DeMarco quickly shrugged his shoulders as he straightened his jacket. "Bitch is crazy," he said to Dylan. "She better watch her herself, or I'll have her ass up on assault charges."

"I never touched you," Fiona said coldly.

"Sure you did. You attacked me. If my own attorney hadn't held you back, no telling what you'd have done." He glanced at Dylan who still gripped Fiona's arm. "What about it, Dylan? We got a lawsuit here or what? At the very least, we can get her disbarred, right?"

Dylan said roughly, "Get out of here, Vince."

"Hey! I'm the injured party here!"

Dylan led Fiona away from the crowd of onlookers who'd gathered to gawk at the spectacle. "What's the matter with you?" he said angrily. "He's right, you know. He probably could get you disbarred."

"I never touched him," Fiona said in outrage.

"And it'll be your word against about a dozen cops. Jesus, Fiona. What were you thinking?"

"I wasn't thinking, obviously. And by the way, thanks for coming to my rescue," she said grudgingly.

"Yes, well, I'm sure I'm the last person you want to be indebted to."

"I can't believe they let him off," she said numbly.

Dylan frowned. "Come on. A part of you had to know they would. Without forensic evidence, it was a lousy case, and you know it. It never should have come to trial. Hardison suckered you into that one."

"I could have said no. But I believed then, and I still do, that DeMarco's guilty as hell. And now I'm afraid he'll go after Kimbra again."

"I'll talk to him."

"And you think that'll do the trick?" Fiona gave a bitter laugh. "Your client's a psychopath, Dylan. A slap on the wrist isn't likely to deter him."

"And I guess you'd know all about psychopaths, wouldn't you, Fiona?"

CHAPTER TEN

FOR DECADES, NORTH AVENUE stood as an invisible wall between Wells and Halstead Streets, a line of demarcation that no one dared cross. To the north, the wealth and privilege of Lincoln Park. To the south, the crime and poverty of Cabrini-Green.

Cabrini was the kind of place tourists were warned not to go to after dark. Chicagoans didn't go there at all unless they lived there. The violence of the neighborhood was so infamous a decade ago that it had become the setting of a popular horror flick.

When Fiona was in high school, she and a couple of her girlfriends took what they thought was a shortcut home from the North Side one night and ended up in Cabrini. She couldn't remember now where they'd been that night or what made them venture into such an unfamiliar part of the city, but when their car died at the corner of Clybourn Avenue and Division Street, she'd known immediately they were in trouble.

Glancing around at the neglected park across the street, the menacing high-rises that loomed against the darkened sky, it had seemed as if they'd strayed into some strange new world.

The auto club wouldn't even send a tow truck into the neighborhood, so Fiona had been forced to call her father, a lieutenant at the time with CPD. He'd arrived with backup. One of the more mechanically inclined police officers had quickly raised the hood on Fiona's car and got to work while the other two kept an uneasy watch for an ambush.

Fiona had never been so frightened in her life, and she'd never seen her father so angry. "Are you crazy? Are you trying to get yourself killed? Do you know what this place is? You're in Cabrini, for God's sakes. *Cabrini.*"

He might as well have said, "You're in hell," because that was certainly the implication.

Times had changed, though Cabrini was still a dangerous place, but in the past few years, parts of the neighborhood had undergone a metamorphosis. Seward Park had been cleaned up, and some of the high-rises were coming down. On Division Street, a new Blockbuster Video and a Starbucks had been built on a patch of land once occupied by battered basketball hoops, and Fiona could see a construction crane just east of the elevated tracks where a new subdivision was going up.

But the cars that passed her—a Lexus, a BMW and a brand-new Land Rover—as she drove along Larrabee seemed to signal the forced changes in the neighborhood even more vividly than the construction and fresh paint.

Maneuvering her own seven-year-old Audi through the heavy traffic, she drove past the redbrick high-rises where snipers had once picked off two off-duty Chicago cops one sultry summer evening, past the fast-food restaurants, past a dark green Chevy pulsing with rap music at the curb.

Children of the Night, the shelter for runaway teens run by Rachel Torres, was located just off Larrabee, on a shady side street that came to a dead end at the next block.

Fiona parked at the curb and made sure her car was locked before hurrying up the cracked sidewalk. Someone whistled from behind her, and when she didn't turn, a voice called across the street, "Yo, baby, whatup? Ya'll one *fine* lookin' bitch. Mmm, mmm, mmm. Red's my color, baby. Looks real good on me."

Welcome to the 'hood, Fiona thought and kept walking toward the shelter. But the come-on was no more or less offensive than the pickup lines she'd heard from some of the highest paid defense attorneys in the city. Not to mention a few judges she knew of.

And don't even get me started on cops.

The long, one-story building had once been a medical clinic that had seen its fair share of stabbings, beatings, and gunshot wounds in its heyday. Now, a decade later, the shelter still retained the clinic's institutional appearance with its antiseptic walls, beige tile floors, and a long, narrow hallway that split the building in two.

To the right, as Fiona entered, was a large gathering room where runaway girls seeking temporary shelter could watch TV, listen to music or sit in a quiet corner and reflect. Down the hallway, closed doors led to what Fiona knew from her previous visits were the bedrooms—cramped, featureless cubicles lined with cots and bunk beds. The rooms afforded nothing in the way of privacy, but they provided something far more important. A haven. A safe night's sleep off the streets.

Rachel's glass-enclosed office was down the hall and to the left. As Fiona started toward it, her gaze was drawn, as it always was, to the dozens of flyers lining the concrete block corridor, known by the girls who came to the shelter as The Wall. The photocopied pictures on the handouts were all different, and yet there was a heart-breaking sameness to the captions: Missing. Have You Seen This Girl?

Someone rapped on the glass behind her, and Fiona

turned. Rachel Torres, phone pressed to her ear, motioned her inside the office and then waved her to a chair.

Rachel was a pretty brunette with sparkling brown eyes and a truly spectacular smile. But her true appeal, Fiona had always thought, was an inner wisdom and strength that complemented her boundless energy. Rachel was fiercely dedicated to what most would consider a thankless job, and deeply devoted to the girls who came to her in trouble.

Once inside the shelter, they were provided clean clothes, a shower, a hot meal and a safe place to sleep, no questions asked. If they wanted to talk, Rachel was always available. If they wanted to call home, she gave them a phone. But the one thing she never did was judge them, and that was why they trusted her. That was why many of them came back night after night. In their eyes, she was one of them.

"Sorry that took so long," she said as she hung up the phone. She rolled her eyes. "Auditors. I think they get off on all those bureaucratic hoops they make us jump through to protect our nonprofit status. I've become quite adept at kissing all those lily-white asses over the years."

Fiona laughed. "And to think, when you were dating my brother in college, you were the hot-blooded hell-raiser who took no prisoners. I think you scared poor Nick half to death. He never knew what you were going to do next."

"Ah, yes, those were the days," Rachel said with a wistful sigh. "Moonlight rides in the back of a squad car, the earthy fragrance of the women's lockup, the midnight phone calls to Nick pleading for bail money. And your dad, that badass cop. Didn't he just love me hanging around one of his boys?"

"He's a little more philosophical now than he was then," Fiona said.

"And how about Nick? Did he ever learn to curb that temper of his?"

"Now that would be asking for too much," Fiona said dryly.

"Still," Rachel said a little wistfully. "I never thought he'd get married, but he did. And they're expecting a kid, I hear." She glanced up at Fiona. "So what's his wife like?"

"Erin's a real sweetheart. The whole family's crazy about her."

"Figures." Rachel shook her head. "And the last Gallagher bachelor bites the dust," she murmured.

"Well, not quite," Fiona said wickedly. "There's still my cousin, Miles."

"The narc?" Rachel quickly crossed herself. "Even *I'm* afraid of him," she said with a shudder. Then her gaze sobered as she regarded Fiona across the desk. "I heard about the verdict. I guess that's why you're here, right?"

Fiona felt that sinking sensation in her stomach all over again. "I'm looking for Kimbra. She was really upset when she left the courthouse. I was hoping she'd come here."

"I haven't seen her. Sorry."

"Do you think one of girls might know where she is?"

"Even if they did, they wouldn't tell you."

Fiona understood. There was an unspoken bond on the street. If someone didn't want to be found, her sisters wouldn't rat her out.

"You have all my numbers," Fiona said as she stood. "If you do hear from her and there's any way you can let me know she's all right without betraying her confidence, I'd be grateful.''

Rachel smiled. "I'll do my best."

"Thanks."

At the door, Rachel said, "Hey, tell Nick I said hello when you see him."

"I will." Fiona waved as she left the shelter and headed for her car.

As she reached the street, she heard rap music vibrating from broken speakers before she actually saw the green Chevy pull around the corner. As it drew even with the shelter, a loud bang, like the backfiring of the car's exhaust, caused Fiona to start violently, and for a moment, she remained frozen on the street, staring into the open windows of the car as it slowly drove past her.

Then something hit her in the back, hard enough to knock the breath from her lungs and send her sprawling to the street. Dimly she heard more shots, two or three at least, but she couldn't be certain. She was too busy gasping for air.

A voice behind her said anxiously, "Are you okay?"

She knew that voice. She was starting to hear that voice in her sleep. She turned her head gingerly and saw Doggett kneeling on the pavement beside her.

"Fiona, are you okay?" he asked again.

She couldn't speak, but it wasn't the shock or the fear that captured her voice. It was…the way he said her name. Fiona. Somehow the syllables seemed to roll up from his chest and vibrate from his vocal chords, sending a shiver of awareness up her spine.

"Are you hurt?"

She nodded.

"Jesus," he muttered. "Where?"

"M-my knees," she finally managed to stammer.

"You were shot in the knees?"

She started to turn over, but he put a hand on her shoulder. Fiona closed her eyes at the unwelcome sensation spiraling through her. She had to be delirious. Half-crazy with pain. Why else would Doggett be affecting her so...powerfully?

"Don't move," he warned. "We need to find out how badly you're hurt first."

She shrugged off his hand and rolled over, then sat up, inspecting her knees where the hide had been peeled away by the pavement.

"You skinned your knees? That's it?" Doggett ran a hand through his hair. "Shit. I thought you'd been hit."

"I was hit," she defended. "You hit me in the back."

"Shit," he said again. He turned away, as if he needed a moment to collect himself. Or to control his temper. Fiona wasn't sure which.

"What are you doing here anyway?" she asked as she struggled to her feet.

He gave her a hand. "Looking for you."

"Are you following me?"

Nine out of ten men would probably have made some lame excuse about being in the neighborhood. But Doggett just shrugged. "Yeah. And it took me awhile to catch up with you."

"How did you know where to find me?" she asked curiously.

"I called your office. Some guy named Milo told me you'd driven to the runaway shelter off Larrabee looking for a client. He was a little concerned about you, and with good reason." Doggett glanced around. "Not a great neighborhood for a woman alone."

Good thing she'd decided to call the office, Fiona thought. Of course, that depended on whether she considered Doggett showing up here was fortunate or not, and she hadn't decided about that yet. "I thought the area had changed. All the new construction—"

He shook his head. "Don't kid yourself. This is still Cabrini."

Rachel came out the front door then and hurried toward them. "I heard gunshots. Oh, God. Is anyone hurt? Fiona?"

"She skinned her knees," Doggett said dryly.

Rachel looked momentarily caught off guard. She glanced from Doggett to Fiona, then back to Doggett.

"Rachel, this is Detective Doggett. Rachel Torres. She runs the shelter."

"What happened to Ellen?" he asked.

"She left seven years ago," Rachel said, busy taking him in. All of him.

He seemed oblivious to her perusal. "It's been awhile since I worked this beat. Some things don't change, though." His gaze moved down the street, to where the Chevy had accelerated out of sight.

"Comes with the territory," Rachel said wearily. "Today was nothing, though. They were just trying to make some noise, let us all know this is still their turf. If the Cobras had wanted to kill someone, you'd both be wearing toe tags tonight."

Comforting thought. "Does this sort of thing happen often?" Fiona asked.

"Not as much as it used to." Rachel glanced down at Fiona's knees. "Are you sure you're all right? Come back inside and we'll put something on those scrapes."

"No, I'm fine. Look, you go back in," Fiona said. "It's probably not safe to be standing out here on the street like this."

"What about you?" Rachel asked.

"She was just leaving," Doggett said.

Fiona arched a brow. "I am?"

He nodded. "There's a coffee shop a few blocks east on Division. You'll see it. It has a big neon cup in the window. If you've got a minute, I'd like to talk to you."

She shrugged. "Sure. But why don't I just follow you over there?"

"I'll meet you there." His gaze scanned the street, then he turned to Rachel. "I'll get a beat car over here and make sure they do a drive-by every so often."

"What about the Chevy?" Fiona asked.

"What about it?"

"Aren't you going to go after it?"

His eyes glinted. "Nah. I gave up high-speed chases my last birthday."

THE LOCAL BANDS THAT PLAYED at Java Jazz, a sixties-style coffeehouse, drew large, hippylike crowds on Friday and Saturday nights, but on a late Wednesday afternoon, the place was nearly empty. Fiona ordered two cups of black coffee and carried them over to a table near the back. She took the seat facing the entrance, but when she saw Doggett come in, she switched places. She didn't know a cop alive who was comfortable sitting with his back to the door.

He sat down and she slid one of the foam cups toward him. "It's just plain black coffee. Hope that's okay."

"That's how I like mine. Simple tastes, remember?" He leaned over the table, as if to peer into her cup. "What, no double latte? No mocha frappuccino?"

She lifted her cup. "I guess I'm not as complicated as you thought."

He gave her the nearest thing to a grin she'd seen since

she met him. Fiona's stomach quivered crazily as their gazes held for a moment.

She still couldn't decide whether she found him attractive or not. In the light of day, his cheekbones were still too prominent, his eyes still that piercing blue. There were lines around his mouth and eyes, a harshness in his features that suggested his life as a cop hadn't been an easy one.

But there was something else in his face. A spark in his eyes that Fiona didn't often see in cops his age. Or maybe it wasn't so much what she saw as what she didn't see—that lazy indifference that suggested he was coasting to his pension. The bitterness and weary resolve of a man whose job had beaten him down. Doggett's eyes still had fire in them. He still liked being a cop. He still believed in what he was doing.

Amazing...

"You said back at the shelter that you used to work in the area." Fiona eyed him over the rim of her cup. "Did you work in the projects?"

He nodded. "My first assignment was driving a beat car in Cabrini."

"How long ago was that?"

"Almost twenty years ago."

"That must have been an eye-opening experience for a rookie," she said with a grimace. "How long did you work in Cabrini?"

"Five years."

"Five years in the baddest 'hood in the city," she murmured. "I'll bet you've got stories."

"A few." He smiled that little half grin that sent her pulse racing. "Don't worry. I won't bore you with them."

Okay, maybe he was a *little* attractive. He was definitely not boring. "Where did you go after you left Cabrini?" she asked curiously.

"Wentworth."

It took her a moment to translate. "Oh, shit. That's the Second District, right? The Deuce. Jesus, that must have been like jumping from the frying pan into the fire." The Second District was the smallest police district in the city, but it maintained the dubious honor, year after year, of having the highest crime rate. It was home to twenty blocks of high-rise projects, burned-out buildings, crack houses and some of the heaviest gang activity in the city.

Fiona took a sip of her coffee. "How long were you there?"

"Eight years, mostly with the tactical unit, and a couple of years in Gang Crimes."

She sat in silent awe. He'd worked the ghettos for a total of thirteen years, which meant he'd seen more violence and misery than most people could even imagine. And he still seemed, for the most part, *normal.* She looked at him with new respect.

"So what made you want to leave all that behind and become a detective?" she teased.

He shrugged, but his eyes glimmered with something that might have been amusement. "Every cop's dream is to be a homicide detective, right? That's where all the glory is. They don't write books or make movies about cops who drive beat cars."

Maybe they should, Fiona thought. Although she couldn't imagine a Hollywood-type getting it right, not unless he or she had walked in Doggett's shoes—and lived to tell it.

"All I can say is, you must like to live dangerously. I'm surprised you didn't decide to go into Narcotics. That's where the real adrenaline junkies go, right?"

He picked up his coffee. "I guess I'm not the thrill-seeking type. I just do my job."

Day in and day out. Fiona would bet he hadn't taken more than a couple of days sick leave the whole time he'd been on the force.

Not that it was any of her business. Not that any of this was her business. Doggett certainly wasn't her business, and maybe it would be better if they just...got down to business.

"So," she said briskly. "What did you want to see me about?"

If he noticed her abrupt shift, he didn't let on. "I wanted to talk to you about Lori and Paul Guest." He frowned. "I'm getting some bad vibes, especially from the stepfather."

"Yeah, I could tell after the interview yesterday that you had some serious reservations about him."

Doggett folded his arms on the table. "It bothers me that he didn't tell us right up-front he was in town when Alicia was murdered. I got the impression he wouldn't have said anything if his wife hadn't given him away. Tell me something." His gaze deepened. "What would you do if you got a call from your spouse telling you that one of your stepdaughters had been murdered and the other one was missing? The same girls you'd supposedly raised as your own? Wouldn't you rush over to their apartment to see if you could find out what the hell was going on? Wouldn't you be out combing the streets looking for your missing kid?"

"Maybe he did go out looking for her," Fiona suggested.

"He didn't go to the apartment. There were cops all over the place. No one saw him."

Fiona studied her coffee for a moment. "You know

what bothers *me* the most? Lori flew into Chicago alone and he couldn't even make time to meet her flight? Now that's cold.''

"I agree. And I wouldn't say he was exactly torn up with grief. Would you?''

"No, but to be fair, people react to tragedy in different ways.''

"Maybe.'' Doggett shrugged, but Fiona could tell he wasn't convinced. "I'm going to do some checking, talk to a buddy of mine on the force down in Houston. But it'll have to be on the QT. I've already caught some heat for the interview yesterday, and if this guy lawyers up, we'll never get near him.''

Fiona frowned. "Why would you catch heat for interviewing the parents? It's standard procedure to talk to the next of kin. Paul Guest is an attorney. He has to know it's routine.''

"I'm sure he does know. But he's making noises like we're focusing solely on the family, on *him*, while we let other leads go cold.''

"That's ridiculous. If you ask me, he's starting to sound a little paranoid.''

"Or nervous.''

The coffee suddenly tasted bitter in Fiona's mouth. "Do you really think he could have had something to do with Alicia's death?'' The thought was almost too horrible to contemplate, but it happened. Every day it happened.

Doggett glanced down, swirling the coffee in his cup. Instead of answering her question, he said, "I talked to the roommate again this morning. She said that Guest would sometimes call when he was in town and ask the girls to dinner, but Alicia would always find an excuse not to go. The roommate had the definite impression that Alicia didn't get along with him.''

"What about Lexi?"

"Evidently she and Guest were on friendly terms, but that's about all Kelly could tell me. She did say, though, that the rift between the sisters over Lexi's married boyfriend ran pretty deep. According to her, they almost came to blows. The tension got so bad in the apartment she thought about asking them to move out. But sometime before Christmas, Lexi agreed to stop seeing the guy, and her relationship with her sister improved."

"I had dinner with them before Christmas," Fiona said pensively. "I would never have guessed anything was wrong between them. They seemed as close as ever."

"Yeah, well, I get the impression both sisters were pretty good at hiding things."

"Apparently so." Fiona pushed her half-finished coffee aside. "Lori didn't seem to know anything about this guy Lexi was supposedly seeing, or about the problems it caused between her and Alicia."

"Maybe she just didn't want to see it," Doggett said.

"What do you mean?"

His gaze lifted. "People have a certain vision of the way they think their life should be. Or the way they want it to be. They tend to bury their head in the sand when something threatens that vision."

"You think Lori knows more than she's telling?"

"I think she's a mother who'll do or say anything to protect her children. Or her vision of them."

"She blames herself for what happened."

Doggett lifted a brow. "She said that?"

Fiona nodded. "She said if she hadn't let the girls come to Chicago, none of this would have happened." She paused. "I'm sure she was still in shock, but she seemed...fatalistic about Lexi being found safe. She kept muttering something about both her girls being lost, and there was no hope for her." Fiona shivered. "God, I feel so sorry for her."

She paused, then glanced up a Doggett. "Do you think Lexi's dead?"

He shook his head. "She's not dead to me until I see a body. But I'd say she could definitely be in some serious trouble."

"What kind of trouble?"

"I don't know." He shrugged. "Married boyfriend kind of trouble maybe."

"Did Kelly say anything else about the sisters' relationship?"

Doggett shoved his own coffee aside. "Only that when the girls came back after the Christmas holidays, Lexi started hanging out with her. She introduced Lexi to the editor of the school paper, a guy named Nick Grable, and I guess he was pretty taken with her. He gave her an assignment and I don't think that sat too well with Kelly."

Fiona glanced up. "Do you think she had a crush on this Nick guy?"

"Oh, yeah. I'm pretty sure she did."

"So if he dumped her for Lexi, that could make for some pretty bitter feelings," Fiona mused. "What does Kelly look like?"

Doggett seemed to know what she was asking. "She's an attractive girl, but she's not in the same league as Alicia and Lexi."

"Do you think she was jealous of them?"

"She didn't strike me as the type of girl who's all caught up in her looks, but if she was dumped by Nick Grable for Lexi, then, yeah, like you said, rejection breeds resentment."

"But that still wouldn't explain why she'd go after Alicia."

"Not unless you remember the way Alicia was dressed the night she was killed," Doggett said grimly.

"Meaning someone could have mistaken her for Lexi." Fiona was silent for a moment. "Have you talked to this Nick Grable yet?"

"I went by the paper earlier, but he wasn't there. A couple of girls hanging out in the office said that was unusual for him. He lives and breathes that paper. When he's not in class, he's almost always there. Even has a cot in the back where he sometimes sleeps."

"You have his home address?"

"I'm working on it." Doggett's tone was very determined. It made Fiona glad she wasn't this Nick Grable person.

Doggett pulled a photo from his pocket and slid it across the table to Fiona. "You recognize this?"

"It's the symbol that was on Alicia's left shoulder, right?" He'd had the picture cropped and the area blown up so that all Fiona could see was the trident.

"Yeah, except the person in this photo isn't Alicia Mercer. This girl's been dead for over a year."

"Oh, my God." Fiona picked up the picture and studied it even more closely. "Two dead girls with the same symbol on their left shoulder. That's not a coincidence."

"I agree."

"So who was she?" Fiona asked.

"I don't know that yet. But Kelly Everhardt said this picture had something to do with a story Grable and Lexi were working on."

"My God, this could change everything." Fiona handed him back the picture. "It could change the focus of the entire investigation. The motive behind Alicia's death might not have been personal at all. At least not in the way we've been thinking."

"I'm hoping Grable can supply some of the missing pieces," Doggett said.

"I hope you're right," Fiona said. "Because this is starting to look more and more like anything *but* a simple homicide."

"We pretty much knew that already, didn't we? A beautiful girl from a wealthy family shot in the back of the head, execution-style. That's never simple."

He was right, of course. And the missing sister only complicated matters. "Look, when you find Nick Grable, do me a favor, will you? Keep him away from Frank Quinlan until I have a chance to talk to him."

Doggett's gaze turned speculative. "You've got a real problem with Quinlan, don't you?"

Fiona had no idea whether her animosity with his commander displeased Doggett or not. His expression didn't give him away. She couldn't even tell if he found her attractive. Not that it mattered, of course.

She glanced at her watch. "Look, I'm sorry to cut this short, but I need to get going. There's someplace I have to be tonight."

He nodded and stood. A thousand other guys would have asked her what her plans were for the night, made some comment about a hot date, but not Doggett. He didn't seem the least bit interested in her private life. And not one come-on the whole time they'd been together.

Not that Fiona wanted him to hit on her. Not that she would do anything about it if he did. It was just...

Oh, hell, she fumed. How pathetic was she?

INSTEAD OF HEADING NORTH toward her apartment, Fiona turned down Radney. She found a parking space on the street across from the alley where Alicia had been murdered and sat for a moment, glancing around the neighborhood. It was nearly seven o'clock in the evening. Most of the offices were closed, but some of the nearby eateries were still open and the streets were crowded. Even after the incident at the shelter, Fiona didn't feel threatened or frightened. In a lot of ways, her job had desensitized her to danger, which probably wasn't a good thing.

She got out of her car and walked over to the squad car that guarded the entrance to the alley. Showing her identification to the officer behind the wheel, she stepped over the crime scene tape and walked down the alley.

The crime scene looked different in daylight, without the fog. Today it seemed like an ordinary alley enclosed on either side by gray-brick buildings painted with graffiti.

The immediate area was still roped off, and Fiona again stepped over the tape and walked to the bloodstained pavement that marked the spot where Alicia had died.

The stain was surprisingly small. Not much blood at all. Once the crime scene tape was removed, no one would ever know that a terrible crime had been committed there.

"Who did this to you, Alicia?" Fiona whispered. Was Paul Guest somehow involved? Was that symbol on her left shoulder somehow the missing link?

Fiona listened for a moment, almost expecting the wind to deliver her an answer, but all she heard was the rattle of a tin can in the gutter.

No answer in the wind, no ghostly revelation against her ear, and yet Fiona suddenly felt chilled. Gooseflesh prickled along the back of her neck as if someone was secretly watching her.

She glanced up, her uneasy gaze scanning the windows that faced the alley, but she saw nothing behind the glass.

Her imagination was getting the better of her, she decided. But the feeling persisted, became so strong, in fact, that she was certain someone had to be watching her.

She glanced up and down the alley, saw no one, but she knew he was there. Somewhere. She could feel him.

David is dead, a little voice reminded her, but the warning was like whistling past the graveyard. It did very little good, because Fiona had already turned to hurry from the alley as fast as she could.

CHAPTER ELEVEN

A LITTLE WHILE LATER, as Fiona surveyed the crowd that had gathered at the Emerald Isle Community Center in Bridgeport to celebrate her uncle's retirement, she wished fervently for the ability to will herself to some other place. *Any* other place.

She'd once enjoyed family get-togethers and social events like this one, but now she merely endured them. It wasn't that she didn't love her family. She did. But...she was no longer the same Fiona that had once been the apple of her father's eye. She was no longer her mother's sweet, innocent daughter, her brothers' adored kid sister.

She was a woman who had fallen in love with a man who'd killed three women. Her family couldn't look at her without thinking about that terrible time in her life. She couldn't look at her reflection in the mirror without remembering, without feeling sick to her stomach at her own culpability.

She wanted to turn back, hoping to make a quick get-away before anyone noticed her, but it was too late. Her mother had seen her from across the room.

Maggie Gallagher waved gaily and started through the crowd, hugging this person and kissing that one, smiling and waving and laughing with friends she'd known all her life.

People had once thought Fiona just like her mother. Hard to believe that now.

Maggie hugged her warmly, kissed both cheeks, then held her at arm's length as she gave her a thorough inspection. "You haven't been getting enough sleep, have you? You haven't been eating properly, either, I see. How long has it been since you've had a decent meal?"

"Nice to see you, too, Mom."

Maggie's smile was rueful. "And I told myself I wasn't going to do that tonight."

"It's okay," Fiona said, then hoping to divert her mother's attention, added, "But, hey, let's talk about you. You look great tonight."

Her mother shook a finger at Fiona. "You are so transparent, Fiona Colleen. I know when a child of mine is trying to change the subject."

"No, it's true. You look beautiful, Mom." And she did. The black pants she wore were stylish and form-fitting, making her look no bigger than a minute, and her soft lavender shell brought out the violet in her eyes and a lustrous sheen in her dark hair.

"Well, in that case, what a sweet thing to say." Her mother wrapped an arm around Fiona's waist. "Come on. Let's go get you something to eat. And I know your dad is dying to see you. It's been weeks since you've been over."

"I know, I'm sorry, Mom. I've been really busy." She started to tell her mother about Alicia and Lexi Mercer, then thought better of it. Tonight was supposed to be a celebration, and besides, Maggie really hadn't known Lori and her parents all that well. In fact, Fiona had always suspected that her mother never really liked Lori, but she had no idea why. It wasn't because of the pregnancy. Her mother's disapproval of the friendship had been obvious long before Lori got into trouble.

"You seem so down tonight, Fiona." Maggie gave her

a squeeze. "I heard about the DeMarco case on the radio. I'm sorry, honey. I know how you tear yourself up over things like that."

A violent rapist was back on the streets because Fiona hadn't done her job well enough to put him away. Yeah, she did tend to brood a little over things like that.

Fiona was instantly ashamed of her thoughts. Her mother hadn't meant to be insensitive. She was the kindest person Fiona knew, and she certainly deserved better from her only daughter. "I'm okay. And don't worry, I'll get something to eat in a little while. I see Gran over there. I want to go say hello."

"Okay, but don't leave without seeing your dad," her mother warned sternly. "And be sure to say something to your uncle. This is his night."

"I will." Fiona disentangled herself from her mother's protective clutches and made her way through the crowd to where her grandmother sat at a small table in the corner. Fiona slid into the chair beside her. "Hi, Gran."

The older woman broke into a smile when she saw Fiona. "Fiona! You came after all! I was so afraid you wouldn't."

Fiona leaned over and kissed her grandmother's cheek. She'd always felt especially close to the older woman, maybe because she was Colleen's namesake and the two of them were the only redheads in the family. "Mind if I join you?"

Colleen took Fiona's face between her hands. "You know I don't. But why would you want to sit here with an old woman when you could be out there dancing with some nice young man?"

"I don't see any of those nice young men beating a path over here to ask me," Fiona said dryly.

"Nonsense. They would if you'd give them half a

chance. And besides." Colleen's eyes twinkled. "I see one who looks like he'd walk through fire if you'd give him a little encouragement."

"What are you talking about?"

"That man over there." Colleen's gaze went past Fiona. "He hasn't been able to take his eyes off you since you sat down."

"What man?" Fiona glanced over her shoulder, and her gaze immediately collided with Ray Doggett's. He was standing in a small group of people who were talking and laughing, but his gaze was on Fiona. He was looking at her with what she'd come to think of as The Stare.

Fiona whipped her head back around to her grandmother. She didn't know why, but the brief eye contact with Doggett left her...almost breathless.

Wait a minute. What the hell was going on here? she asked herself desperately. First that odd stomach quiver when she'd been with him earlier, and now a shortness of breath? This was getting serious. And scary. Maybe she was coming down with something.

"Do you know him?" Colleen asked.

"His name is Ray Doggett," Fiona heard herself answer. "He's the lead investigator on one of my homicide cases."

"Well, don't look now, but he's coming over here."

"What?" Sure enough, Doggett was making his way through the crowd toward them. Why this should disturb her, Fiona had no idea. She'd left the man not two hours ago. They'd had a fairly long and intense discussion about Alicia Mercer's murder and Lexi's disappearance. And now she was nervous because she and Doggett had turned up at the same party?

Her gaze drifted over him in spite of herself. He'd changed from the suit he'd had on earlier to jeans and a soft-looking gray T-shirt that made his eyes seem even lighter. He looked…

Whoa. He looked *good*.

She looked up nervously as he approached the table.

"Hello," he said.

Before Fiona could greet him, much less introduce him, her grandmother extended her hand. "I'm Colleen Gallagher, Fiona's grandmother."

He glanced at their hair. "I can see the resemblance," he said, then took Colleen's hand and shook it warmly. "Ray Doggett."

"Won't you join us, Ray?"

"For a minute maybe. If it's okay with your granddaughter."

Fiona shrugged and waved toward the chair across from her. She didn't know what had come over her, but she seemed completely incapable of speech. And that wasn't like her. Not at all.

"Fiona tells me the two of you are working together on a case."

He glanced at Fiona. "Yes, ma'am, we are."

Colleen looked thoughtful for a moment. "Doggett. Why do I know that name? Have we met before, Ray?"

He shook his head. Almost grinned. "I don't think so." His gaze went back to her impossibly red hair. "I think I would have remembered."

Colleen gave a delighted laugh. "Aren't you nice?" She snapped her fingers. "I know where I've heard your name. You used to be Joe Murphy's partner, didn't you?"

Doggett looked startled. "That was twenty years ago. How in the world did you know that?"

Colleen smiled. "Joe's mother, Irene, lives down the street from me. She and I have been widows for a good many years. We don't have anything better to do than sit around gossiping about our families these days.''

Fiona shuddered at that thought.

"Joe always speaks very highly of you," Colleen told Doggett.

"Joe's a good guy."

"I remember when you were shot a few years back—" She broke off, looking concerned. "Unless you don't want to talk about that."

Doggett glanced at Fiona, then shrugged again. "No, it's okay."

Colleen nodded. "Everyone, including the doctors, had just about given up on you, but Joe wouldn't. He stayed by your bedside night and day, leaving only when he had to go to work. Did you know he was there?"

Doggett suddenly looked uncomfortable. He wouldn't like talking about himself, Fiona thought. Not something this personal. "On some level, I guess I knew." He glanced around. "Is Joe here tonight?"

"Yes, I saw him a little while ago," Colleen said.

"If you'll excuse me, I think I'll go see if I can find him."

She nodded graciously. "Of course. It was very nice meeting you, Ray."

"You, too, Mrs. Gallagher."

"You can call me Colleen."

He stared down at her for a moment, then smiled. "No, ma'am. I don't think I could do that."

He turned then and walked away, and Fiona let out a breath she hadn't realized she'd been holding. She hadn't said a word the whole time he'd been sitting there.

"What a nice young man," Colleen murmured.

Doggett was forty if he was a day, but Fiona's grandmother thought anyone under the age of sixty was young, and anyone with polite manners was nice.

"You were awfully quiet," Colleen accused.

Fiona shrugged. "You were chatty enough for both of us." She paused. "What's this business about him being shot?"

"It was a long time ago," Colleen said. "I only remember it because he was in the hospital the same time I had my gallbladder surgery. Irene came to visit me one day and she told me that Joe had brought her because he'd gone to sit with Ray. Joe was really torn up because the doctors didn't think Ray was going to make it."

"But he did."

"He must be tough," Colleen said. "I like that in a man. I think he's very attractive, too." She glanced around Fiona as if to get a second look.

Fiona glanced around herself. "You think he's attractive?"

Colleen's eyes glittered. "Yes, and sexy. I doubt he's been kicked out of any beds lately."

"Gran!"

"Gran what?" she asked innocently. "Would you rather we sit here and talk about my arthritis? Or maybe you'd like to exchange cheese doodle recipes?"

The woman had a point. "I don't even know what a cheese doodle is," Fiona admitted.

Her grandmother patted her hand. "No reason you should, dear. Now, where were we? Oh, yes. Ray Doggett. Do you know who he reminds me of?"

"I haven't a clue," Fiona said helplessly.

"The actor who was in the second 'Terminator' movie. I saw it just the other night on cable."

Okay, the revelation was disturbing to Fiona on two levels. First, that her grandmother actually had cable, and secondly, that she thought Doggett even remotely resembled—

"Arnold Schwarzenegger?" Fiona asked incredulously.

Colleen looked slightly appalled. "No, not Arnold. I've never been a fan of bodybuilders. The other one. The man with the piercing eyes. Like Ray's."

"Well, then, you must mean the cyborg killer," Fiona said with irony.

But it was lost on Colleen. She leaned toward Fiona and lowered her voice. "He took all his clothes off in that movie."

Fiona just stared at her. "Okay, Gran, you do realize it wasn't actually Ray Doggett in the movie, right?"

Her grandmother's eyes sparkled maddeningly. "You should go rent that video, Fiona. I know I plan to."

Kill me. Kill me now. "What has gotten into you, Gran?"

She lifted her chin. "What's wrong, Fiona? Am I not acting grandmotherly enough for you? Well, if you and the rest of the family expect me to go quietly to my just reward, you are in for a very big surprise. I mean to go out with a bang."

"I can see that. At the rate you're going, you'll probably outlive us all," Fiona muttered. And have a hell of a lot more fun in the bargain.

"I should hope not," Colleen stated firmly. "I've lived a long and happy life, and I want the same for you. Isn't it time you found yourself some nice young man, got married and started having me some redheaded grandchildren?"

"Oh, well, sure, Gran. I'll get right on that."

"I recognize sarcasm when I hear it, young lady. And I don't find it at all becoming."

"Sorry."

Colleen stared into the crowd. "Do you and Ray see each other often? In regards to the case, I mean."

Fiona saw right through her. She narrowed her eyes. "Don't go getting any ideas, Gran."

Colleen's eyes widened. "You mean about you and Ray? You thought I was inferring that the two of you—" She broke off, shaking her head. "Oh, no. No, no. Ray Doggett is not the right man for you, Fiona."

Well, no, of course, he wasn't. But why not? Fiona wondered.

"Why not?" she blurted. "I mean, just to see if your reason is the same as mine."

"Because obviously he's never gotten over his wife," Colleen said matter-of-factly, and folded her arms on that little bombshell.

Fiona felt something go very cold and still inside her. Something that might have been her heart. "His...wife?" she stammered. "He's married?"

"Was. He's a widower. Why do you look so surprised?" Colleen asked. "Most men his age have been married at least once. The ones worth having, anyway."

Never mind that with the exception of John, Fiona's brothers hadn't married until they were well into their thirties. And Fiona, herself, at the ripe old age of thirty-three, hadn't yet made a trip to the altar. "So...when was he married? Recently?"

"No, this was back when he was still partners with Joe Murphy. Irene told me all about it. He and his wife were very young, I gather, and she was very beautiful but she had problems."

"What kind of problems?"

"Drugs, for one thing. She and Ray grew up in Indiana, and Ruby—that was her name—ran away from home.

Irene said Joe never knew for sure about her background, but he got the impression from Ray that Ruby had been abused as a child. That's why she left home. Ray followed her to Chicago, and he found her living on the street. She was already into drugs and God knows what else, but he wouldn't give up on her. He found them a place to live, got her off the street and then he married her. Joe said he was crazy about her, but things were never right between them. She had too much baggage, I guess. Poor thing. She'd just up and take off, and Ray wouldn't hear from her for days. He'd go crazy looking for her, and then when he found her, things would be okay for a while. Then she'd take off again.''

"Gran," Fiona said. "If you and Irene Murphy discuss such intimate details about people you don't even know, what do you say about your own families? You don't talk about me, do you?"

Colleen's gaze slid away. "Of course not, dear."

Right. The scandal with David Mackenzie would probably provide rich fodder in the neighborhood for at least another ten years. Fiona hated to think about her life being dissected the way Doggett's apparently had been. She despised gossip. Loathed it with a passion.

"So tell me what happened to his wife."

Colleen leaned closer. "She was murdered."

"Oh, my God." Fiona stared at her grandmother in shock.

Colleen nodded. "They never found who did it, either. Can you imagine being a cop and having to live with something like that? It's so obvious he's never gotten over her. He's never remarried, you know. That kind of loyalty is so rare these days."

OTHER THAN HIS HAIR BEING a little thinner and his waistline being a little thicker, Joe Murphy hadn't changed much in the nearly two decades since he and Doggett had gone their separate ways. His face split into a wide grin when he saw Doggett, and then he grabbed him and clapped him on the back. "How've you been, kid?"

"Not bad," Doggett said. "And you?"

"Feeling no pain." Murphy grinned and held up his beer. "Buy you a drink?"

"Maybe later."

Murphy nodded. "Still on the wagon, huh, kid? How long has it been? Twenty years?"

"Something like that."

"Never met anyone as disciplined as you," Murphy said, his words slightly slurred. He glanced around the crowded room. "Barb's here somewhere. I'll catch holy hell if I let you leave without saying hello to her."

"I'll go find her before I leave," Doggett promised.

"You do that, because she's got a bone to pick with you already," Murphy warned.

"What about?"

"You haven't been over for dinner in nearly a year. She was asking me just the other day why you don't come around anymore."

"I've been meaning to call. I've just been busy." A lame excuse, and they both knew it. Murphy was the closest thing to a friend Doggett had in the department, and he'd been lousy at keeping in touch. "You know how it is," he muttered.

"Yeah," Murphy agreed. "I know how it is. I heard about the transfer."

Doggett scowled. "News always did travel fast in the department."

"Faster than a speeding bullet." Murphy took Doggett's arm and drew him away from the group of cops he'd been talking to. When they were in a secluded corner, his gaze narrowed. "So what gives with the transfer, kid?"

Doggett shrugged. "Nothing gives. I just decided it was time for a change."

"And so you put in for Area Three?"

"They had an opening."

Murphy shook his head as if he wasn't buying it. Not for a minute. "And the fact that Quinlan is the unit commander over there didn't have anything to do with your decision?"

Doggett's expression tightened. "That's right, it didn't."

"Well, that's good." Murphy gestured with his beer bottle. "Because, you know, I was afraid it did. I was afraid, after all these years, you might still be carrying around a grudge against Frank Quinlan."

"Well, then, you thought wrong."

"On account of he was the lead detective in Ruby's homicide investigation, and he let the only suspect he had slip through the cracks," Murphy continued, as if Doggett hadn't spoken at all. "Be understandable if you did still hold it against him."

"I don't."

Murphy gave him a long, hard look. "Then things sure in hell have changed because you and I both thought something was fishy about that investigation. Something smelled to high heaven when Marcus Tate skated."

At the mention of Tate, Doggett felt something burn inside him, the bitterness and resentment and hatred that had been festering for years. Marcus Tate was a lowlife drug dealer and pimp who'd run a seedy bar where Ruby had worked. Doggett had never been able to prove it, but he was certain that Tate had been the one to get her hooked on drugs. And that was only one of the reasons Doggett hated the man.

"Last time we talked, you still thought that maybe a deal had been cut under the table between Quinlan and Tate. We both did. Maybe Tate bought off Quinlan, or maybe he had something on him. Whatever it was, nobody ever did any time for Ruby's murder." Murphy paused, his gaze narrowing again. "I kind of figured that had been eating away at you all these years, kid, and that maybe it got worse after you were shot. You were in the hospital a long time. Had a lot of time to think while you were laid up."

Murphy swayed toward him and put a hand on Doggett's shoulder to steady himself. "Maybe you even went back and looked over the old case files. Maybe you started asking a few questions on the sly. Putting two and two together on your own." Murphy squinted one eye. "Any of that sound familiar?"

"Yeah. I think I saw a movie like that once," Doggett said dryly.

"Then you know how the rest goes down," Murphy said. "The beat cop, who's now a hotshot detective, has gotten himself a little clout over the years. He lets it be known to the right person that he's ready for a transfer, and the next thing he knows, he's working with Quinlan, who, after all that time, probably doesn't even remember him from jack. The detective probably figures that if he can't prove Quinlan cut a deal with his wife's murderer, then he'll get him on something else. Still sound familiar?"

Doggett shook his head. "I must have walked out on that part. So how does it all turn out, Murph?"

Murphy shook his head. "Not good, kid. Not good at all. Yeah, because see, the detective made a big mistake going after Quinlan. He didn't count on how powerful Quinlan was, what a guy like him would do if he was cornered.''

"Sounds like the detective wasn't such a hotshot after all.''

"No, he was good,'' Murphy said. "One of the best I ever saw. But he had what you might call a fatal flaw.''

"Yeah? What was that?''

Murphy's expression turned grim. "He played by the rules, kid. And Quinlan never did.''

Doggett almost smiled. "You know something, Murphy? You don't know me as well as you think you do.''

CHAPTER TWELVE

THE LAST PERSON DOGGETT expected or wanted to see that night was Clare Fox. From what she'd told him in the past, she was hardly in tight with the Gallaghers, and now that she was deputy chief of detectives, it wasn't her style to rub elbows with the rank and file.

But Doggett was hardly in a position to criticize. He hadn't exactly been issued a personal invitation from the Gallaghers, either, but he'd seen the flyers around the station about the party tonight and some of the cops he'd worked with at Wentworth were from Bridgeport. They'd talked him into coming down here with them.

He hadn't needed all that much persuading, truth be told. Doggett usually avoided these kind of things, but he'd been curious to see Fiona. He wanted to see her in a more personal setting, find out how she interacted with her family and friends, what she'd be wearing.

He hadn't been disappointed. The sleeveless green dress she had on was a very simple style that did great things for her body. And the color made her hair look on fire. She'd worn it clipped back as usual, and Doggett was still itching to see it loose. But he figured that gave him a little something to look forward to.

But if he'd been hoping she'd express some sign of pleasure at his presence tonight, he might as well get over himself. Fiona hadn't said two words to him when he'd sat with her and her grandmother. Scratch that. She hadn't said *anything* to him.

Which told him a great deal more than he wanted to know. He wasn't going to be seeing her hair down anytime soon.

He tried like hell not to make comparisons as he watched Clare approach him. That wouldn't be fair. Clare had a good twelve or thirteen years on Fiona, but even so, she was no slouch in the looks department. She was still pretty damn fine, with her thick, dark hair and sultry brown eyes. And nobody, not even a woman half her age, could wear a skirt the way Clare did. Doggett's gaze dropped inadvertently to her amazing legs, and when he looked up again, she was smiling at him.

Clare made him nervous when she smiled.

She'd come a long way in the years since they'd first met, but he knew her well enough to know that she wasn't satisfied being deputy chief of detectives. Clare was never satisfied. Unless he missed his guess, she had her eye on the top cop position, and if she made it, she'd be the first female superintendent in Chicago PD history. She'd like that, making history. Clare had always had a healthy sense of her own self-worth.

But rumor had it, she wasn't exactly going to cruise into the superintendent's office. Doggett had heard that John Gallagher, Fiona's older brother, had some heavy-duty clout behind him, too, which could make things interesting. Politics didn't get any uglier than in the Chicago PD, and Clare Fox against the Gallaghers was a dogfight Doggett wanted no part of.

"Hello, Ray," she said in that throaty voice of hers.

He made sure he kept his eyes on her face. "Clare."

Her gaze seemed knowing. "I'm surprised to see you here. I had no idea you even knew Liam Gallagher."

"I came with some buddies of mine."

"I had no idea you even had friends." Her tone mocked him.

"Oh, one or two."

"Like Joe Murphy?" She glanced over her shoulder. "I saw you talking to him earlier. You two go way back, don't you?"

Doggett shrugged.

"I've always been curious about something, Ray."

"What's that?"

She eyed him for a moment. "Did you ever tell Murphy about us?"

He'd never told anyone about the monumental mistake he'd made with Clare Fox. He always figured the fewer people who knew about it the better off they'd both be. "I don't recall your name ever coming up."

"I think I've just been insulted," she said with a frown.

"Don't be too offended." Doggett glanced down at her. "I doubt you ever told anyone about us, either, did you?"

"No, you're right about that. It's always been our secret. And speaking of secrets." She moved in closer and lowered her voice. "We need to talk."

Doggett fought the urge to step back from her. It didn't do to let Clare think she had the upper hand. "I don't think we have anything to talk about."

She smiled. "You're wrong about that. We've got plenty to talk about. You asked me to help you with a transfer to Area Three, and I got it done. No questions asked." Her smile disappeared. "But you had to know I'd want something in return, didn't you?"

FIONA HAD THE STRANGEST feeling when she saw Doggett with Clare Fox. It wasn't jealousy or anything like that.

No way. She barely knew Doggett. It was just...strange seeing him with a woman like Clare.

She hardly knew Clare Fox, either, but what she did know of the woman she didn't like. Years ago, when Tony had first made detective, Clare had been his partner and mentor and—Fiona had always suspected—his lover. The personal side of their relationship must have ended badly because when the partnership dissolved, Clare turned on Tony with a vengeance. She even tried to derail his career while hers had skyrocketed.

She'd always been an ambitious, arrogant, sometimes vicious woman, the kind Fiona knew to avoid.

She didn't seem like Doggett's type, but of course, Fiona had no idea what his type was. Nor did she care.

He and Clare were certainly engrossed in an intense conversation, though. Well, Clare looked intense. As usual, Fiona didn't have a clue how Doggett felt or what he was thinking. His expression never seemed to change.

Oh, shit. He'd caught her staring at him. And he was staring right back. Shit!

Their gazes held for the longest moment and try as she might, Fiona couldn't tear hers away. He didn't smile, he didn't nod, he didn't acknowledge her presence in any fashion, but suddenly Clare turned and her gaze swept over Fiona in a sort of arrogant dismissal before she turned back to Doggett.

All right, go, leave, get the hell out of here! The next thing you know, he'll think you're interested in him, and you're not. You are definitely not interested in Ray Doggett.

Not in any way. Not on any level. Not even if he really was a naked cyborg assassin, and she was the buff chick who stood between him and mankind's total destruction. She might sneak a peek, but that would be *it*.

Okay, a graceful exit was in order, just in case Doggett, or more important, Clare was still watching.

Fiona turned and collided with her brother, Nick, who grabbed her arms before she went sprawling.

"Damn, Fiona. Don't you ever watch where you're going?"

So much for the graceful exit. "Sorry."

"Hey, I was kidding." Nick cocked his head, staring down at her. He was Fiona's middle brother and the most conventionally handsome of the three, with his coal-black hair and dark blue eyes. He had a temper on him, too, but he'd mellowed since he married. He gave Fiona a curious look. "What's the matter? You look like you just lost your best friend."

She shrugged. "No, just a case."

"Well, you can't win them all."

"Thanks, Nick, for that pearl of wisdom."

"Ouch," he said.

She heaved a deep sigh. "Sorry, again."

"I heard about the DeMarco case," he said with genuine sympathy. "Tough break."

"Yeah, my day pretty much sucked after that, but on the upside, I ran into one of your old girlfriends. She told me to tell you hello."

He looked intrigued. "Which one?"

"Rachel Torres."

"Ah, Rachel…"

"Who's Rachel Torres?" his wife demanded as she suddenly appeared by his side. Erin was petite, pretty and very pregnant. She also had absolutely nothing to worry about. Nick was crazy about her.

"No one." He drew her against him and wrapped his arms around her stomach.

"Wow, I'm impressed," she said, glancing up at him. "I wasn't sure you could still get your arms around me."

"What did I tell you last night? Where there's a will there's a way," he murmured, nuzzling her neck.

Okay, *that* was a mental image Fiona really didn't need. "I think I'll get some air," she murmured and walked away.

"We'll see you later," Erin called after her.

Fiona turned. Her brother's hand was on his pregnant wife's ass so, no, they would definitely not see her later. Not if she saw them first.

Outside, she walked past the smokers on the terrace, past the kids playing in the grass, all the way to the back of the grounds and the cheesy white gazebo that was sometimes used for weddings. Fiona was surprised and not ungrateful to find the place empty. She sat down on the steps and buried her face in her hands. God, what a day. What a perfectly hideous mother of all bad days she'd just lived through, and she couldn't even have a drink.

"I thought I saw you come out here," a male voice said from the darkness.

Fiona lifted her head. Then she slumped. "Oh…it's you."

Her brother Tony sat down on the steps beside her. "You were expecting…?

Fiona shrugged. "No one."

He was dressed in his usual faded jeans and grungy T-shirt, and as always, looked as if he hadn't shaved in two days. Honestly, Fiona had no idea what Eve saw in him. But then, Tony had never had a shortage of women in his life, including Clare Fox, who was inside at that very moment undressing Doggett with her eyes. For

God's sake, couldn't she just rent *Terminator 2* as Fiona and her grandmother planned to do?

Tony rested his forearms on his knees. "I saw Nick inside. He said you were kind of bummed tonight. I heard about the DeMarco case."

"Yes, everyone's heard about the DeMarco case," Fiona said. "Everyone's sorry. Everyone feels really, really bad that I let a rapist go free."

"Cut it out, Fiona."

"Cut what out?"

"The smartass attitude."

She opened her mouth to retort, then thought better of it. This was Tony, after all. The guy who'd once put his life on the line for her. "Easier said than done," she muttered.

"Well, try."

She gave him a sidelong glance. "You know your attitude must really stink when you start getting lectures from the black sheep of the family."

He grinned. "I'm reformed, haven't you heard?"

Her gaze took in his attire. "Yeah, I can tell."

"Okay, let's just cut to the chase here." He turned his head to stare at her for a moment. "I know what's really eating you tonight. You want to talk about it?"

She glanced away. "There's nothing to talk about."

"It's not your fault, you know. You weren't responsible for that girl's rape."

Fiona stared furiously into the darkness. "I might not have been responsible for the rape, but it was my duty to put her rapist behind bars. And I failed."

"But that's not what you're blaming yourself for, either, is it?" he asked softly.

She gave him an angry glare. "And since when did you take up pop psychology? You, of all people?"

He ignored her dig. "Deep down, you're blaming yourself because you didn't have the power to stop him in the first place."

"That's ridiculous."

"Is it? It seems to me you've been blaming yourself for every crime that comes across your desk because you weren't able to stop David Mackenzie from killing those three women."

Fiona sucked in a sharp breath. She and Tony never talked about this. It was an unspoken agreement. An unbreakable trust. "I should have been able to stop him," she said on a whisper. "I should have known."

"Why?" Tony asked harshly. "*I* didn't know. I'm a cop, and I didn't know. He was my best friend for years. He used to come to our house and eat Sunday dinner with us. Mom was crazy about him. He was like another son to her. So why do you think you should have known something that the rest of us didn't?"

She closed her eyes. "Because I was in love with him."

"Love doesn't give you any special insight into another person's psyche. If anything, it can cloud your judgment."

Which was exactly why she was still alone after all these years, Fiona thought miserably.

Tony stared off into the darkness. "You've got to stop beating yourself up like this, Fiona. You've got to put all that behind you somehow."

"I wish I knew how to do that." She shoved her hair from her face. "Sometimes I think if we'd handled things differently that night...if we'd told the truth..."

"Don't."

"But if we *had* told the truth," she insisted, "Maybe that would have somehow assuaged my guilt. If I'd owned up to my responsibility, if I'd confessed that I was the one driving the car—''

"Shut up, for God's sake," he said furiously. He glanced around.

"You were the one who wanted to talk about this," she reminded him angrily.

"Not about *that*." He cast another glance around the darkened grounds. "Look, I did what I thought was best that night. If I was wrong, I'm sorry. But we can't go back and change it now. It's done, Fiona, and you've got to find a way to live with it. If the truth came out now, it wouldn't just be my career on the line. It'd be yours, too. Don't give up everything you've worked so hard for all these years. Don't let David Mackenzie destroy you all over again."

He got up from the steps and walked off without another word. Fiona stared after him for a moment, then got to her feet. She wasn't sure if she'd meant to follow him or not, but a movement in the darkness drew her up short. She glanced around, saw nothing at first, and then, almost in slow motion, a shadow moved toward her.

Fiona's breath stalled in her chest.

She couldn't see his face, couldn't make out any of the man's features in the shadows, but she knew it was him. She'd come to know that walk, the shape of his body, the way he carried himself. She knew when he finally stood in front of her that he would stare down at her so intently she would wonder if he was trying to see into her very soul.

Oh, God, she didn't want to be attracted to Ray Doggett. That was the last thing she wanted. She didn't like the fact that her stomach became a quivering mass whenever he was near her, or that she felt tongue-tied, her insides all in knots, at the very sound of his voice.

She suspected she wasn't the only woman he had this effect on. She'd seen the way Clare looked at him earlier. He wasn't the kind of man women would notice if he passed them on the street, or the kind they'd whisper about behind their hands in a restaurant if he was seated nearby. He wasn't smooth and sophisticated, not edgy and dangerous. He was just Doggett, a man who would be impossible to get over once he got under your skin.

Fiona watched him approach with a wariness perfected over the years.

His gaze met hers in the darkness. "I saw you come out here."

"So you followed me?" Amazing how normal her voice sounded with all that banging her heart was doing.

He shrugged. "Seemed like a good idea at the time. But then I saw you with your brother and I didn't want to interrupt. I didn't figure Tony'd take too kindly to that."

Fiona glanced at him curiously. "You said something the first night I met you about my brother. I got the impression then that the two of you had had some kind of problem. What happened?"

Doggett shrugged. "No problem. Just a difference of opinion."

"Yeah, Tony has a lot of those," she said dryly. "So do you know my other brothers, too?"

"I've met John a couple of times. He seems like a straight-shooter."

"He is. What about Nick?"

"I only know Nick by reputation."

"I didn't realize he was that famous," Fiona said.

Doggett gave a ghost of a smile. "Well, he did shoot a superintendent. But I never was too clear on the details."

"Difference of opinion," Fiona said.

"Yeah, I figured it was something like that."

The conversation fizzled, and Fiona glanced around, trying to think of something clever to say. "Are you enjoying the party?" Oh, that was extremely clever.

"What's not to like? Good food, plenty of beer—"

"But you don't drink."

He lifted a brow. "What makes you think that?"

"When you were at my apartment the other morning, I got the distinct impression that you don't drink and you don't approve of people who do."

He frowned slightly. "I'm not a Boy Scout, if that's what you're asking. It's not my business what anyone else does."

"You seemed to think it was your business the other morning."

He stared at her for a moment. "That was different. I don't have a problem with people having a few drinks. Or even getting shit-faced, for that matter. Like I said, it's not my business. But I get a little concerned when I find the prosecutor assigned to one of my cases wasted at four o'clock in the morning."

Anger trickled through her. She eyed him coldly. "And if I told you that morning was an isolated incident?"

He shrugged. "I guess I'd wonder if it was the truth."

"Well, it is," she said flatly. "I went home that morning and had a couple of drinks because I'd just found out my friend's daughter had been murdered. I'd just seen her body lying in an alley where her executioner had left her. And maybe I was wondering how I was going to tell her mother what had happened. Maybe I needed a drink or two for courage."

"And did it help?" His gaze on her was relentless.

"No," she admitted. "But it made all of it go away

for a while." She paused. "Not that I owe you an explanation, but for the record, I don't have a drinking problem."

He nodded. "People who drink alone at four o'clock in the morning never think they have a drinking problem."

"Now, look…" Her voice trailed off. "Okay," she conceded, surprising even herself. "Maybe you have a point. But I had a couple of drinks that morning because I wanted them, not because I had to have them. There is a difference. And until then, I hadn't touched a drop in six months."

"Are you trying to convince me or yourself?" He was suddenly standing so close, Fiona could almost feel the rumble of his voice in his chest. Even in the darkness, she could see his eyes staring at her, through her, and she wondered again what he was thinking. If he was attracted to her.

"I don't have to drink, you know."

"As easy as that, huh?"

She'd never said it was easy. "Can I ask you something else?"

"Why not?"

"You said I reminded you of your mother. What did you mean by that?"

"Did I say that?" His gaze dropped, lingered for a moment on her neckline and then on her hemline before lifting to meet hers. "What was I thinking?" he muttered.

Fiona's heart started to pound a quick, uneven rhythm against her chest. She took a moment to steady her resolve. "Was your mother an alcoholic?"

"Where I came from, she was known as a drunk."

Fiona winced at his harsh words. "Was your father an alcoholic, too?"

"No. He was just a plain old son of a bitch."

And just like that, he'd told her more about himself than he'd probably ever intended. He'd had a lonely, unhappy childhood, by the sound of it. Fiona wondered if anything had changed now that he was an adult. Somehow she didn't think so, and the loneliness of her own life, the isolation she'd come to hate was suddenly a powerful bond between them. "Did you have siblings?"

"No," he said with a bitter edge. "At least they got that part right."

"Is your mother still alive?"

"If you can call it living. She's in a nursing home."

"And your father?"

"Dead." He didn't elaborate, and Fiona sensed it was better to leave it at that.

"Anything else you want to know?" His deep voice vibrated in the silence, making Fiona wonder what he would sound like in the morning before his first cup of coffee. Before he got out of bed.

"I'm curious about your wife," she said.

His mouth went thin. "How the hell—"

"Irene Murphy." She smiled sympathetically. "Evidently no topic is off limits between her and my grandmother. But if it helps, they're not trying to be malicious. There isn't a mean bone in my grandmother's body. She genuinely cares about people."

"Yeah, I got that."

"She said your wife was very young when she died. How old were the two of you when you got married?"

He was silent for a moment, and Fiona didn't think he would answer. She wouldn't have been surprised if he'd told her to mind her own business, and she wouldn't have blamed him if he had. If someone probed into her life the way she was probing into his—

"Ruby was eighteen, and I was twenty-one," he finally said.

God, they'd been kids. No wonder he'd never gotten over her. Ruby had probably been his first love, and she'd died before the passion had burned itself out. In Doggett's eyes, she would always be eighteen, beautiful, and tragic. That would be a hard act to follow. Not surprising he'd never remarried.

"Okay," he said, his gaze still on her in the darkness. "Now it's my turn."

"Your turn?"

"To ask the questions."

"Uh, no, sorry." Fiona shook her head. "I'm the lawyer, remember? I get to ask the questions."

He lifted a brow. "Oh, so that's the way it works? I spill my guts, and you get to keep all your secrets. Doesn't seem fair somehow. Especially since there's something I really need to know about you."

He sounded so serious. Fiona immediately stiffened. How much had he heard of her and Tony's conversation? Had he heard... Oh, God, did he know about David?

"I'll allow one question," she tried to say lightly, but her heart was beating so hard and so fast, she felt suddenly faint. If he asked about David, what would she tell him? If he asked about that night seven years ago, would she be able to keep up the cover?

"All right, it's a deal," he said.

"So...what do you want to know?"

He was standing very close, and even in the darkness, Fiona could see something in his eyes that she'd never seen there before. For the first time, she thought that he might actually be attracted to her, that he might actually be contemplating kissing her.

And she wanted him to. Oh, God, she wanted him to.

Don't ask about David, she silently prayed. *Just kiss me. Kiss me like you mean it. Kiss me like there's no tomorrow because who knows if there will be?*

He gazed into her eyes for the longest moment, as if he were trying to read her thoughts, and then he smiled. A real smile. A smile that made him look young and handsome and, yes, sexy. *You were right, Gran. Oh, boy, were you right.*

That smile did unseemly things to Fiona's insides. "Just ask the damn question," she said on a breath.

His gaze flickered over her. "Why don't you ever wear your hair loose?"

CHAPTER THIRTEEN

THE TWO-FLAT DOGGETT RENTED was on the fringes of a ghetto, in an old, run-down neighborhood that was showing signs of a comeback. A new subdivision was going up a few blocks over, and Doggett still hadn't gotten used to seeing the old row houses surrounded by the modern glass and brick dwellings that were selling for close to half a mil.

In Cabrini, a lot of the longtime residents had moved out when the new construction began, and they'd never come back, but in Doggett's neighborhood, most of the old-timers, including his landlady who lived in the other flat, had stubbornly refused to budge.

Doggett didn't know why he'd hung around for as long as he had. He could afford something better now, in a safer neighborhood, but he had no desire to move. Besides, the two-flat was like a palace compared to the dump he and Ruby had lived in.

It bothered him still that he hadn't been able to afford a better place for her. After he'd finished his training at the academy and his six-month probationary period on the force, Doggett had figured on looking for a nicer apartment, in a better neighborhood. He and Ruby had managed to put away a little money, and they'd even talked about buying a house someday, having a family.

Even then, Doggett had known it was a pipe dream. Ruby's past, the awful things she'd lived through, horrors that she hadn't been able to talk about, even to him, wouldn't let them have a happily-ever-after.

But back then dreams were about all they did have. It was pleasant to lie in bed at night and contemplate a better future. Until the nightmares came back. Until Ruby's past would start haunting her again, and she'd take off. Stay gone for days at a time, and Doggett, sick with worry, would comb the streets looking for her. Except for the last time.

Doggett was never certain why he hadn't gone to look for her then. Maybe he'd gotten fed up or maybe he'd just given up, but he'd left her out there all alone. Three days later, her body had been found in an alley. He'd had to live with that.

He'd had to live with a lot of things, not the least of which was the fact that Ruby's killer was still out there. Nor the fact that, in all this time, he hadn't been able to give her the one thing that could have made things right. For twenty years, justice had eluded them.

Doggett got out of the car and locked the doors, then crossing the tiny front yard, let himself into the apartment. Flipping on a light, he winced. The place was grim. No getting around that. The kitchen, living and dining areas were all crowded together, and a dark, narrow hallway led to the bathroom and two bedrooms, one of which he slept in and the other he used as a junk room-slash-office.

He hung his gun and holster on a coat hook just inside the front door, but later, when he went to bed, he'd take the weapon with him. Home invasions were commonplace in the neighborhood, although Doggett's gun was about the only thing of value he owned. The stereo was cheap, the television secondhand and the furniture tattered beyond repair. He wondered what Fiona would think if she saw where he lived, and it bothered him that she probably wouldn't be all that surprised.

Would she be surprised to know that he had a healthy bank account? he wondered. That he had a stock portfolio that had actually made money while high-tech billionaires had gone belly-up?

The nest egg he'd put away over the years didn't give Doggett any particular sense of security or satisfaction. It was just something he did out of habit, and besides, what the hell else was he going to spend his paycheck on? His rent was cheap, his car was paid for, and he sure as hell didn't socialize. He didn't go to bars or clubs as a rule, didn't smoke, drink, or do drugs. He was a frugal man, but not by design and no longer by necessity. That was just what life had made him.

Getting a soft drink out of the refrigerator, he walked out back to the concrete slab his landlady generously called a patio. He'd dragged a couple of plastic chairs out there a few summers back, and now he dropped down in one and propped his feet on the other. Letting his head loll back against the seat, he closed his eyes and thought about the Mercer case.

Almost forty-eight hours since that girl's body had been found, and he still didn't have much to go on. The case was fast becoming what cops called a mystery. A case with no solid leads, few clues and no viable suspects.

And the other sister still missing.

He thought back over everything he'd learned from the interviews he'd conducted the past two days. He still had a bad feeling about the stepfather, Paul Guest. The man had money and he had clout, but what he didn't have was an alibi. He claimed he'd been in a meeting for most of the evening, and had returned to the hotel at around ten and turned in. He couldn't prove that he hadn't gone out again, but then, Doggett couldn't prove, yet, that he had.

There was something about him…about that whole relationship with his stepdaughters…

Kelly Everhardt had said that Alicia didn't like him, that she made up excuses not to see him when he was in town. On the other hand, Lexi didn't seem to have a problem with him.

Okay, just put it all out there, Doggett told himself grimly. *Quit skating around the issue and face it head on.*

Was it possible that Paul Guest was the married man Lexi had been having an affair with?

Creepy thought.

But there it was.

And if so, was "affair" even the right word? Had he abused the girls while they were still living at home, under his care? Had the mother known?

It happened. It happened so often Doggett wasn't about to discount the possibility. Maybe Alicia and Lexi had come all the way to Chicago to get away from him. But if that were the case, why would Lexi continue to see him, unless, of course, he had some kind of hold on her? And that happened, too. An abuser who continued to have psychological power over his victim even after she was an adult. He knew all about that.

Maybe Alicia found out and confronted him…

But if that were the case, where the hell was Lexi?

Okay, stick to the facts, he warned himself. But the facts, so far, were precious few. What he did have was a stepfather who hadn't come clean about being in Chicago until his wife had given him away, a roommate who may or may not have been jealous of either one or both of the Mercer girls and a possible boyfriend Doggett had yet to track down.

Then there was that symbol, a trident that seemed to connect Alicia's death with a girl who'd died over a year ago.

Like Fiona, Doggett couldn't seem to wrap his mind around the emergence of a second victim and what it could mean to the investigation. He'd been starting to get a real feel for the stepfather as a viable suspect, and then that damn trident had turned up on another body.

And what in the hell did any of that have to do with Lexi Mercer's disappearance?

Contrary to what he'd told Fiona earlier, Doggett wasn't at all certain the girl was still alive.

The phone inside the apartment rang, and he thought about letting the machine pick up, but then he had a strange notion that it might be Fiona.

Yeah. Like she would be calling him at home at this hour.

Unless, of course, it had something to do with the Mercer case…

He'd better grab it.

He walked inside and picked up the phone. "Doggett."

"Ray, it's Clare."

Shit. He tamped down an unreasonable disappointment that the caller wasn't Fiona after all.

"Ray, are you there?" Clare asked impatiently.

"Yeah, I'm here." But he wished he wasn't. "What do you want, Clare?"

"I told you earlier, we need to talk."

"Does it have to be tonight? It's been a long day, and I'm beat."

"This won't take long. I'm parked right outside your apartment. I didn't want to get out of my car until I knew for sure you were home. Christ, Ray. This neighborhood is as crappy as it ever was. What are you still doing here?''

He smiled thinly at her disapproval. "I like it here."

He hung up the phone and walked over to the front door. He watched as Clare got out of her car and headed toward him. She looked as if she'd just come from the Gallagher party. She wore the same short skirt she'd had on earlier, the same silky blouse opened at the neck. She was a sexy woman, no doubt about it, but as Doggett watched her, he thought about Fiona.

The simple green dress she'd worn tonight shouldn't have been sexy or provocative, but on her, it was both. She was a beautiful woman. Not voluptuous like Clare, but still with enough curves to make a man want to touch them.

And Doggett had wanted to touch her. Like crazy.

Earlier, when they'd spoken outside the community center, there'd been a split second when all he could think about was hauling her against him and kissing her until they were clawing at each other's clothes. And if he'd gotten a signal from her, a hint that she might have been thinking the same thing, he would have been all over her.

"Why don't you ever wear your hair loose?"

"I don't like it loose."

And just like that, the moment had been gone. Doggett had had to pretend that he felt nothing. Pretend that the desperate urge churning inside him was nothing more than hunger pains.

Yeah, he was hungry all right. Starved, in fact. But not for food.

Clare walked past him into his apartment and he closed the door. She stood glancing around for a moment, then laughed. "Gee, Ray. I like what you've done with the place."

He shrugged. "It suits my needs."

"Your needs have always been pretty basic," she agreed. She glanced toward the tiny kitchen. "You got anything to drink?"

"No."

"Blunt as always." She sighed. "Can we at least sit down?" She didn't wait for him to answer, but instead walked straight over to the battered sofa and sat. When he took a chair across from her, she leaned back, smiled and crossed her legs. "It's been a long time, Ray."

"You didn't come all the way over here to reminisce," he said gruffly. "What do you want, Clare?"

She frowned. "You keep talking to me in that tone, I might just have to insist you call me Deputy Chief Fox."

"I'll call you whatever you want," he said with a weary sigh. "Just get to the point."

Her mouth tightened. "Six months ago you asked me to make sure you got a transfer to the Area Three Detective Division that you put in for. I did that. Now I need something from you."

"So you said."

She regarded him for a moment. "I didn't ask you why you wanted that transfer, but I had a pretty good idea. I always kind of figured you carried a grudge against Quinlan, and with his recent troubles, I figured you thought now might be a good time to move in for the kill."

"Go on." Jeez, was he that transparent? First Murphy, and now Clare. With that kind of subtlety, it was a wonder Quinlan hadn't already put a bullet in his back.

"I decided to just sit back, watch and wait to see what you were up to. You're good, Ray. I have to hand it to you. You've fit in well over there. The other detectives like you, for the most part, and Quinlan seems to trust you. Which is exactly why I'm here."

So they were finally getting down to the nitty-gritty. Good. At least he'd know then what he was dealing with. "I'm listening."

"You and I both know Quinlan should have been kicked off the force years ago. He's dirty. He's up to his eyeballs in filth, but he's got so much clout, no one has been able to touch him. And his men sure as hell won't rat him out. It's only a matter of time before a suspect turns up dead after one of his tune-ups, and after all the shit that's gone down in the department in the past ten years, we don't need that kind of PR nightmare. Morale is bad enough as it is."

"So you want me to spy on Frank Quinlan," Doggett said with a frown. "Is that it?"

She sat back. "I want you to do exactly what you've been doing. Keep your eyes and ears open. But if you see or hear anything, you don't take care of it yourself. You bring it to me. No one else. To me. I'll handle Quinlan."

Doggett's gaze narrowed. "Why do I get the feeling we're talking about more than just Quinlan's interrogation practices here? You've got something else on him, don't you?"

Clare shrugged. "Let's just say, I have my suspicions, but I can't do jack without proof. I need an eyewitness, one of his own cops who'll be willing to testify against him."

"Do you know what you're asking me to do?"

She returned his stare. "I'm asking you to break the first cardinal rule in police work. Go against the brotherhood."

"You want me killed, Clare?"

She smiled. "No. But I want to make sure you'll keep this conversation just between us, Ray."

THE FIRST THING FIONA DID when she got home that night was grab the bottle of Scotch on the table and pour the contents down the kitchen drain. She had a couple of bottles of beer in the refrigerator, and she dumped them out, too. Then she threw the empty containers in the trash and dusted her hands, as if it were indeed going to be that easy.

But easy or not, she'd gotten a wake-up call from Doggett tonight, a swift kick in the butt that she'd sorely needed. She'd glimpsed herself through his eyes, and the image hadn't been pretty.

She hadn't lied to him when she'd said that drinking alone at four o'clock in the morning wasn't the norm for her, nor had she lied when she'd told him that she hadn't had a drop in over six months. That was all true. But what she hadn't told him was that there'd been a time when drinking alone at four o'clock in the morning was all too normal for her. And at two o'clock in the afternoon. At eight o'clock at night. Anytime she'd needed to take the edge off the horror and guilt she'd felt in the aftermath of David Mackenzie.

She hadn't developed a physical dependency on alcohol, thank God, but she'd definitely used it as a mental crutch. But she was stronger than that now, and she didn't want to fall back on old, dangerous habits that could ruin her career and reputation, everything she'd worked so hard for. She was a better person than that. She was a better prosecutor than that, and smart enough to realize that there might come a time when a drink at four o'clock in the morning could make a difference in a case. Impair her judgment. Take the edge off her sharpness. Fiona didn't want that on her conscience, along with everything else.

Besides, she didn't much relish the notion that Ray Doggett thought of her in the same context as his mother.

Although…he might be over that now.

There'd been a moment tonight when he'd looked at her in a way that made her stomach tremble and her breath quicken.

"Why don't you ever wear your hair loose?"

"Why don't you loosen it?" she'd wanted to invite him, but she'd held back. Something had spooked her. That spark in Doggett's eyes that told her maybe, just maybe, she was playing with fire. So she'd backed off, Doggett hadn't kissed her, and Fiona had been left with an odd sense of relief, disappointment and…loneliness.

She still felt lonely and restless so she went in search of her cat. She found him asleep on her bed, and Fiona curled up beside him. She'd only close her eyes for a moment, she told herself, but it felt so good lying atop the soft covers with a warm body next to her.

Kicking off her shoes, she settled in for the night. The last thing she thought about before drifting off to sleep was Doggett's wife.

What kind of woman could hold a man under her spell twenty years after her death?

HELL, DOGGETT THOUGHT as he closed the door behind Clare. The night was shot now. Might as well turn in.

But as he walked down the hall toward his bedroom, he stopped and glanced inside his office. Turning on a light, he went over to the desk, unlocked the bottom drawer, and removed a copy of a police file that was grimy with age, the pages inside dog-eared from constant turning. Doggett sat down and opened the folder, but he didn't bother skimming the contents. He knew the police and autopsy reports by heart.

Ruby had been shot in the head with a .38 caliber slug, but the hit hadn't been clean like the one that killed Alicia

Mercer. Ruby had still been alive when her killer left her, and she'd tried to crawl for help as the blood slowly pumped from her body.

She'd been found in an alley outside Marcus Tate's sleazy club. The gun used to kill her had been traced to an ex-con named Danny Walker who worked for Tate as a bouncer and pusher. Two days after the murder, Walker's body had been found floating in the Chicago River. He'd been shot with the same .38, and his hands and feet were tied with a nylon cord. The gun was never found.

A woman named Shannon Ferris, who worked as a dancer at Tate's nightclub, claimed to have seen Ruby and Tate arguing on the night Ruby was murdered. The day after the police questioned her, she disappeared, too.

Doggett had tracked her down a few years later. She was living in Evanston with a husband and two kids, and she hadn't been exactly thrilled to find Doggett on her doorstep. But she did remember him.

"You're Ruby's husband," she said, her dark eyes narrowing with suspicion. "What do you want?"

"I want to talk to you about Ruby's murder."

"That was a long time ago. I told the police everything I knew."

Doggett put a shoulder to the door so she couldn't slam it in his face. "Then why'd you disappear like that? Why'd you run off after talking to the police?"

She hesitated. "Because I thought it was better that way."

"Better for who?"

She drew a deep breath. "I guess you'd better come in before my nosy neighbors start looking out their windows."

When they were settled in her living room, Doggett

leaned toward her. "Do you have any idea what Ruby and Marcus Tate were arguing about that night?"

She looked nervous, all of a sudden, and glanced away. "No. But I always figured it had something to do with you. Tate didn't like it when Ruby got married. He had a thing for her himself. I thought he was in love with her, but looking back, I think it was more like an obsession. He thought he owned her."

"Did you ever see him get violent with her?"

She shrugged. "Tate got a little rough with all the girls now and then. That's just the way he was, but nobody ever got hurt, and we were all pretty grateful to him for our jobs. Most of us had been on the street one time or another, just like Ruby."

"Was there anyone else at the club who might have had it in for Ruby? Did you ever see anyone give her a hard time?"

The woman frowned. "Some of the girls were jealous of her because she was Tate's favorite and because of her looks. Tate wasn't the only guy who had a thing for her. Men used to come into the club just to see her dance."

It was Doggett's turn to frown. "She…danced?"

Shannon's brows lifted. "You didn't know that?"

"I thought she was a cocktail waitress."

"She was at first. Then, sometimes when she would come back, Tate would talk her into dancing. She was good, too. She had this quality about her. She seemed innocent and sexy at the same time. Men ate that up."

"Did you ever see any of the customers come on to her?"

Shannon laughed. "Almost all of them."

"Was there anyone in particular you might have noticed?"

She thought for a moment. "There were a couple of cops that came in to watch her."

Doggett glanced at her in surprise. "Do you remember their names?"

"I didn't know their names at the time, but I saw one of them at the station when they brought me in for questioning. I got the impression he was, you know, the head honcho or something."

"Was his name Quinlan?"

Her shrug was noncommittal. "Could have been."

Doggett described Quinlan, and Shannon said, "Sounds about right."

"What about the other cop?"

"I never saw him again. But there was this other guy who used to come in. He wasn't a cop. He was some kind of professional, I think. He always had on a suit, like he just came from the office, and he wore glasses. Clean-cut type. Sometimes they're the worst." She winced, as if she'd just had a bad memory. "Anyway, this guy used to come in to watch Ruby. He'd sit in one of the back booths where none of the other customers could see him. Tate had the place designed that way. The girls could see everyone from the stage, but the booths were very private. This guy always came in alone, he'd have a couple of drinks while he waited for Ruby, then after she danced, he'd leave."

"Did you ever find out who he was?"

"No, but the odd thing was, I saw him down at the police station, too. He wasn't a cop. I know that much. I think he might have been a lawyer, or maybe a D.A. Something like that. When he saw me, he turned away, like he was afraid I'd recognize him."

"Did you say anything about him to the detectives who questioned you?"

She shook her head. "They didn't ask me the kind of things you're asking me. They mostly wanted to know about Ruby's relationship with you."

What did you tell them? Doggett wondered, but he knew better than to ask a question he might not want to hear the answer to.

"Look," Shannon said impatiently. "My kids will be getting out of school soon. I don't want them to find you here. They don't know anything about my life back in Chicago. I'd like to keep it that way."

Doggett had never tried to contact Shannon Ferris after that day, but he'd never forgotten what she'd told him. Now, with the memory of their conversation rolling around in his mind, he rifled through Ruby's file until he found what he was after. He'd torn the page from a yellow legal pad and written three names across the top: Marcus Tate, Frank Quinlan and Guy Hardison. He'd drawn a line beneath the names, scrawled the word *suspects* in big letters, and traced arrows pointing to each name.

Marcus Tate's connection to Ruby was obvious. He'd owned the nightclub where she worked, and Doggett had always suspected that Tate supplied her with drugs. According to Shannon, Tate had also been in love with Ruby, or at least obsessed with her, and the two of them had argued on the night she was murdered.

Frank Quinlan had been the lead detective on the case. He'd always been the type of cop who bragged about how good he was, how many cases he'd closed. And if old rumors and recent allegations were true, he was also the type of cop who wouldn't think twice about torturing a suspect in order to get a confession. How and why had a detective that driven let a guy like Tate slip through his fingers?

Guy Hardison had been the assistant state's attorney

assigned to the case. Doggett had never been able to prove it, but he'd always figured Hardison was the clean-cut guy Shannon had seen at the nightclub and later at the police station. Why else would he have let Tate squirm off the hook unless he, too, had something to hide?

Those three names had nagged Doggett for twenty years, but what really ate at him wasn't just the fact that Ruby's killer was still out there somewhere. What infuriated him was the notion that her killer might have actually prospered since her death.

From what Doggett had heard, Marcus Tate now owned and operated a nightclub in the Rush Street area, Frank Quinlan had been promoted to commander of the Area Three Detective Division, and Guy Hardison was first assistant to the state's attorney, with political ambitions of his own.

That was what bothered him about the Mercer case, too, Doggett realized. Whoever killed that girl was someone who expected to get away with it. Someone who planned to carry on with his life without an ounce of remorse for what he'd done.

Doggett stared down at the names he'd scratched across the paper, and a cold chill shot up his spine. He suddenly noticed something he'd never seen before.

"Holy shit," he muttered.

The lines and arrows he'd drawn to connect the three suspects formed a trident, not unlike the one that had been stenciled on Alicia Mercer's left shoulder.

And in a flash, Doggett knew where he'd seen that symbol before. And what it meant.

CHAPTER FOURTEEN

NEPTUNE'S PALACE was located on the trendy, upscale end of Division, only blocks from Cabrini, but a world away in terms of culture and prestige. Doggett didn't hold out much hope of finding anyone around at ten o'clock in the morning, but luck was with him for a change. A delivery truck was backed up in the alley adjacent to the club, and Doggett could see a couple of workers going back and forth hauling in boxes of liquor.

He pulled into the alley and got out of his car. The side door of the club was propped open, and glancing around, Doggett stepped inside. One of the guys from the delivery truck saw him and nodded. "You looking for Jimmy? He's in the storage room. Right through there." He pointed toward a narrow hallway, and as Doggett started down it, a man suddenly appeared out of nowhere and blocked his path. "Hold it, buddy."

The guy looked as if he might have been in training for the WWF with his bulging arm muscles, thick neck and long, dark hair pulled back into a ponytail. He seemed so stereotypical of a nightclub bouncer than Doggett almost laughed.

"You Jimmy?"

The man narrowed his eyes. "Who wants to know?"

Doggett got out his ID. "I'm Detective Doggett, Chicago PD. Are you the manager of this place?"

The man folded his arms, unimpressed. "I might be."

"I need to ask you a few questions."

"You gotta search warrant?"

"I just need to ask you some questions, that's all." Doggett glanced up at him. The guy had a good five inches on him. "No need to get defensive. Unless, of course, you've got something to hide." When Doggett reached into his jacket pocket, the man automatically tensed. "Relax. I'm just getting out a couple of photographs I want you to take a look at." He showed him a picture of Alicia Mercer. "Have you seen this girl before?"

Jimmy barely glanced at the picture. "No."

"What about this one?" He held up one of the autopsy photos Kelly Everhardt had given him.

"No."

"You're sure?" Doggett got out a third picture. "Because they're both dead, and I have reason to believe they each came into this club before they died."

"A lot of girls come into this club," Jimmy said.

Doggett showed him the close-up shot of the trident. "You recognize this symbol?"

Jimmy's gaze flickered, but he didn't say a word.

"It's a trident," Doggett said. "You know what a trident is, Jimmy?"

"It's a three-pronged weapon carried by the Roman god of the seas," a voice said from a doorway farther down the hall. "Neptune."

Doggett hadn't heard Marcus Tate's voice in nearly two decades, but he would have recognized it anywhere. Every muscle in his body tensed at the sound, and for a moment, the anger that rushed up from somewhere deep inside him threatened to overpower his self-control. But then he reminded himself that there was more at stake here than just the past. A hell of a lot more.

His gaze rested on Tate. He was about Doggett's height, and his physique was still trim beneath a light gray suit that had probably cost more than two month's pay on the force. His hair had gone almost completely gray, but his glaucous eyes held the same cynicism, the same degeneration that had always made him seem as if he'd just slithered out from some place unpleasant. A diamond stud flashed in one of his earlobes, but the jewel didn't give him any class. Nothing could do that.

"Ray Doggett," he said, his smile about as charming as an oil slick. "How long has it been? Twenty years? I'd like to say you haven't changed a bit, but to tell you the truth, you look a little worse for the wear."

"Right back at you," Doggett said.

Tate grinned, flashing milk-white teeth that looked sharp enough to rip out a man's heart. "Let's let Jimmy get back to his work. Come on out to the bar and I'll buy you a drink. For old time's sake."

Doggett followed him down the long, dim hallway, past several closed doors, into the main area of the nightclub. The place was cavernous and luxurious, with marble floors, curtained booths, and huge exotic fish tanks recessed into the walls. In one of the larger tanks, a woman in a mermaid costume practiced erotic underwater dives. She waved when she saw Tate and blew him a kiss that sent bubbles floating to the surface. Her long, red hair reminded Doggett of Fiona, and he watched the girl for a moment longer than he should have.

"Her name's Jada," Tate said as he stepped behind the carved bar and got out a bottle of Scotch and two glasses. "You wouldn't believe the things she can do underwater." He pushed one of the glasses across the bar toward Doggett.

Doggett shoved the glass right back. "It's a little early for the hard stuff."

"It's never too early for good Scotch." Tate poured himself a drink and lifted the glass. Light flashed off the diamonds in his rings. "Here's to your late wife," he said, and downed the Scotch.

Doggett ignored the toast and glanced around the club. "Not much like your old place," he said. "At least on the surface."

"Times change. At least for me. But you're still a cop, I see. Frankly I never could understand what Ruby saw in you. A farm boy from Indiana with no imagination and no prospects. And I was right. After twenty years on the force, you've risen no higher than the rank of detective."

"And yet I'm the one she married."

A muscle began to throb in Tate's cheek. He wasn't quite as blasé about this meeting as he would have Doggett think. "Somehow I don't think you came here to talk about Ruby."

Doggett slid the picture of Alicia Mercer across the bar. "Ever see this girl in here?"

Tate picked up the picture and studied it. "She's a knockout, but we get a lot of beautiful girls in here. You should drop by some time, Doggett. I might even waive the cover charge for you."

Doggett took his finger and slid the autopsy photograph toward him. "What about this girl?"

Tate sipped his Scotch. "What happened to her?"

"She met with an untimely death after she left your nightclub. As did the other girl."

Tate glanced up. "How do you know either of these girls came in here?"

"Because of this." Doggett slid the third picture toward Tate. "Recognize this?"

"As you said, it's a trident. We stamp our customers hands with a symbol very much like this when they come through the door."

"These symbols were stamped on both girls' left shoulders."

Tate shrugged. "Sometimes the doorman gets a little creative." He glanced at the pictures again. "I don't deny these girls might have come in here at one time or another, Doggett, but I can assure you, I had nothing to do with their deaths."

"Just like you had nothing to do with Ruby's?"

Tate smiled. "So you did come here to talk about her after all. That's what this is really about, isn't it? You using a new case to resurrect an old vendetta?"

"What this is about," Doggett said, leaning across the bar, "is putting a murderer behind bars. No matter how long it takes."

The muscle continued to throb in Tate's cheek. "A word to the wise, Doggett. You couldn't touch me back then, and you can't touch me now."

"We'll see." Doggett straightened and gathered up the pictures. "It was nice talking to you, Tate. I have a feeling I'll be seeing you again real soon."

He started for the exit, but turned when Tate called out his name.

"Let Ruby rest in peace, Doggett. You go digging up the past, you might find yourself buried right along with her."

"Thanks for the warning," Doggett said. "But you better hope that I don't. Because when I go, I'm taking you with me."

"I'M AFRAID YOU CAME ALL the way over here for nothing," Rachel Torres said with an apologetic shrug. "Kimbra was here when I called, and she did agree to see you. But I guess she changed her mind. She left just before you got here. I'm sorry, Fiona.''

"It's not your fault.'' They were standing in front of The Wall, and Fiona's gaze was drawn time and again to the posters. The image of all those missing girls had stayed with her since she'd left the shelter the day before. She'd even dreamed about them last night

She turned back to Rachel. ''Did Kimbra happen to mention where she was going or when she'd be back?''

Rachel shook her head. She looked especially pretty today with her dark hair falling about her shoulders and a shade of red lipstick that matched her dress and complemented her olive skin tones. ''She didn't say anything to me before she left, but that's not unusual. The girls don't have to check in and out. They come and go as they please. We only have one rule around here. The doors are locked at eleven o'clock at night and no one is allowed in or out until seven o'clock the next morning.''

"When did Kimbra come in?''

Rachel thought for a moment. ''Sometime after nine this morning, I think. I saw her in the gathering room talking to some of the girls, and that's when I asked her if she'd mind if I gave you a call. She said it was okay, but then she must have changed her mind for some reason.''

Fiona sighed. ''Obviously she's still upset with me, and I don't blame her. She trusted me to put DeMarco away and I let her down.''

Rachel gave her a sympathetic smile. ''You didn't let her down. You did the best you could. That's all any of us can do.''

But that was the part that troubled Fiona, nagged at her day and night. Had she really done her best? There must have been something else she could have done. Something else she could have said. There was always something...

"I don't suppose you have any idea when she might be back?" she asked hopefully.

Rachel shook her head. "I never know when any of the girls walk out that door if they'll ever come back."

"How do you stand that?" Fiona blurted. How did Rachel care about the runaways as passionately as she did, become as emotionally involved in their lives as she did, and then watch them walk away, knowing the dangers they faced on the street. Knowing she might never see them again. At least not alive. Fiona shuddered.

"I stand it because someone has to," Rachel said quietly. "If I don't care about them, who will?"

The eloquent simplicity of her words moved Fiona. "Do any of them ever stay in touch once they've left the shelter?"

Rachel shrugged. "Not often. I've gotten cards and letters from some of the girls who've gone back home to their families. They write to let me know they're okay. Or sometimes, to tell me that they're not okay. Occasionally, the beat cops will notify me when they've picked up one of my girls, usually on possession or solicitation charges, and I'll try to arrange for bail and an attorney." Her expression turned grim. "The worst, though, is having to go to the morgue to make an identification."

Yes, Fiona thought. That would be just about as bad as it could get, especially considering how young they all were. Some of them looked no more than twelve or thirteen. Others a little older, but still juveniles.

Fiona stared at all those innocent faces, all those lost souls, and she wondered how many of them might already be dead. She thought about Alicia Mercer, lying in that alley and her sister, Lexi, still missing. They weren't runaways, and yet they'd met with the same tragic fate as some of the girls on that wall. One was dead and the other had simply vanished.

Rachel touched Fiona's arm. "Look, since you're here, there's something I'd like to talk to you about."

Her serious tone immediately alarmed Fiona. "Of course."

"Let's go into the office."

Once inside, Rachel closed the door. She hesitated before she spoke, as if she wasn't quite sure she was doing the right thing. "You're right to be worried about Kimbra," she finally said. "She is scared. She's terrified of something, but I don't think it's DeMarco."

Fiona frowned. "Then what?"

Rachel cast a furtive glance toward the window that looked out into the hallway, as if she wanted to make sure they wouldn't be overheard by any of the girls. She lowered her voice. "I don't know what she's so afraid of, but she's not the only one. A lot of the girls are jittery, and more secretive than usual. Something's going on out there."

"On the street, you mean?"

Rachel nodded. "I don't know what it is, but I don't mind telling you I'm pretty spooked. Some of the regulars haven't been back in weeks."

"But you said that's not unusual," Fiona reminded her. "When they leave, you never know if and when they'll be back at all."

Rachel's dark gaze grew even more troubled. "I know, but this is different. These girls just seemed to have disappeared off the street. Vanished without a trace."

Fiona's thoughts immediately went back to Lexi. But she wasn't a runaway. She didn't live on the street. She had an apartment, a family, a bright future ahead of her.

Her disappearance couldn't be connected to any of this, and yet a shiver traced up Fiona's spine just the same.

"Have you reported their disappearances to the police?"

Rachel gave a helpless shrug. "What can the police do? These girls are runaways. When they disappear, they don't leave a trail." She sighed, her hand going to the tiny gold cross she wore on a chain around her neck. "I don't even know why I'm telling you all this. There's nothing you can do, either, but you're obviously concerned about Kimbra. The fact that you took the time to come all the way over here just to talk to her is probably more consideration than she's had from anyone in years. Maybe in her entire life."

And didn't that just put her own life into proper perspective? Fiona thought as she left the center.

Mindful of the Chevy from yesterday, she glanced around warily as she hurried to her car. Climbing in, she locked the doors and started the engine, but instead of pulling away from the curb, she sat staring at the shelter, her mind still on Kimbra, on all those missing girls.

When Fiona was growing up, her own home life hadn't exactly been a fairy tale. Her parents had fought bitterly, and lying in bed at night, listening to them rip into each other, she'd sometimes fantasized about running away, spent hours playing out the whole "then they'll be sorry" scenario in her mind.

And later, as a teenager, when her father had been so overprotective, her mother so hovering, her brothers so macho toward her boyfriends…Fiona shuddered. God, her dating years had been a *nightmare*. And like any normal teenager, she'd rebelled and again entertained thoughts of running away.

But she never had and for one simple reason. She always knew she was loved. She knew, no matter how crazy her family drove her at times, she could always count on their support. Even now, in her thirties, she knew that if she were ever in trouble, her family was just a phone call away. Especially her brothers. They'd do anything for her. Tony had even risked his life for her.

And yet Fiona had taken all that for granted, and she was suddenly ashamed of the way she'd pulled away in recent years. Ashamed of all the excuses she'd made for not attending the birthday parties, the baby showers, the anniversary celebrations that meant so much to her family.

She loved them. She did. But the problem with families was that they knew you too well. They knew too much about you. Fiona could never look at her parents or her brothers and their wives without seeing the same question in all their eyes: *How could you not have known?*

It wasn't like she hadn't asked herself that same question a thousand times since the night David Mackenzie died, but even after all these years, Fiona still had no good answer.

As she merged with the heavy traffic on Larrabee, a horn sounded somewhere behind her, and she glanced in her rearview mirror. As she did so, a movement in the back seat startled her, and then as she took a second glance, she gasped. Someone was in her car!

Without thinking, Fiona hit the brakes. The car behind her almost hit her, and then the driver laid on his horn as he angrily cut around her in the other lane. He flipped her off, but Fiona barely noticed. Somehow she managed to pull off the street and park without further mishap.

She whirled, her hand going to her heart. "What do you think you're doing? You nearly scared me to death! I could have gotten someone killed!" Namely, herself.

"Sorry," Kimbra mumbled, but she didn't look apologetic in the least. In fact, her dark eyes glittered with what might have been amusement. It was the first hint of humor Fiona had ever seen from the girl.

"How did you get in here anyway?" Fiona asked, trying to calm her shattered nerves. "I know I locked my doors."

"Ain't no car I can't get in if I need to," Kimbra stated proudly.

"Okay. Maybe the better question is, why are you in here?"

"I wanted to talk to you."

Fiona's brows soared in surprise. "Then why did you leave the shelter when you knew I was coming?"

Kimbra cast a stealthy glance out the back window. Her furtive movement reminded Fiona of Rachel's. "We can't be seen together no more, Miss Lawyer."

Fiona frowned. "Why not?"

"They could be watching us."

"Who?"

The girl shrugged.

"Kimbra, what's going on?" Fiona demanded. "Why shouldn't we be seen together?"

She shot another clandestine glance out the back window, then Kimbra leaned forward and handed Fiona a newspaper. She'd folded it in quarters so that only a portion of the front page was exposed.

Fiona glanced down. The headline read, Houston Family's Nightmare. One Daughter Dead, The Other Missing. Beneath was a photograph of Lexi and Alicia Mercer.

"Why are you showing me this?"

Kimbra eyed her for a moment. "I seen that girl, Miss Lawyer."

Fiona's heart skipped a beat. "Which one?"

Kimbra leaned over the seat and pointed to the photo of Lexi Mercer.

Fiona grabbed her arm. "Are you sure it was her?"

Kimbra scowled and pulled away. "Yeah, I'm sure."

Fiona tried to calm her excitement, tried to remind herself that in these situations, leads more often than not didn't pan out. "When?"

Kimbra shrugged.

"Last Thursday. She hangin' on Division with some sisters from the shelter."

"Do you know the other girls' names?"

Kimbra shook her head, but not because she didn't know, Fiona suspected, but because the code of the street prevented her from naming names.

Fiona's mind raced furiously. "This is very important, Kimbra. Did you see this girl after Thursday?"

She shook her head again.

"Okay, then tell me about when you did see her. She was on Division hanging out with some other girls, you said. What was she wearing?"

"I don't know. Jeans and shit, I guess."

That was very helpful. Fiona forced herself to curb her impatience. "Okay. Do you remember what color her shirt was?"

"Black, maybe."

"Anything else you remember about her appearance?"

Kimbra thought for a moment. "She didn't look much like that picture, but she didn't look like she been on the street that long, neither. You can tell by they hair," she said with a wisdom that seemed older than time. "And by they teeth."

God, Fiona thought. What had happened to Lexi? Had she been in some kind of accident? Did she have amnesia and couldn't remember who she was or where she lived?

It sounded far-fetched, but it wasn't impossible. And it was the only explanation Fiona could come up with at the moment that made any sense.

"Did you talk to her?" Fiona asked.

"I axed her and the sisters if they seen Capri lately. They said she done leave Division and head over to Madison."

"What happened to this girl?" Fiona pointed to Lexi's picture. "Did you see her leave?"

"While we standin' there, a car pulls up, she gets in, and they drives off." Kimbra shrugged, as if that were that as far as she was concerned.

"Did you see the driver?"

"No, Miss Lawyer."

"Do you remember what the car looked like?"

Kimbra gave a scornful laugh. "Wasn't no chariot, I can tell you that."

"Kimbra, there's a detective I want you to talk to. I need you to tell him exactly what you just told me."

She chicken-necked at Fiona, her eyes wide. "You kiddin' me, right? Talk to Five-O? After what they done to me?"

"I know it'll be difficult for you, but I'll be with you the whole time. I won't leave you, even for a second. You have to do this, Kimbra," Fiona insisted. "This girl's life could be in danger."

But Kimbra wasn't persuaded. She reached for the door handle. "You may as well forget that skit, okay? I ain't talkin' to no *po*-lice."

"Kimbra—"

"Look here, Miss Lawyer. I done tol' you everything I know, okay? Now I'm gettin' my ass outta here."

"Kimbra, wait! Lexi Mercer could be in big trouble, and you may be the only one who can help us find her."

The door was open, but Kimbra paused, glancing back. "You still don't get it, do you? Why you think I won't talk to Five-O?" She looked around, then leaned toward Fiona. "It was a cop done took that girl, Miss Lawyer."

The blood in Fiona's veins turned to ice. "How do you know? You said you didn't see the driver."

Kimbra glared at her. "I didn't have to eyeball no driver 'cuz I know an unmarked cop car when I see one. I go shootin' my mouth off to the *po*-lice, what you think gonna happen to me? I'll end up dead just like that girl's sister, that's what."

CHAPTER FIFTEEN

THE *HILLSBORO FREE PRESS* was located a few blocks off campus on the ground floor of a building owned by the university. The same girl Doggett had spoken to the day before was seated behind the counter, and she looked up with a wary frown when she saw him walk through the door.

"You're back," she said unhappily.

"Jennifer, right?" When she nodded, Doggett glanced around the office. "Nick here today?"

She rose. "Wait here. I'll go check."

Doggett had heard that one before, which was why he'd made damn sure before he came in that there were no back entrances to the place.

While the girl was gone, he walked around the counter and glanced through the folders she'd left on her desk. After a few moments, a door opened at the back of the room, and a tall, lanky young man who looked to be around twenty ambled out.

The kid had grungy blond hair, a goatee and was dressed in a black T-shirt and jeans that rode so low on skinny hips, Doggett wondered how he kept them up.

He flashed his ID. "Nick Grable?"

"Yeah."

"I'm Detective Doggett, Chicago PD."

The kid gave him a sleepy-eyed appraisal. "Jen said you wanted to talk to me about Alicia Mercer's murder?"

He nodded toward the blond girl who'd followed him back out. She was seated behind the computer again, trying to look busy, but Doggett noticed that her gaze kept straying to Nick. "Look, man, I don't know what I can tell you. I didn't really know Alicia. I only met her a couple of times when she came by here looking for Lexi."

"I understand." But Doggett wasn't letting him off the hook that easily. "Is there somewhere we can speak privately?"

Nick rubbed the back of his neck. "I guess we can use the office."

He led Doggett to a small, cramped cubicle in the back littered with books, papers and stacks of files. There was an unmistakable aroma in the air, and Doggett glanced around. "Damn, kid. What've you been smokin' back here?"

Nick idly scratched his arm. "So'd you come here to bust me or what?" If this was the kid's first encounter with the police, he seemed pretty damned relaxed about it. For now.

"That depends on how much cooperation I get," Doggett advised.

Swiping some of the newspapers aside, Nick cleared a chair for Doggett, then took a seat behind the battered desk, folding his arms on the surface. "What do you want to know?"

"When was the last time you spoke to Alicia Mercer?"

Nick took a second to consider. "She came by on Monday looking for Lexi. She said Lexi hadn't come home last Thursday night."

"Did she seem worried?"

Nick shrugged. "More pissed than worried."

"Why was she pissed?"

"She didn't say and I didn't ask."

Doggett switched gears for a moment. "Okay, when was the last time you saw Lexi?"

"One day last week."

"Which day, exactly?"

"I don't remember, *exactly*."

"Try." Already Doggett was sick of this kid.

Nick ran a hand through his messy hair. "Look, I don't take notes when people come in and out around here, okay? I think it was on Thursday. She used the computer for a while and then left."

"Did you talk to her?"

"Not really. We put the paper to bed on Friday night, so it gets kind of crazy around here by the end of the week."

"When Alicia came by on Monday, what did you think when she told you that Lexi had been missing for nearly four days?"

Something flickered in Nick's eyes, but he quickly glanced away. "I guess I figured she'd hooked up."

"Hooked up?"

"Yeah, you know, with a guy? On second thought, maybe you don't know." The kid actually had the nerve to sneer.

Dumb ass. "You know," Doggett said, glancing around, "Be a shame if I have to get Narcotics over here because those guys can be pretty thorough with their body cavity searches. Especially the ones with the big hands."

Doggett gave the kid a minute for the visuals to take effect, then he leaned forward, "Were you and Lexi Mercer romantically involved?"

For the first time, Nick actually looked a little rattled. "Why the third-degree about Lexi? I thought you were investigating Alicia's murder?"

Doggett sat back, studying him. "I'd appreciate it if

you'd just answer my questions. I'm starting to wonder why you're being so evasive."

Nick stared sullenly at the desk. "Lexi and I went out a couple of times, okay? But it didn't go anywhere. She didn't want it to. She said she'd been involved in a serious relationship last semester, and I got the feeling she was still hung up on that guy. When her sister said she hadn't come home, I figured she'd gone back to him."

"Do you know his name?"

Nick shook his head. "She never mentioned him by name."

"You didn't find it strange that she didn't talk about him?"

He shrugged. "I don't talk about my old girlfriends. Chicks don't like that."

And you'd know all about what chicks like, wouldn't you? Smooth guy like you. "What kind of story was Lexi working on for the paper?"

"What does that have to do with anything?"

Doggett sighed. "Just answer the question, kid."

Nick looked as if he wanted to refuse, but wasn't quite prepared to deal with the consequences. He actually squirmed in his chair. "She was doing some investigative reporting on runaways. I got the idea from a girl I went out with last year. Her name was Gwen Bertram. She transferred to Hillsboro from a private college in Kentucky because her sixteen-year-old sister had run off to Chicago. Gwen wanted to find her."

"Doesn't sound like much of a story," Doggett said. "Girls run away from home all the time."

Nick glanced up. "Yeah, but this one had a different twist."

"How so?"

"I'd rather not say."

"Oh, you'd rather not say?" Doggett got up.

Nick looked alarmed. "Look, man, you don't understand. There's a lot riding on this story, okay? It could mean a Pulitzer—"

Doggett was around the desk in a flash. He hauled Nick up by his shirt and shoved him back against the wall. "Listen to me, you smug little shit. I don't care if there's a friggin' Nobel Prize involved, *okay?* One girl's dead and another one's missing, and if you don't start being a little more cooperative, you'll be typing out your police brutality story with your toes. You get what I'm saying?"

Nick was looking a little green around the gills. "Okay, okay. I get it. Just…lighten up, man."

Doggett swiveled the chair around and pushed Nick down in it. "Let's try it again. Tell me about this story you and Lexi were working on."

Nick sprawled in the chair, trying to regain his cool. "Gwen's sister liked to hang out in the Rush Street area with some of the other runaways. She told Gwen once about this guy who would sometimes come around and offer them money. Not all of them, but the hot ones, like Gwen's sister, Sarah. He bought them new clothes and took them to a nightclub where they were supposed to make nice with some of the male customers."

"What nightclub?" Doggett asked sharply.

"I don't know. I swear, she never said."

"Sounds like they were running a call girl ring," Doggett said with a frown. "That's not exactly groundbreaking reporting, either, kid."

"Yeah, except these girls weren't asked to perform sexual favors. They were just supposed to walk around looking hot. Or innocent. Whatever the guy told them to do. Some of the girls were invited back, some of them were told to get lost, and some of them just disappeared. Gwen thought there was something strange about her sister's story, but when she pressed her about it, Sarah wouldn't say anything else. Then a few days later, Gwen got word that Sarah was dead.''

"So you and Lexi were trying to find out what happened to Sarah Bertram?''

Nick scowled. "Not exactly. After she turned up dead, Gwen went back to Kentucky, and I pretty much forget about the whole thing until I ran across something on the Internet one day that got me to thinking. A reporter in Houston broke a story about runaways being bought-and-sold on the black market. The girls were taken to some nightclub in Houston where all these rich dudes, mostly foreigners, could bid on the ones they liked. The police found a tunnel network beneath the club where they kept the girls in chains, sometimes for weeks at a time, until they could smuggle them out of the country.''

Something cold slithered up Doggett's spine. "Are you talking white slavery here, kid?''

Nick nodded grimly. "They had what they called scouts, as in talent scouts, guys who hung out at bus terminals and on street corners looking for runaways. They tried to get them before the girls had been on the street too long because once they get on crack or some shit like that…'' He trailed off on a grimace. "Sometimes a client would even give a specific order—blond, blue eyes. Tall, short, whatever. The scouts would go out and find a girl matching that description. After I read about the Houston story, I got to thinking that maybe that's what happened to Sarah Bertram.''

"That's some pretty heavy reporting for a college paper,'' Doggett said.

Nick's expression turned defiant again. "Anybody can

report on cheating or date rape or some shit like that. That's not what we do here.''

"So how did Lexi get involved in all this?''

"She understood where I was trying to take the paper, and she wanted to be a part of it. Plus, she had the kind of looks that I knew would get her noticed. So she started hanging out in the Rush Street area posing as a runaway. After a while, people accepted her as part of the scene.''

"Did she ever make contact with one of these scouts?''

Nick hesitated. "No, I don't think so.''

"You don't think so? Wouldn't she have told you?''

Nick scowled. "I thought so, but now I'm not so sure. The plan was for her to make contact, then call and let me know which nightclub she was being taken to. I was to meet her there. She was never supposed to carry it any further than that.''

"And if she couldn't call?''

"She was never supposed to put herself in a dangerous situation,'' Nick insisted. "That wasn't part of the plan.''

Un-frigging-believable. "Why didn't you call the police when you found out she was missing?''

"I didn't know she *was* missing until Alicia showed up here on Monday looking for her. And like I said. I figured she'd gone off with an old boyfriend.''

Doggett stared at the kid in disgust. "She's hanging out on street corners, trying to get herself picked up, and when she disappears, your first assumption is that she's gone off with an old boyfriend?'' He shook his head. "Sorry, kid, but I'm not buying that.''

Nick looked suddenly indignant. "It's the truth! It's what Alicia thought, too.''

"Yeah? Well, you know what I think?'' Doggett leaned toward him. "I think you didn't report her missing because you didn't want someone scooping your story.''

The kid had the decency to at least blush.

"It never once occurred to you that she might have gotten in over her head? That she might end up like this?" Doggett pulled out the autopsy photos Kelly Everhardt had given him and spread them across the desk. "Is this Sarah Bertram?"

Nick's face went pale. "Where did you get these?"

"Doesn't matter where I got them. What matters is where you got them." When the kid didn't answer, Doggett planted his hands on the arms of his chair. "Hey, Woodward, you don't feel comfortable talking here, we can always go down to the station. And maybe while we're there, the narcs can come over and start tearing this place apart."

Nick muttered something under his breath. "Okay, you've made your point. But you've got some serious attitude issues, dude."

This little creep had put an eighteen-year-old girl on the street to pose as a runaway in order to infiltrate a white slavery ring, and Doggett was the one with issues?

"You were telling me where you got these photos," he said.

"I know somebody who moonlights at the morgue, Okay? I talked him into making copies for me. But before you even ask, I'm not going to tell you his name. There is such a thing as journalistic integrity."

The kid was unbelievably arrogant, and Doggett would have liked nothing more than to haul his ass to the station and put him in a lineup, just to take him down a peg or two. "I'm going to need all your files and notes, everything you've got on this story," he said instead. "Oh, and one other thing." He straightened and stared down at Nick Grable. "Don't even think about leaving town."

A LITTLE WHILE LATER, Fiona headed over to Area Three headquarters on Belmont for a hastily arranged powwow between the state's attorney's office and the police investigators involved in both of the Mercer cases. Passing through the metal detector in the lobby, she took the stairs to the second floor and made her way to the conference room—a small, windowless space that contained an oval table, metal chairs and a large blackboard adorned on either side by the Illinois state flag and the United States flag.

Several of the detectives working the cases, including Doggett, Skip Vreeland and Jay Krychek, were already seated while Frank Quinlan and Deputy Chief of Detectives Clare Fox jockeyed for the position of power at the head of the table. Frankly Fiona's money was on Clare. For all his power and clout, Quinlan was no match for a woman with a dream.

Fiona wondered if Clare's interest in what otherwise should have been routine homicide and missing person investigations was solely self-serving, or if Paul Guest was already starting to pull some pretty heavy-duty strings.

As Fiona moved to take an unobtrusive seat at the far end of the table near Guy Hardison, two things occurred to her. One, that Doggett hadn't looked up when she entered the room, hadn't given her so much as a brief nod. He sat halfway down the conference table, quietly going over his notes as he waited for the meeting to start. Fiona could have been the Invisible Woman for all the notice he paid her.

The second thing she realized was that this was the first time she'd been face-to-face with Guy Hardison since Milo had made his outrageous accusations while they'd been en route to the crime scene. And outrageous might even be an understatement considering the vague, disinterested smile Guy gave her when she sat down.

Like Doggett, he seemed totally oblivious to her presence, much less her sex appeal, which made Fiona start to seriously reconsider her brand of deodorant.

But in actuality, Guy's attitude toward her hadn't changed. His interest in her had never been anything but professional. What had changed was Fiona's attitude toward him. Since Milo—bless his paranoid little soul—had planted the notion of Guy's secret infatuation for her in her head, Fiona was suddenly self-conscious of the way her blouse formed a deep V beneath her suit jacket, of the way her slim skirt rode to midthigh when she sat. Which were pretty ridiculous concerns for an invisible woman, she decided.

Guy was a happily married with two grown kids, and even though a wedding band didn't stop some creeps from fooling around, he seemed too disciplined, too focused to risk everything on a fling.

Not that he probably hadn't had his chances, Fiona thought. He wasn't *her* type, but he was an attractive man. In his late forties, she would guess, but he looked much younger. His hair had only a strand or two of gray, and the wire-rimmed glasses he wore gave him an earnest, boyish demeanor that belied his almost fierce ambition.

He had a mild-mannered, Clark Kent look about him, but Fiona doubted very seriously that a Superman persona lurked beneath his conservative suit. In spite of Milo's dire warnings to the contrary, Guy just didn't seem the type to have a wild side.

Fiona's gaze drifted unaccountably to Doggett. He was probably younger than Guy by several years, but his face was lined with a thousand stories, his features hardened by all his time on the street. And his eyes...oh, man, those eyes. Laser blue and relentless, they could pierce you to the very core.

Unlike Guy, there was nothing mildly attractive about Doggett. There was nothing mild about him, period. He was the kind of man a woman would either dismiss on sight or find wildly irresistible. There would be no in between.

And beneath his suit? Superman?

Somehow, Fiona thought he just might be.

With a start, she realized he was staring back at her. His gaze narrowed, as if he were reading her thoughts, and Fiona felt a blush touch her cheeks. And damn it all, she hadn't blushed in years!

What was it about him anyway? He wasn't her type anymore than Guy Hardison was her type. Actually, *no* man was her type. Fiona didn't trust any of them. Didn't particularly care for any of them. As far as she was concerned, they all had the potential to be another David Mackenzie. Or Vince DeMarco.

But with Doggett she knew better. There was something almost…noble about him.

God, Fiona. Could you be any more sickening?

Doggett would probably be the first to scoff at such a description, but sentimentality aside, it was true in a way. There was something admirable about a white cop who felt compelled to work the ghettos for as long as Doggett had. Something virtuous about a man who still grieved, even in a quiet way, for a wife he'd lost twenty years ago.

But he wasn't *completely* chaste, unless Fiona had badly misjudged him.

And that wouldn't be the first time she'd misjudged a man, now would it?

But she didn't think she was wrong about Doggett. There was a darkness inside him, a hint of something

Fiona had seen before, and that scared her to death. That alone should have sent her screaming for the exit.

And she might yet run if she thought there was a possibility Doggett would chase her. But with the exception of that one brief moment at her uncle's retirement party when she thought he might actually kiss her, Detective Ray Doggett had been the very picture of propriety. The very epitome of a gentleman. He'd been every bit as intent—and maybe more so, damn him—as she on keeping their relationship professional.

And that was for the best. It really was.

Fiona might even have managed to convince herself of that fact if not for Doggett's eyes. Those eyes taunted her with the unspoken message, *Baby, you don't know what you're missing.*

Okay. But who needed a night of wild sex anyway? Fiona had her cat for company, her cable for entertainment, her imagination for...

Never mind how she used her imagination.

None of those things was a very good substitute for a warm male body to cuddle with.

Cuddle? Yeah, that's what she wanted to do. She wanted to cuddle Doggett's brains out.

"Fiona?"

She started.

"Are you okay?" Guy's stare was quizzical. "You look a little flushed?"

"What? Oh." Fiona's face went even hotter. "I, uh, think I may be coming down with something." Like a bad case of the stupids.

She shot Doggett a glance, but he was looking the other way. Staring at Clare Fox. What was up with *that?*

Fiona forced her attention back to Guy. "Listen, I need to talk to you about something I just found out—"

She had to leave the sentence dangling because the door to the conference room burst open at that moment and Superintendent Demetrius Booker blazed in, flanked by deputy superintendents and a couple of bodyguards bringing up the rear. His black eyes snapping with fury, his posture as ramrod straight as the day he'd left the Marine Corp thirty years ago, Booker, at six feet six, was a handsome, imposing figure.

Clare and Quinlan couldn't scramble to their feet fast enough.

"Superintendent Booker," Clare said almost breathlessly. "We didn't know you were coming, sir."

"That was kind of the point." His contemptuous gaze swept the conference room, making everyone present feel like an elementary school student being taken to task by the big, bad principal.

"Sir…"

He silenced Clare with one look. She folded herself back into her chair, leaving Quinlan standing all alone. He glanced around, didn't seem to know quite what to do with himself, then he sat as well. It was interesting to see him and Clare in situations that had them at a disadvantage. Fiona suspected it happened so rarely.

She settled in, preparing to savor the moment.

"I just came from a meeting with the mayor." Booker's deep voice all but quivered with suppressed rage. "Suffice it to say, he is not happy about the events of the past three days. He's been on the phone with Mayor Canfield from Houston, who happens to be a close, personal friend of Paul Guest's. As is the governor of Texas, who also called to express his concern, along with a number of congressmen, assemblymen and a goddamn U.S. senator."

No one dared say a word at this point. Quinlan and

Clare's expressions were comically identical. They might have been bookends.

Fiona couldn't remember when she'd enjoyed herself more. She caught Doggett's eye, and something that might have been amusement glittered in those blue depths. And for some reason, the moment suddenly seemed intimately charged, as if the two of them had just shared something deeply personal.

Or maybe she was reading too much into it, Fiona decided. Maybe Doggett just enjoyed as much as she did seeing Quinlan and Clare having to eat what they both dished out so generously.

"In another twenty-four hours, this case will go national, and Chicago is going to look like *shit*." Booker's dark eyes fairly bulged with disdain over the unimaginable incompetence he had to endure. "One girl dead, her twin sister missing, and what do we have? No leads, no suspects, not one concrete piece of evidence. And what are you people doing about it besides sitting around with your thumbs up your asses?"

Fiona's gaze shifted to Clare, who had once again risen. "With all due respect, sir, Commander Quinlan has assured me that his detectives are handling both cases according to departmental protocol." Neatly done, the way she'd shifted the blame to Quinlan while all the time looking as if she were defending him.

Fiona glanced at Quinlan, who was scowling. Hmm, no love lost there.

"Alexis Mercer is still technically a missing persons case," Clare said. "We have no evidence, at this point, suggesting she met with foul play."

"I'd say the fact that her sister turned up dead in an alley three days ago might at least give you a *clue*," Booker said snidely. "The girl's been missing for nearly a week. I hope to hell you people manage to have a suspect in custody by the time *her* body turns up.''

Fiona was surprised to find herself rising to her feet as well. But unlike most everyone else in that room, Booker didn't particularly intimidate her, and for one good reason. He wasn't her boss. He had no power over her.

''I have some information regarding Lexi Mercer's disappearance that I haven't had a chance to share with the detectives working the cases. You might like to hear it as well, Superintendent Booker.''

She could feel Doggett's gaze on her, but she refused to look at him. She forced herself to remain focused on Booker.

''Sir, this is ASA Fiona Gallagher,'' Clare said. ''You may have read about her…exploits in the paper recently.'' She cut a cold glance toward Fiona.

Booker eyed her curiously. ''Yes, I know who she is. Your reputation precedes you, Counselor. I'd be curious to know who your PR person is.'' His tone was friendly enough, but there was an undercurrent of something she couldn't quite define in his voice. ''You're the only one in city government who seems to generate any favorable press these days.''

''I wouldn't know about that,'' Fiona said with an uneasy smile. ''My concern at the moment is in finding Lexi Mercer alive.''

''Then, by all means, tell us about this information that has come to your attention.''

She had no idea if he was mocking her or not. ''I talked to a witness earlier today who claims to have seen Lexi Mercer on Division Street the night she went missing. According to this witness, Lexi got into a car with someone and they drove off.''

''Who is the witness?'' Booker asked curiously, but his

gaze gleamed in a way that finally did manage to intimidate Fiona. She couldn't help remembering Kimbra's last words to her. *"I go shootin' my mouth off, what you think gonna happen to me?"*

Fiona swallowed. "I'm not at liberty to say." She didn't dare glance at Doggett. She knew he was giving her The Stare, and that kind of pressure she didn't need at the moment.

"May I ask why not?" Booker's voice had gone curiously gentle. The calm before the storm, no doubt.

"Because divulging that information might place the witness in danger."

"Then we'll offer your witness police protection," Booker said.

"That won't work in this case, I'm afraid."

"Why not?"

Fiona did glance at Doggett then, and his gaze seemed to go right through her. With just that stare alone, he managed to do what Demetrius Booker hadn't been able to do with all his bluster—reduce Fiona to a quivering mass of jelly.

"I repeat, why not?" Booker's tone took on an edge of steel now, and Fiona slowly lifted her gaze to his.

"Because this witness has reason to believe that the person Lexi Mercer drove off with was a police officer."

CHAPTER SIXTEEN

"ARE YOU HEADED BACK to the office?" Guy Hardison asked Fiona a few minutes later as they walked down the hall toward the stairs.

"I'd like to talk to Detective Doggett first," she said. "But it won't take long."

Guy nodded. "As soon as you get back, call my secretary and have her make some time in my schedule this afternoon. You and I need to talk."

An alarm bell went off at his tone. "What about?" Fiona tried to ask casually.

"Your little performance back there, for one thing."

Fiona's heart skipped a beat. She'd ticked Guy off more times than she cared to remember, but there was something in his tone this time she'd never heard before. "What do you mean?"

"A mysterious witness who's afraid of the police? Come on, Fiona. You've always had a flair for the dramatic, but that was a little over the top even for you. But I have to hand it to you. Booker seemed impressed by the time you were finished." Behind his wire-rimmed glasses, Guy's eyes flickered with anger. "Of course, I suspect that was the whole point, wasn't it?"

"I don't know what you're talking about," Fiona said with a frown. But that wasn't altogether true. She had her own suspicions, and the way she saw it, Guy's irritation probably had a lot more to do with the attention she'd received from a man who could help the next state's attorney get elected than with what she'd actually said.

"So who is this witness?" he pressed. When she hesitated, he slanted her a glance. "You can't even tell me?"

"I'd rather not. Not yet."

He stopped at the top of the stairs and turned to face her. "This is all just bullshit, isn't it? If you actually thought this witness was credible, you'd have her brought in for questioning so fast her head would spin."

"Wait a minute," Fiona said slowly. "I never said the witness was female." In fact, she'd been very careful not to be gender specific.

"You didn't have to." Guy smiled. "I heard about your little visit to the runaway shelter this morning. Doesn't exactly take a psychic to figure out who you went to see."

"I didn't know you were keeping such close tabs on me," Fiona said bitterly.

"Your actions lately seem to warrant it."

"And what's that supposed to mean?"

"This strange attachment you seem to have developed for Kimbra Williams, for one thing."

"I care about her," Fiona defended. "I care what happens to her. And given the outcome of the trial, I don't think that's so hard to understand."

Guy studied her for a moment. "You honestly believe she saw Lexi Mercer on Division Street the night she disappeared?"

Fiona shrugged. "Why would she lie about it?"

"I don't know. Because she thinks it might get her a little more attention from you, maybe? Or maybe she's telling you exactly what you want to hear." He paused, his gaze darkening behind his glasses. "Considering your recent press, some people might leap to the conclusion that you're buying into Kimbra Williams's story so eagerly because it incriminates a cop. And it's good PR to go after cops these days, isn't it? At least for you. First Quinlan, then DeMarco and now this."

"*That's* bullshit," Fiona shot back. "You're the one who dumped the DeMarco case in my lap because you didn't want to prosecute it yourself."

His mouth tightened. "It was your decision to prosecute. You could have had the charges dropped once you saw how weak the case was."

"Oh, and wouldn't the press have loved us for that? The state's attorney's office has one kind of justice for cops, another kind for the projects. But maybe that's what you wanted. Maybe you thought the heat would all come down on me."

"Don't say something you'll regret," he advised.

Fiona drew a breath, reminding herself that where Demetrius Booker had no power over her, Guy Hardison literally held her future in the palm of his hands.

And as if to prove his power, he said in a low voice, "You've developed a disturbing tendency lately of getting emotionally involved in your cases. To the detriment of everyone concerned, I might add. Considering your history with the family, I think it would be a good idea if you recused yourself from the Mercer case."

He couldn't have slapped her across the face and stunned her any more. Fiona actually staggered back a step.

"You're already too involved," he said grimly.

"Look," she said through gritted teeth. "You're the one who sent me to the scene. You're the one who got me involved. And now that I am, I'm not quitting."

"Then back off," Guy warned. "Back off this investigation and let the police do their job or I will take you off the case."

He spun to hurry down the stairs, and Fiona was left reeling with shock over his unexpected attack. What was *that* all about?

In spite of his warning, she had no intention of backing off, especially in light of what she'd learned from Kimbra. If a cop was involved in Lexi's disappearance, a cover-up wasn't inconceivable, and Fiona wasn't about to let that happen.

She turned away from the stairs, eager to find Doggett, but Frank Quinlan was suddenly blocking her path. He'd come up behind her so stealthily Fiona hadn't heard his approach.

"Excuse me." She tried to move around him, but he side-stepped in front of her again. Fiona gave him the coldest stare she could muster, which was pretty damn frigid considering she was still highly pissed. "*I said* excuse me."

He didn't budge, and it suddenly occurred to Fiona the precarious position she found herself in. She stood at the top of the stairs, her back to the lobby, her heels at the edge of the top step. She wanted to reach out and clutch the banister for support, but she didn't want to give Frank Quinlan the satisfaction of knowing he made her nervous.

He moved closer, forcing Fiona to back up until her heels were hanging off the edge of the step. She did grab for the rail then, and he gave her a nasty grin.

He wouldn't dare push her down the stairs in a police station. Even Frank Quinlan didn't have that kind of nerve.

Or did he? Maybe, on second thought, this would be the perfect place to do her in. A dozen cops around to eagerly swear they'd seen her trip and lose her balance.

Fiona's heart pumped wildly inside her chest. She wanted nothing more than to turn and flee down the stairs and out the door of the station and not look back, but she would never give into Quinlan's intimidation. She'd learned on the playground of St. Anne's that it didn't pay to run from a bully. That only made them worse.

So she forced herself to hold her ground, forced herself to look Frank Quinlan straight in the eye. "Get the hell out of my way."

"Hey," he said. "No cause to take that tone. I just thought you might like to hear about the little office pool we've started around here."

Fiona lifted a brow. "Let me guess. You're taking wagers on who gets to kiss Booker's ass first. You or Clare Fox."

Quinlan's face went beet-red with anger. Fiona's hand instinctively tightened around the banister.

"We're taking bets all right," Quinlan managed to choke out, "but they don't have anything to do with the superintendent. The jackpot goes to the first cop who nails you."

Something curdled in Fiona's stomach and the sour taste rushed up to her mouth. "You son of a bitch."

He grinned, satisfied that he'd finally gotten to her. "Yeah, I put my money on DeMarco, but it looks like Doggett may have the inside track. Now who would have thought that?" He ran his hand up her arm. "Maybe I should have put myself in the running."

Fiona's skin crawled beneath the long sleeve of her suit jacket. "You take your hand off me, or I'll have your ass up on harassment charges so fast you won't even have time to wave bye to your pension."

"You think you can take me on, Gallagher?" His smile sent a chill up and down Fiona's spine. "You're on my turf now. Your brothers may own the South Side, but up here, I'm the man. You'll remember that if you know what's good for you."

He brushed past her then and headed down the stairs, and Fiona let out a relieved breath. She could hold her own with Quinlan, no problem, but it took something out of her. Her knees were shaking as she turned and made her way back to the conference room, looking for Doggett.

He was still there. He and Clare Fox. Clare was sitting on the conference table, her back to the door, but Fiona knew it was her. She recognized the way the woman's dark hair curled wantonly over her shoulders, the seductive way she crossed her legs. And Fiona recognized the look on Doggett's face as he stared down at Clare.

Every instinct told Fiona to back quietly away from the door and make a speedy exit before they knew she was there. But some sort of sick fascination rooted her to the spot. She couldn't seem to move. And then it was too late to leave because Doggett's gaze lifted and met hers.

His stare was suddenly so intense that Fiona found it a little scary. And a lot sexy. *Damn* him.

FIONA WAS HALFWAY ACROSS the lobby when Doggett caught up with her. He took her arm, and she wanted to sling it off, but she was mindful of all the cop stares around. *The jackpot goes to the first cop who nails you.*

"Hey," he said. "What's the rush?"

She removed her arm from his hand. "I've got things to do." Better things, her tone implied, than stand around lusting after you.

His gaze flickered, as if he didn't quite get what was going on. "You got a minute? I need to talk to you."

"It'll have to wait," she said tersely. "I'm in a hurry."

In a hurry to figure out just what the hell was going on between him and Clare Fox.

Doggett scowled down at her. "What's the matter with you?"

What's the matter with me? What's the matter with me? I'm not the one who looked as if I might start tearing my boss's clothes off at any second and going at it on the conference room table. What's the matter with me? What the hell's the matter with you? "Nothing."

He brushed a hand through his close-cropped hair. "Look, if this has something to do with Clare—"

She gave him an incredulous look. "Clare? You mean Clare Fox? Why would you think I have a problem with Clare Fox? Believe me, I don't. I barely know her. Why would I even give her a second thought?" Oh, crap.

Doggett looked thoroughly perplexed by that little tirade. "You didn't have a problem with what she said to the superintendent?"

Fiona had the sudden notion that she might burst into hysterical laughter at any moment. Or hysterical tears Honestly, didn't this guy know *anything* about women? Why didn't he just kiss her already and put her out of her misery?

Because even now, even knowing about that damn office pool, even having caught Doggett in—to her mind— a compromising position with Clare Fox, all Fiona wanted to do was drag her mouth across his, plunge her tongue down his throat—

Damn it!

She put a hand to her feverish forehead. "I'm sick. I'm really, really, really sick."

"You do look a little flushed," Doggett observed.

"I have to go." *Now!*

"Okay, I'll catch up with you later." Doggett gave her another strange look, then he turned and walked off. Fiona forced herself to do the same.

CHAPTER SEVENTEEN

FIONA HAD OUTSIDE appointments after lunch and didn't get back to the office until almost three. As soon as she stepped off the elevator on the twelfth floor in the Administration Building, one of the secretaries, Gina Ribisi—a fiery, fortysomething Italian—let her know she had two visitors waiting to see her in the conference room.

"I don't have any appointments," Fiona said with a frown. "How'd they get past the receptionist?"

"Same way they got past me, I guess." Gina grinned. "You know I'm a sucker for a pretty face."

"So who are they?" Fiona asked as she rifled through her messages.

"They wouldn't give me their names or tell me why they wanted to see you." Gina lowered her voice. "But they said it was a matter of life and death."

Fiona glanced up. "That's a little melodramatic, isn't it?"

"Yeah, and normally I would have had them tossed out on their backsides for wasting my time, but there was something about these two." Gina absently adjusted the ruffled neckline of her polka-dot blouse. "They're young, for one thing. Not much older than my kids. And to tell you the truth, they did look as if they'd had the you-know-what scared out of them recently. I felt sorry for them."

Fiona sighed. "Okay, I'll talk to them. Give me a couple of minutes to freshen up, then I'll meet them in the conference room.''

A few minutes later, after a pit stop in the ladies' rest room, Fiona opened the conference room door and stepped inside.

She didn't recognize the couple at the table, and as she crossed the room, she made a quick appraisal. Even though he was seated, she could tell the young man was tall and thin, probably around twenty, with scraggly brown hair and a motley goatee. The woman, by contrast, was neatly groomed in a T-shirt and jeans, her dark hair pulled back into a tidy ponytail. She had gorgeous eyes, Fiona noticed and a beautiful complexion.

''I'm Fiona Gallagher. I understand you need to see me?''

The young man half rose and took her extended hand. ''Nick Grable.''

''Oh, yes. You edit the college paper at Hillsboro University, right?''

He looked startled. ''You know who I am?''

''I've heard your name mentioned in conjunction with Alicia Mercer's homicide investigation.''

Nick Grable looked extremely discomfited by this information, and not a little disturbed. He exchanged a glance with the young woman seated to his right, and she nodded encouragingly before she turned to Fiona. ''You've probably heard my name mentioned, too. I'm Kelly Everhardt. Lexi and Alicia's roommate.''

''How do you do?'' Fiona shook the girl's hand and then sat down across the table from them. ''So what can I do for you?''

''We came here because we thought we should talk to someone other than the police,'' Kelly said anxiously.

Fiona frowned. "You do understand that I'm not a defense attorney."

The girl nodded. "We don't need an attorney. We haven't done anything wrong. We just need to tell someone else...what we've already told the police."

Fiona lifted a brow. "Why me?"

"Because Lexi and Alicia liked you. And because I read about you in the newspaper recently, about how you went after that cop who beat those prisoners into confessing."

"Allegedly beat them," Fiona clarified. "He was cleared of all charges."

"Still," Kelly insisted. "You weren't afraid of him."

Fiona was completely at a loss. "No, I wasn't afraid of him, but I still don't understand why you're here."

Kelly turned to Nick. "Go ahead," she urged in a low voice. "Tell her."

Nick leaned toward her, as if he were afraid someone might be listening in. His movements were so furtive that Fiona resisted the urge to glance over her shoulder. "I talked to a cop this morning. A detective named Doggett."

Fiona's heart gave a funny little flutter at the mention of Doggett's name. "He's the lead investigator on Alicia's homicide investigation."

"Yeah, that's what he told me," Nick agreed. "But most of his questions were about Lexi." His gray eyes regarded Fiona closely, as if he expected this information to surprise her.

She shrugged. "We haven't ruled out the possibility that Alicia's murder and Lexi's disappearance are related. I'm not surprised some of his questions pertained to Lexi."

Nick paused, glanced at Kelly and she put her hand on his arm. *"Tell* her."

When he still hesitated, Fiona said, "Look, something has obviously upset you. Why don't you just tell me what it is? Maybe I can help."

"We're not upset," Nick corrected. "Scared shitless is more like it."

"Nick," Kelly scolded.

He gave Fiona a sheepish shrug. "Sorry."

"Your being afraid has something to do with your conversation with Detective Doggett?" Fiona prompted.

Nick leaned in even closer. "I told him about the story Lexi and I are working on. It's an investigative piece on runaways who are being sold on the black market."

"Black market?" Fiona frowned. "What are you talking about?"

"You've heard of white slavery, haven't you?"

Fiona's stomach lurched. She had a sudden vision of The Wall at the shelter and all those pictures of all those missing girls. What was it Rachel had said earlier? *"These girls just seemed to have disappeared off the street. Vanished without a trace."*

She shuddered. "You have proof of this?"

"We were working on getting proof," he said.

"How?"

"Lexi was pretending to be a runaway."

"She went undercover," Kelly added. "She started hanging out on the street with other runaways."

Fiona sat back in her chair and stared at them. She couldn't believe what she was hearing. "That girl is only eighteen-years-old, and she's led a very sheltered life. She doesn't have a clue how to survive on the street. Do you have any idea the trouble she could be in?" When Kelly and Nick exchanged another glance, Fiona said, "Wait a minute. That was the whole point, wasn't it? To get herself into trouble. She was *trying* to get picked up. Is that what happened to her?''

Nick looked very nervous. "No. I mean, we don't know what happened to her.'' He ran a hand through his tangled hair. There was something about his tone, something in his frightened eyes that made Fiona want to cringe away from the rest of what he had to tell her. In some parts of the world, selling young girls into sexual bondage was a very lucrative business, and it would be easy to pretend that such a brutal enterprise could only happen in exotic locales like Hong Kong or Bangkok.

But Fiona had seen so many atrocities in her own city, she was no longer capable of burying her head in the sand. She'd once prosecuted a young woman who'd nearly severed her newborn's head with a pair of scissors, another who'd left her five children in an abandoned warehouse in the middle of winter to freeze to death, and still another who'd shot up her two-year-old with heroin in order to have an uninterrupted afternoon with her lover. If mothers did those things to their own children, then it wasn't hard to imagine total strangers taking young girls off the street and selling them for profit.

But the knowledge of what one human being could do to another still had the power to chill Fiona's blood.

She stared at Nick Grable for a moment, then said in a firm voice, ''I think you'd better start at the beginning.''

He told her then how he'd come to know Gwen and Sarah Bertram and about the article he'd read on the Internet, how he'd started to think a similar ring might be operating in Chicago. When he told her about Lexi taking to the streets to try to attract the attention of the ''scouts,'' Fiona could feel something rising inside her, a mixture of outrage, horror and nausea. For a moment, she could hardly breathe, and the only thing she could think was that Doggett had known about this and he hadn't said a word.

"You say you told Detective Doggett everything you just told me?" She was surprised by the trembling in her voice.

"Well..." Nick's gaze went to Kelly, then back to Fiona. "There was one thing I didn't mention to him. That's actually the reason we're here. Cops were involved down in Houston. They were involved big time. The reporter who finally broke the story was intimidated and harassed and so much of his evidence went missing in police custody that he couldn't get a decent paper to publish the article. They even went after his witnesses, and then his reputation. The cops did everything they could to shut him up. That's why he had to take the story to the Internet."

The words hung suspended in the space between them, like a bird trapped in a windstorm. *"The cops did everything they could to shut him up."*

"It was a cop done took that girl, Miss Lawyer."

Fiona felt the bile rise in her throat. She tried to swallow it away, and then realized her hands were shaking.

Damn.

Why hadn't Doggett said anything in the meeting this morning?

Not because he was involved. Fiona refused to believe that. Not Doggett. He was a clean cop, a straight arrow, a man who could never be party to something so horrendous. But he was still a cop. And if Fiona knew anything about cops, it was that they protected their own.

According to Nick Grable, it had taken a reporter to expose the ring in Houston.

She didn't like the direction her thoughts were taking,

but she knew firsthand the powerful bond police officers formed. Doggett was a loner, but he was still a cop.

He was still a cop.

Her gaze went back to Nick. "Is that why you're both so scared? Are you afraid the police will start harassing you?"

"I think they already have," Nick said grimly. "Detective Doggett already threatened me with a bogus narcotics charge, and he tried to confiscate all my files. I told him it would take me some time to gather up everything. A lot of my notes were at my apartment. He said he'd be back in a few hours. I had a couple of classes after that so I didn't make it back to the paper until after lunch. When I got there, someone had broken in and trashed the place. They even took the hard drive off my computer."

"And you think Detective Doggett had something to do with the break-in?" Fiona asked, her heart pounding.

Nick shrugged. "Except for Lexi and me, he was the only one who knew anything about this story."

"But it doesn't make sense that he would break in looking for your files when you'd already agreed to hand everything over to him," Fiona argued.

"Unless the point wasn't to gather evidence, but to get rid of it."

"That's why we came here," Kelly put in. "If the police know that you have this information as well, there'll be no reason for them to come after Nick."

But what's going to stop them from coming after me?

Fiona wished Kelly and Nick would just leave so that she could be alone to think. But if there was more to the story, she had to hear it. For Lexi's sake. For Lori's sake. Even for her own sake.

She turned to Kelly. "When did you find out about all this?"

"Nick called me a little while ago and told me the whole story. He was pretty shaken up by the break-in and I don't blame him. I suggested we come straight here to see you." The way she cast Nick a sideways glance told Fiona that the girl still had a very big crush on him. And she was more than a little thrilled that he'd called her for help.

But Nick seemed oblivious to the girl's infatuation. To be fair, he obviously had other things on his mind at the moment, but Fiona had a feeling the kid was a user. As long as he needed Kelly's help, he'd keep her around, but when someone more interesting came his way—like Lexi Mercer—*adios*.

"Are you sure Alicia didn't know about this story?" she asked Nick.

"I didn't tell her," he said with a shrug. "But it's possible she could have found out some other way."

"What other way?"

Kelly slid a business card across the table toward Fiona. "I found this in a jacket Alicia borrowed from me."

Fiona looked down at the card. It was from Simon Byrd Investigations, a private detective firm. The address was just north of Chinatown.

"If she had a private investigator following Lexi around to find out who she was sleeping with," Nick said, "Maybe he figured out what Lexi was up to. Maybe Alicia confronted her, and Lexi told her the truth. Or some of it at least."

Enough that someone had wanted her dead. But who?

FIONA PLAYED PHONE TAG with Simon Byrd for the next two hours until finally she caught up with him in his office just before five. "I'll be here until six," he told her. "If you can make it before then, fine. We can talk. Otherwise, we'll have to set something up for next week. I'm going out of town tomorrow and I won't be back until Monday.''

Fiona glanced at her watch. She'd be fighting rush hour traffic all the way, but if she left now, she could probably just make it, barring any unforeseen complications. It was worth a try, she decided. She certainly didn't want to have to wait until the following week to find out what kind of investigative work Simon Byrd had been doing for Alicia.

Professional P.I.s, like lawyers, entered an implied confidentiality agreement with their clients, but Fiona hoped Alicia's murder might be enough inducement to get Byrd to talk.

On the drive to his office, she thought back over everything Nick and Kelly had told her. She still couldn't understand why Doggett hadn't said anything in the meeting at Area Three headquarters about his interview with Nick. The information could be extremely critical to both cases, but Doggett hadn't said a word.

And speaking of that meeting, Fiona thought unhappily, what about his cozy little tryst with Clare in the conference room?

Every time she saw Doggett with Clare, Fiona had the disturbing notion there was something going on between them. She'd seen the way Clare looked at Doggett, and Fiona knew that look. There was an intimacy between them that couldn't be denied, and she wondered if the two of them had been lovers at one time. If they were still lovers.

The image of Doggett and Clare together tied Fiona's stomach in knots, made her want to pull over and lose the remainder of her late lunch, but she told herself she was being ridiculous about the whole thing. She had no claim on Doggett. They barely knew each other. They'd never even kissed. He could see whomever he pleased. But Clare?

Face it, she was prejudiced against Clare Fox because of what she'd done to Tony. And even worse, Fiona didn't trust the woman. Clare Fox had her own agenda, and God help anyone who got in her way.

She just didn't seem like Doggett's type, but then Fiona had no reason to believe that she was, either.

Byrd's office was located in an old high-rise that reminded Fiona of the Cabrini-Green towers with their narrow windows and bleak, redbrick facade, but the interior was a pleasant surprise. Walls had been removed to create more spacious office suites and huge skylights had been installed in the roof to flood the atrium lobby with natural light.

Fiona rode the glass elevator to the ninth floor and, following the suite numbers and arrows posted prominently at each corner, located Byrd's office at the end of a long, bright hallway.

A lot of the offices in the building already looked deserted for the evening. The lights had been lowered and the blinds drawn at the plate-glass windows overlooking the hallway. But as Fiona walked briskly down the carpeted corridor, she noticed several people behind the glass walls, still busy at their desks.

A woman in the office next to Byrd's looked up and smiled as Fiona passed, then she went back to work at her computer.

The blinds were drawn across the windows of Byrd's office, and there didn't seem to be any lights on inside. Fiona tried the door, then glanced at her watch. It was barely after six. She must have just missed him.

She started to knock in case he was working in a back office, but before she could do so, the knob turned beneath her hand, and she was startled when the door was drawn back suddenly.

A huge man stood in the dimly lit office staring at her with strange, glassy eyes. He was dressed in slacks and a dark shirt, and was at least six feet three and probably weighed well over two hundred pounds—a giant, imposing figure of a man. His hair was gray, as was the thick mustache that curled above his upper lip, but he didn't look that old, forty-five at the most.

The way he kept staring at Fiona without saying anything unnerved her. She thought at first he might be drunk. He leaned heavily against the door, and she wavered for a moment, before stepping inside the office.

"Mr. Byrd?"

He didn't say anything, just continued to stare at her so silently and so intently, Fiona felt a chill crawl up her spine.

From the inner office, she heard a noise that sounded like a file drawer being closed very softly, and her gaze darted back to Byrd.

Something was wrong here. The hair at the back of Fiona's neck stood on end as she stared at the man clinging to the door. He put out a hand toward her, and then, without warning, pitched forward, literally collapsing into her arms.

His bulk dragged Fiona to the floor with him.

And that's when she saw the blood. She gasped and tried to scream but the weight of the man's limp body cut off her air. She struggled for several frantic seconds, trying to get out from beneath him, and then, over his shoulder, she saw the door to the inner office open.

A shadow stood silhouetted just inside the doorway, and Fiona had the brief impression of a tall, lithe figure, eyes gleaming through the narrow slits of a ski mask. A dark arm lifted in her direction. She couldn't see the gun, but she knew it was there and instinct told her to duck.

She flattened herself against the floor, and heard the *spit spit* of a silenced weapon just before the first bullet hit the man lying on top of her, causing him to jerk violently. The second buried itself in the door frame just behind her, splintering the wood into a thousand tiny projectiles.

Terrified and working on pure adrenaline, Fiona shoved the prone man the rest of the way off her and scrambled on hands and feet into the corridor.

He grabbed her ankles and hauled her viciously back into the office. Fiona didn't go quietly. Nor easily. She fought every inch of the way. Clawing at the floor. Twisting her body first one way and then the other.

She rolled to her back, kicking with her feet, trying to dislodge the killer's hold on her. He did let her go then, but he was on her in a flash, one hand closing around her throat, his eyes peering down at her through those eerie slits as he lifted the gun to her head.

Those eyes…

Fiona's purse was still strapped over her shoulder, and she groped frantically in the bag until she felt the metal canister of pepper spray. In the split second before she knew he would have pulled the trigger, she lifted the can and fired directly into the killer's eyes. He grunted in outrage and immediately fell back, clutching his face.

She'd only bought herself a few seconds, but Fiona made the most of them. Heaving herself backward, she rolled out the door and struggled to her feet in the hallway. And then she ran.

Glancing over her shoulder, she saw the killer stumble into the hallway, rubbing frantically at his eyes as he lifted the gun. He fired in her direction, and a glass wall shattered beside her.

Someone screamed inside the office. Fiona had a brief glimpse of a woman's white face staring at her through the broken window before she yelled, "Get down!"

The woman dived under her desk. Fiona lunged around a corner and grabbed for her cell phone, pushing the button for 911 as she sprinted down the hallway. When she heard Doggett's voice, she stumbled in shock before realizing she'd hit his cell phone number on her speed dial by mistake. But that was probably for the best. He could get a squad car there faster than a 911 operator.

Fiona's breath was coming so fast and furious she could hardly speak. "Someone...trying to...kill me..."

"Fiona? What's going on? Where are you?"

His deep voice helped to steady her. Fiona glanced over her shoulder, saw that she wasn't being followed, but slackened her pace only slightly. Over deep gasps, she managed to give him the address of the building and to explain, very briefly, the situation she found herself in.

"Find cover," he barked, "And for God's sake, don't try to be a hero, okay? Just keep yourself alive."

He didn't have to tell her twice. Fiona saw an open doorway and ran toward it.

CHAPTER EIGHTEEN

BY THE TIME DOGGETT ARRIVED on the scene, squad cars, unmarked vehicles, and an EMT van were parked at the curb in front of the building. He pulled in behind them and then raced inside, ignoring the large group of spectators who'd gathered on the street.

Let her be okay. Just...let her be okay. I don't ask for much, right? But this one time—

Doggett's heart was pounding so hard he actually felt a little light-headed as he showed his ID to the officer stationed at the front door. He asked for a quick assessment of the situation and was told that the scene was secure, but the suspect had fled. One man was confirmed dead on the ninth floor. No other reported casualties, but witnesses saw the shooter fire at a woman.

Let her be okay.

Doggett took the elevator to the ninth floor, and by the time he got off, the adrenaline pumping through his veins made his heart feel as if it were about to explode. The people still working in the offices at the time of the shooting had undoubtedly been advised to stay put until the detectives had a chance to interview them. Doggett could see them peering anxiously through the plate-glass windows or standing in open doorways waiting to be told they could go home.

There were cops all over the place, and at least two

detectives from Area Four. Doggett flashed his ID as he approached the one standing nearest him.

"I'm looking for a woman," he said. "A tall redhead. Good-looking."

The detective nodded. "The ASA? Gallagher, right? Yeah, she's over there."

The moment Doggett saw Fiona seated on a bench in the hallway, he let out a breath of relief. She held a white cloth to her head, but other than that, she looked unharmed.

He couldn't believe how shaky his legs felt as he walked over and sat down beside her on the bench. "Hey, you okay?" He saw the blood on her clothes then, and his heart rolled over. "Do we need to get you to a hospital? Where are the paramedics?"

She turned then, her face pale but her eyes glittering and alert. "I'm okay. This isn't my blood." She removed the cloth from her head and saw that it was dotted with red. "Well, most of it's not."

"Have they checked you out?" Doggett asked worriedly, studying the cut near her right temple.

Fiona seemed a little surprised by his tone. "It's just a scratch. I've had worse paper cuts."

"You're tough. I'll give you that."

She shook her head. "No, I'm not. I'm usually a total wuss about these things. I think I must be in shock. When reality sets in, I'll be blubbering like a baby." She was dead serious, but somehow Doggett doubted that she'd let herself fall apart. She'd find a way to cope first. He hoped it wasn't by drinking.

"So what happened?" He was surprised to hear how gruff his voice sounded. Maybe he was the one about to fall apart, he decided, and that notion didn't sit well with him at all. He cleared his throat. "Who's the victim?"

He nodded toward the open doorway, where the crime scene techs were already busy gathering evidence.

"His name is Simon Byrd. He's a private investigator."

"He worked for you?"

"No. I have reason to believe he worked for Alicia Mercer."

The revelation surprised Doggett. "Why do you think that?"

She looked away then, as if he might see something in her eyes she didn't want him to. "Kelly Everhardt found his business card in a jacket Alicia borrowed from her."

Doggett frowned. "She didn't say anything to me about a business card."

Fiona's gaze was on the open doorway, and Doggett thought he saw her shudder. "It seems a lot of people have been keeping secrets in this case," she said cryptically.

"Meaning?"

She hesitated, and when she finally turned to face him, her eyes were dark with suspicion. "Why didn't you tell me about your interview with Nick Grable?"

There was no mistaking the accusation in her tone, and Doggett's frown deepened. "I haven't had a chance to. You were too busy to see me this morning, remember?"

"You could have said something in the meeting."

"What are you getting at, Fiona?"

Her gaze held his. After everything she'd just been through, Doggett marveled at her steadiness. "After your interview with Nick, the paper was broken into. Did you know that?"

"No, I didn't know that." Doggett swore. "The place was deserted when I went back over there. I thought the kid was doing the fade on me. Why the hell didn't he report the break-in?"

"Because he was afraid to."

"*Afraid* to?"

Fiona's expression hardened. "He told you about the story he and Lexi were working on? Well, what he didn't tell you was that cops were involved in Houston. That's pretty much why the story was kept under wraps so well. The police department lost evidence, hushed up witnesses and even went so far as to try to intimidate and discredit the reporter who finally broke the story. After Nick's office was broken into, he decided he needed to tell someone other than a cop what he'd learned."

"Wait a minute." Doggett sat forward. "Are you saying he thinks I had something to do with the break-in?"

"I guess the possibility crossed his mind."

"That's crazy. He'd already agreed to turn over his files to me."

"Yes. But as he pointed out to me," Fiona said slowly, "maybe the intent was never to collect evidence but to get rid of it."

Doggett couldn't believe what he was hearing. She actually thought that about him?

He'd had his share of complaints over the years. He wasn't denying that. Every active officer did. You made collars, people got pissed, tried to blame the arresting office for their troubles. Sometimes they even went so far as to file bogus charges.

But in over two decades on the force, no one had ever accused Doggett of being dirty. Until now.

His gaze narrowed. "So what about you, Fiona? You think I had something to do with the break-in?"

"…no…" But she'd hesitated a little too long.

Anger shot through him, and he dragged a hand through his hair. "I don't believe this. What the hell have I done, besides being a cop, to make you think I'm dirty?"

"I never said I thought that."

"The hell you didn't."

"I didn't say it," she said hotly, "and I don't think it. But I've been around cops all my life. I know the code of the brotherhood. I know how far some officers will go to protect their own. I've seen it."

He took a moment to try and curb his temper. "Let's get one thing very straight. I had nothing to do with that break-in. And not that I owe you an explanation, but I didn't bring up Nick's interview in the meeting this morning because I wasn't sure I even bought it. He read it off the goddamn Internet, okay? I had to check it out for myself. That's how it works and you know it. I don't bring the prosecutor every scrap of evidence I find unless I know it'll help build a case."

Her gaze faltered slightly, as if she might have had a moment's doubt. Then she said almost defiantly, "And did you check it out?"

"I tracked down the reporter. He swears by every word of his story."

"Including the part about the police department's involvement and cover-up?" When he nodded, Fiona said, "Did you believe him?"

Doggett shrugged. "Let's put it this way. I didn't hang up on him." He paused. "Look, I don't know what went on down in Houston, but I've seen enough cover-ups here in Chicago to know that they happen. Cops watch each other's backs. That's the way it is. But if you think I'd look the other way in a murder investigation, much less a black market flesh ring, then you don't know me very well. You don't know me at all."

Their gazes held for the longest moment, then Fiona glanced down at her hands. "You're right. I'm sorry."

He shrugged. "You *don't* know me. I understand that.

But you know your own family, don't you? Would you believe this of any of your brothers?''

She shook her head. ''No. And I shouldn't have jumped to conclusions about you. I know better than anyone that there are plenty of good cops. And I know you're one of them. It's just—''

''Easier to believe I'm one of the bad guys?''

She put her hands to her head and shoved back her hair. ''God,'' she whispered. ''If I don't know you at all, how is it that you know me so well? We only met four days ago.''

He shrugged, but he wanted to tell her that sometimes it only took a split second to make a connection. It had happened to him before. Not the same as with Fiona, but the instant bond he'd felt with the ten-year-old kid who'd died in his arms, the victim of a drive-by shooting, had been no less powerful. Or with the grandmother who'd flagged down his squad to turn in her only grandson because she thought his chances for survival in prison were greater than in the projects.

Those connections Doggett still carried with him. They would be with him forever. And the one with Fiona? It was partly sexual, yeah. A lot sexual, maybe. He'd be a fool to deny the attraction. But it was more than that, and they both knew it. And that was why she was scared. That was why she was looking for excuses not to trust him. Doggett understood her so well because she was a lot like him.

''I am sorry.'' Her blue eyes glittered against her pale face, and Doggett thought that, blood-splattered and on the verge of shock, she'd never looked more beautiful.

''Let's just forget it.'' He glanced toward the office across the hallway. ''Tell me what happened when you got to Byrd's office?''

"He'd already been shot, but I didn't know it at first. Somehow he managed to get to the door and let me in, and then he collapsed."

"Where was the shooter?"

"In the back office, going through files. He came out when he heard us. The rest of it happened pretty fast. I don't remember a lot of it, but I know he shot at me. I managed to crawl out into the hall and call for help, but he dragged me back inside the office. He didn't want witnesses, I guess."

Doggett's blood went cold at the images going through his head. "How'd you get away from him?"

Fiona lifted her chin, but her bottom lip quivered slightly, giving away her nerves. "I pepper sprayed his ass."

And if there had been any doubt before about his feelings for her, there were none now. Doggett was a goner and he knew it.

AS SOON AS FIONA GOT HOME, she stripped off her bloody clothes and climbed in the shower, standing under water as hot as she could stand it. After awhile, the trembling stopped, and she was able to think a little more clearly, but the Mercer murder and disappearance were mysteries that were getting murkier by the minute. If anything, Simon Byrd's murder only added to the confusion.

Who had wanted him dead?

Fiona supposed that any number of people could have wanted to get rid of him. It was his job to dig up dirt. On a cheating spouse? A dishonest employee? Throw in the criminal element, and the possibilities were endless.

Could it be just a coincidence that he'd been murdered so soon after Fiona had learned he might have been hired by Alicia to follow her sister?

And if it wasn't a coincidence, what had Simon Byrd found out about Lexi that had frightened someone into killing him?

Had Byrd shared with Alicia something he'd learned concerning either Lexi's affair with a married man or her undercover assignment for the paper? Had that information gotten them both killed?

And what did either of their deaths have to do with Lexi's disappearance?

The questions running through Fiona's mind were so chaotic that by the time the water grew tepid, she'd developed a splitting headache. Getting out of the shower, she quickly dried off and then, gulping down two aspirin, she walked into the bedroom, resisting the urge to crawl into bed and pull the covers up over her head. But her cat was sound asleep in the middle of her coverlet, lying on his back, paws crossed, the very picture of contentment, and Fiona didn't have the heart to disturb him.

Besides Doggett had promised to let her know if he found out anything else at the crime scene, and Fiona had no idea if he would call or show up at her door as he had a few nights ago. To be on the safe side, she forced herself to get dressed again in a fresh skirt and cotton blouse.

Carrying a blanket out to the living room, she curled up on the sofa, with no idea that she would ever be able to sleep. Not after the close call she'd had. But from exhaustion or some internal defense mechanism kicking in, Fiona promptly dozed off. When the doorbell pealed sometime later, she came instantly awake, as if her subconscious had been waiting for the sound all night.

She threw off the cover and crossed the room to look through the peephole.

Releasing all the dead bolts, she opened the door for

Doggett. He scrutinized her carefully as he stepped inside. "You okay?"

"I'm fine." She closed the door and quickly turned to face him. "So what did you find out at the crime scene?"

"Not much more than we already knew," he said with a weary sigh. "The office was ransacked. File drawers were ripped out, papers scattered everywhere. The destruction was overkill. Whoever shot Byrd was trying to cover his tracks. He didn't want anyone figuring out what he was looking for."

Fiona motioned Doggett to the sofa, and they both sat, he at one end and she in the middle, one leg curled beneath her.

"We've contacted Byrd's secretary," he said. "She's agreed to go through all the papers and see whether or not she can determine which files are missing."

"What about the shooter?" Fiona asked anxiously. "Did anyone besides me get a look at him?"

"We have two witnesses on the ninth floor who saw a tall, thin, armed man dressed in dark clothing and a ski mask run into the stairwell. Presumably he was able to get out of the building before the squads arrived."

Fiona frowned. "What about witnesses on the ground floor? Most of the offices face the lobby. Someone must have seen him before he left the building. A man dressed from head to toe in black on a mild summer evening doesn't exactly blend with the crowd."

"According to the witnesses, he was carrying a briefcase. My guess is that he ripped off the ski mask in the stairwell and probably changed his clothes before calmly walking out of the building."

"Then he must have been caught on the security cameras," Fiona said.

"We're looking into that. There are cameras at all the

ground floor exits, but nothing on the ninth floor, unless Byrd had his own hidden surveillance cameras, which is pretty likely, given his line of work. But we haven't located them yet. In the meantime, we'll go over the lobby security tapes and pinpoint the people who arrived and left the building during our time frame.''

"Tall and thin," Fiona mused, mentally matching that description with what she'd seen for herself. "I guess that pretty much eliminates Frank Quinlan as a suspect. He's neither tall nor thin.''

He looked surprised. "Frank Quinlan? Why did you think the shooter was Frank Quinlan?''

She shrugged. "When Nick told me the story about cops scouting out runaways to be sold on the black market in Houston and the possibility of a similar operation here in Chicago, I admit, Quinlan was the first person I thought of. I guess it's no secret that I'm hardly a fan of his.''

"I'm not a fan of his, either," Doggett said. "But being an asshole doesn't make him a criminal.''

"I realize that." Why was he defending a guy like Quinlan? Because he was a cop? Fiona rubbed her forehead. "Look, have we gotten way off track in this investigation? Do you really think those kids stumbled onto a sex slave trade here in Chicago, or have we allowed ourselves to be led on a wild goose chase?''

"I don't know," Doggett said honestly. "All I know for sure is that one girl is dead, her sister is still missing, and half the time I feel as if I'm walking around in a damn fog.''

Fiona could sympathize. "But if there is a black market flesh ring, as you called it, that means Lexi deliberately put herself in a position to be taken by these people. She's a smart girl; would she really take such a risk?''

"You answered your own question earlier. She and

Nick are kids. So, yeah, it's been my experience that someone her age might take that risk, especially with a little sleaze like Grable egging her own. He has delusions of journalistic grandeur, and he probably managed to convince Lexi she could be the next Ashleigh Banfield.''

''Have you told Lori about any of this?''

''I haven't spoken with the Guests since our initial interview.'' He shot Fiona a glance. ''And I'd just as soon they not hear about this angle of the investigation. Not at this stage.''

''Any particular reason why not?''

''I'm still not willing to eliminate Paul Guest as a suspect. My gut tells me there's something not exactly kosher about that guy.''

''You still think he's the married man Lexi was involved with, don't you?'' Fiona shuddered. ''God, I hope you're wrong. After everything else she's been through, I'm not sure Lori could survive finding out something like that.''

''It'd be rough,'' Doggett agreed. ''About as bad as it gets.''

Fiona pulled the blanket over her legs to ward off a sudden chill. ''You know, in a twisted sort of way, I guess I can understand how he could be infatuated with Lexi. She's so completely gorgeous, and she's not his real daughter. Seeing her day in and day out—'' Fiona broke off on another shudder. ''This is so sick. I can't even believe I'm trying to justify it. But even assuming it's true, how does it connect Paul Guest with everything else that's happened?''

''Think about what Booker said this morning. Guest is a close personal friend of Houston's mayor, and of the governor of Texas. He has some powerful connections down there. Let's assume for a moment that he was involved in the operation in Houston and that the ring down there is connected to the one here in Chicago.''

"That's a pretty wild assumption," Fiona said.

"Granted. But stay with me for a minute. Supposing he and Lexi weren't having an affair. Supposing he came on to her and she rejected him, maybe even threatened to tell her mother. A man like Paul Guest would find another way to get what he wanted."

"By *buying* her? His own stepdaughter?" Even after everything Fiona had seen in her years as a prosecutor, Doggett had still managed to shock her. "Look, this wild speculation is getting us nowhere. We don't have one shred of evidence tying Paul Guest to Alicia's death or to Lexi's disappearance, much less to the black market sex trade in Houston or Chicago. As you said about Quinlan, being an asshole doesn't make him a criminal."

"If that were the case—"

"Half the population would be in prison," she finished for him.

He gave her that little half grin that set her heart to pounding. "I might even have to do some hard time myself."

"You think?"

It was a relief to lighten the mood. Their previous conversation had disturbed Fiona more than she wanted to admit. She was used to having to crawl through muck to get at the truth, but it still sometimes left her feeling as if she needed a shower and a good disinfectant.

"Can I ask you something?" she said on impulse.

"About the case?"

"No. It's...personal."

Doggett hesitated. "Sure. Go ahead."

"What's going on between you and Clare Fox?"

"What do you mean?" Was it her imagination or had alarm flickered ever so briefly across his face?

Fiona drew up her legs and wrapped her arms around her knees, blanket and all. "I've seen the way she looks at you. It's as if she knows you very well. One might even say intimately."

"Just ask your question, Fiona."

She drew a breath. "Are you and Clare lovers?"

He shook his head. "No. No way."

"But you...were?"

He glanced away, as if he could no longer meet her gaze. "Clare and I were married for a while."

CHAPTER NINETEEN

FIONA'S BREATH LEFT HER lungs in a painful rush. "Married?" she all but gasped. "When?"

"A long time ago."

"How long?"

He still couldn't look at her. "It was a couple of years after Ruby died. Clare was involved with the investigation, and she kept me informed, which was more than I can say for Quinlan."

"Quinlan?" Fiona asked in surprise.

Doggett nodded. "Frank Quinlan was the lead investigator on Ruby's case."

"He never made an arrest?"

"No."

It was amazing how much bitterness one little syllable could contain. Fiona stared at Doggett for a long moment, trying to figure him out. The man was a total enigma. Married to Clare Fox? She never would have guessed that. She felt as if the defense had just blindsided her with a surprise witness at the eleventh hour. "What happened with the investigation?" she finally asked.

"Nothing happened. He had a suspect in custody, and he let him get away."

"*Let* him?"

Doggett turned to face her, his expression shuttered once more. "That's all water under the bridge now."

And yet Fiona knew that it wasn't. A cop who couldn't

solve his own wife's murder. It was the stuff of nightmares. And nightmares were something she could well understand.

She suddenly remembered what her grandmother had said the night of her uncle's retirement party. Doggett had never remarried, she'd told Fiona. *"That kind of loyalty is extremely rare these days."*

If you only knew, Gran.

"I don't really like talking about this, but since you asked…" Doggett trailed off on an uncomfortable shrug. "Like I said, Clare was a good friend to me after Ruby died, but we should have left it at that. The marriage was a big mistake from the start. We weren't right for each other." He grimaced. "We're lucky we both got out alive."

"How long did it last?"

"Six months." He glanced at her. "Not many people in the department even know about this so I'd appreciate it if you'd keep it just between us."

Fiona nodded, but she was still having a hard time dealing with the image of Doggett and Clare…of the two of them together…

"Is that why you don't like my brother, Tony?" she asked suddenly. "Because he got involved with Clare?"

"You've got it wrong," Doggett said. "Your brother's the one who has a problem with me. Or at least, he did. When I heard about him and Clare, I said some things I probably shouldn't have."

"Such as?"

"I warned him he didn't know what he was getting into. Clare's…not an easy woman to deal with."

That could well be the understatement of the year, Fiona thought. "Let me guess. Tony didn't exactly take kindly to the advice."

"He took it the wrong way, and he's held it against me ever since."

"That's a Gallagher for you," Fiona said dryly. "We do hang on to our grudges. Just ask the O'Roarkes. On second thought, don't." She paused, her gaze on Doggett, but he still seemed to have a difficult time looking her in the eye. Did he regret his marriage to Clare that bitterly? Somehow, it made Fiona feel a little better to think so.

"So how old were you when you married Clare?" she asked curiously.

"Twenty-five."

"You were married twice by the time you were twenty-five? Wow," she teased softly. "That's some record, detective."

"Not one I'm proud of," he agreed. "But I've been single for over fifteen years. That should count for something, right?"

He did look at her then, and something went all still inside Fiona. She couldn't remember when she'd been so attracted to a man. He wasn't her type, and she was all wrong for him. They didn't belong together, and yet when their eyes met, Fiona could think of nothing but kissing him.

"So now it's my turn," he said. "And don't tell me that since you're the lawyer, you get to ask all the questions. It's not going to work that way tonight."

She swallowed. "It isn't?"

He shook his head, his gaze on her very determined. Now it was Fiona who looked away. She rested her chin on her knees. "What exactly do you want to know?"

"Tell me about you and David Mackenzie."

So there it was. The moment of truth. It was bound to come sooner or later, Fiona thought. And after she told him what he wanted to know, it would be Doggett's moment of truth.

"You probably know most of the story from the papers," she said. "Tony and David Mackenzie went to college together, and they both ended up in love with the same woman, although Tony didn't know that at the time. He and Ashley were high school sweethearts. Everyone thought they'd get married someday. But somewhere along the way, she started seeing David behind Tony's back. She got pregnant, and, according to David, she was supposed to tell Tony the truth the night she was murdered.

"David secretly believed that Tony had flown into a rage and killed her, and that my uncle and my father, who were the first detectives on the scene, had covered up evidence that would have incriminated him. David was right about that." She glanced at Doggett. "They did withhold evidence. So you see, I know all about how cops look out for each other."

Doggett said nothing, just continued to regard her with the same steady, nonjudgmental stare. She was grateful for that.

"Anyway, a man named Daniel O'Roarke was convicted of Ashley's murder, but David continued to believe that Tony was the real killer. He plotted his revenge while still pretending to be Tony's best friend. Years after Ashley died, he killed three women and tried to frame Tony for the murders."

"What about you?" Doggett asked quietly. "Where do you fit into this picture?"

That was the hard part. "I was in love with him," she said just as quietly. "And I never suspected a thing."

"Why would you?"

"Because I should have known."

"How?"

"He would leave me and go out to kill those women," Fiona said harshly. "What kind of person wouldn't have known?" She put her hands to her face, closing her eyes briefly. She felt Doggett's hand on her arm, and she opened her eyes to find him watching her intently.

"You didn't kill those women," he said.

"I know."

"So why the guilt?"

"You didn't kill Ruby, but you still have your guilt."

"That's different."

"No, it's not. Not really. Look, I know I'm not responsible for what he did. But if I'd picked up on the signals sooner, if I'd just listened to my instincts, maybe those women would still be alive."

"And just what makes you think you're so special?"

She gazed at him in shock. "I don't."

He leaned toward her. "Then why do you think you should have seen something in this guy no one else did? Someone who plans out his kills the way he did is by nature cunning and deceitful, and a guy like that usually conceals it by being charming and outgoing. Look at Ted Bundy."

"But David wasn't a serial killer."

"Some of the same characteristics still apply. My point is, professionals sometimes misread these guys. I've sat across an interrogation table from men I would have sworn were guilty as sin, and they turned out to be innocent. I saw a widow once whose grief nearly ripped my insides out, and then I found out later she was the one who had cut her husband's throat. We're all fooled at one time or another."

Fiona sighed. "I know. I've told myself the same thing a thousand times, but that's not going to stop me from questioning my judgment in any relationship I ever have."

He frowned. "Maybe you're being too hard on yourself."

"Maybe." She wrapped the blanket more snugly around her legs. "I know David didn't really care about me. His being with me was just another way to get at Tony. But he never slept with me. I worried back then, before I knew the truth about him, that it was because I wasn't attractive or sexy or sophisticated enough for him. But I like to think now that maybe it was because there was something decent left inside him. And it was that small part of him that I fell in love with."

"I can buy that."

Fiona drew a ragged breath. "Wow. I got that all out and lightning didn't strike me dead. I'm still here, and I feel...I don't know. I think I actually feel better."

She glanced at Doggett. "You don't know what a big step that was for me. In the seven years since David died, I haven't told anyone what I just told you except for the psychologist I saw right after it happened. He made all the correct shrink noises, of course, but I never really believed he understood how I felt. But you do, don't you? How is that?"

"Because we're not so different, Fiona."

She loved the way he said her name. His deep voice was like an intimate caress along her spine. "Sometimes it almost seems as if you can tell what I'm thinking."

"Maybe I can."

Her breath quickened as she gazed up at him. "Can you tell what I'm thinking right now?"

"I hope so. Because if I'm wrong, I may be about to get my face slapped."

He kissed her then, not gently as she had expected, but

with his lips hard against hers, his tongue plunging deep, deep inside her mouth. And it was actually just what she wanted, she realized. Who needed gentle when Doggett was making her melt, making her lose her natural inhibitions by the second?

Her heart started to pound as she wound her arms around his neck and pulled him close. He tasted so good, a little like Juicy Fruit chewing gum only a million times better. She pressed herself against him, her hands in his hair, and he kissed her even harder, kissed her until she could hardly breathe. When they finally broke apart, she put her hands on either side of his face and stared into his eyes. "Oh, man, you kiss good."

He gave her that little half grin. "Do I?"

She took his hand and held it to her heart. "Feel that?"

His hand slipped to her breast. "Yeah." His gaze turned deep and dark and hot then as his lips came crushing down on hers. Her mouth opened readily for him and he groaned as he pressed her back against the couch. He kept right on kissing her until somehow Fiona ended up on her back with him lying over her.

"What are we doing?" she whispered.

"Isn't it obvious?"

"No, I mean, *what are we doing?* You don't want to get involved with me." She reached up and touched his face. "You have no idea how truly screwed up I am."

He turned his mouth into her hand. "Maybe that's what I like about you."

She closed her eyes. "God. That probably means you're as sick as I am."

"Probably." He hesitated. "You know, we don't have to take this any farther. We could stop right now and it would just be a kiss."

But it wasn't just a kiss and they both knew it. Fiona

had experienced mediocre kisses before. She knew when a kiss was just a kiss. And that kiss had been anything but. That kiss had been—face it—a prelude to some pretty hot sex.

"I've dreamed about that kiss," she admitted.

"Yeah? Tell me more."

"The dream always starts off just this way. You lying on top of me with your tongue down my throat..."

"God."

"Ray. In case you hadn't noticed, you don't exactly need to pray here." All he had to do was kiss her again, and she would be his for the taking.

And he did. His hands slipped under her, lifting her hips to press her more firmly against him as his tongue flicked over her lips, then dipped inside. For a moment, Fiona almost resisted. What the hell *were* they doing? This couldn't be a good idea. But for the life of her, she couldn't come up with one good reason why she should send Doggett packing. It felt too damn good, whatever it was they were doing.

She plunged her fingers through the soft, short strands of his hair, then trailed her hands over his shoulders, down his back.

And all the while, he never stopped kissing her. He undid the buttons on her blouse, so quick it made Fiona's head spin, and then he spread the fabric wide, deftly unfastening the front hook of her bra. His hands flattened on her breasts, and Fiona gasped in pleasure. The man obviously knew what he was doing. Had she ever once doubted it?

She tried to reciprocate, but her fingers were not nearly so clever or nimble. She fumbled with the buttons on his shirt until finally, in frustration, she jerked the two sides apart. Buttons flew everywhere, but Doggett didn't seem to mind. She wasn't even sure he noticed. One of his hands had left her breast to shove up her skirt, and then his fingers were inside her panties.

Doggett made it impossible for her to think at all. His hand was doing mind-blowing things to her body. She pushed against him, moving her hips back and forth...

Her panties were in the way. That bit of silk had to go. Doggett's fingers twisted in the delicate elastic, and the fabric resisted for just a moment, then *poof!* Problem solved. He was that good.

But she wasn't. She struggled with his belt and zipper until Doggett shifted his weight, trying to give her some maneuvering room. Before she knew what was happening, they rolled off the sofa, and his head banged against the hardwood floor.

Fiona was astride him, reaching behind her, sliding her hand into his pants. "I don't care how badly you're hurt, don't you dare lose your concentration," she said. Her fingers closed around him.

He was breathing as if he'd just run a marathon. "A nuclear blast couldn't make me lose my concentration right now."

Fiona slid back until they were touching as intimately as they possibly could without—

"Tell me you brought something," she gasped.

Doggett went completely still. "Damn."

"It's okay." She scrambled off him. "Don't move. Maybe I have something." She'd better have something.

Fiona ran into the bedroom and started tearing through drawers. Nothing in the nightstand. Nothing in her lingerie drawer.

Why in the world had she thought she'd have a spare condom lying around? She hadn't had a man in her apartment in yea   She hadn't had *sex* in years. But there'd been that defense attorney she'd had dinner with a few times last fall. She'd thought something might be developing, but—

"Found one!" *Yes!* She raced back to the living room, then skidded to a halt at the end of the hallway. Doggett was kneeling, pants fastened, shirt open, phone to his ear. Expression grim.

Not good.

Fiona knew from his face it wasn't going to happen. Not tonight.

Talk about a letdown.

He hung up the phone, his gaze on her, all over her. She resisted the temptation to straighten her clothing. It seemed a little late for modesty.

"I have to go," he said, getting to his feet.

She wanted to ask him if he'd come back later and finish what they'd started, but decided that might be a little forward even for her. "So...you'll call me?"

His gaze dropped to the panties lying in the middle of her living-room floor. "You can pretty much count on that."

CHAPTER TWENTY

"HEY, DOGGETT, WE'VE GOT TO stop meeting like this," Meredith Sweeney told him the next morning when he stopped by the morgue. "It's been, what...? All of five hours since I last saw you."

Meredith had been called out last night to the crime scene as well, and they'd both been tied up for hours. By the time Doggett finally got away, it had been too late to call Fiona, much less to go back to her place and finish what they'd started.

But he'd been tempted.

When he'd finally gotten home, he'd lain awake thinking about her instead of the case, which wasn't like him. A fresh homicide usually gave him tunnel-vision, but not last night. Not after Fiona.

God, she'd been so...*hot*. That was the only way to describe her. Hot in his arms, hot against him, hot for him...

Who would have ever thought that?

"What's so funny?" Meredith demanded.

"What?"

"You had the biggest shit-eating grin I ever saw on your face, and that's not like you. In all the years I've known you, I don't think I've ever even seen you smile. So what gives?"

"Nothing."

Meredith narrowed her eyes. "Hey, you don't have the hots for Fiona Gallagher, do you?"

Doggett stared at her in shock. What the hell was she, a damn psychic or something? "I hardly know Fiona Gallagher."

"That's not what I asked. I asked if you had a thing for her."

"Why would you think that?" He tried to make his expression innocent looking.

"Oh, I don't know. Maybe because I saw sparks fly between you two back in that alley a few nights ago. I figured it was just a matter of time."

He shook his head. "Must have been your imagination."

"My imagination, huh? I don't *think* so. The way you two were looking at each other, I figured you'd be going at it by now." She paused and gave him a long perusal. "Want a piece of advice, Doggett?"

"About my case?"

"No, about your love life."

He sighed. "Would it do any good if I told you no?"

"None whatsoever." She leaned toward him. "Watch yourself with Fiona Gallagher."

That surprised him. "What do you mean?"

"How well do you know her brothers or her old man?"

He shrugged. "I had a couple of run-ins with Tony Gallagher. The others I know only by reputation."

"And here I thought everybody knew the Gallaghers," she said dryly.

"CPD is a big place," Doggett said. "Besides, I don't exactly move in the Gallaghers' circle."

"And if you're smart, you'll keep it that way."

Doggett frowned. "What's your point, Meredith?"

"My point is this. You pull any crap with Fiona Gallagher and her brothers will be all over you like white on rice. I know what I'm talking about, too. I used to be married to John Gallagher. Talk about the ultimate big brother complex. You get out of line with her, he'll kick your ass six ways to Sunday.''

''I'll keep that in mind,'' Doggett said. ''Now can we please get down to business?''

She grinned. ''If you insist. But if you're here for the postmortem on the floater your guys pulled out of the river last night, you're wasting your time.'' She motioned toward the stack of paperwork on her desk. ''Looks like he's going to be on ice for a couple of days.''

''That's not what you said last night.''

''Last night I didn't know a lunatic would go on a rampage and shoot up some South Side dive. We've got bodies up to here.'' She put a hand underneath her chin. ''There's got to be a full moon out.''

''What about the middle-aged Caucasian male that was shot in Chinatown yesterday?''

''The P.I.? Murray's got that one. You'll have to talk to him.''

''Okay,'' Doggett said. ''One last thing.'' He got out the autopsy photographs of Sarah Bertram and tossed them onto Meredith's desk. ''Can you pull up the autopsy report that goes with these photos? The victim's name was Sarah Bertram. According to the time stamp, she would have come through here a little over a year ago.''

Meredith leafed through the photos. ''Why don't you just check the police report? Isn't that where you got these?''

''No. And for reasons I don't want to go into right now, I'd just as soon keep this between us.''

Her gaze lifted. ''Why?'' When he didn't answer, she

said, "You don't want someone to know you're looking into this, is that it?"

"No more questions, Meredith."

"Okay. If that's the way you want to play it." She shrugged, then swung around to her computer, touched a few keys, and said, "Spell the name for me."

"Sarah with an *H. B-E-R-T-R-A-M.*"

Meredith typed in the information, and while she waited for the file to load, she picked up the photos again. When she came to the one that showed the symbol on the girl's left shoulder, she paused. "Hello. I've seen this before. On the body found in that alley Tuesday morning, right? The Mercer girl."

Doggett nodded.

Meredith studied the picture. "Two girls with the same weird symbol on their bodies but killed more than a year apart. Correct me if I'm wrong, but you're probably not thinking that's a coincidence."

"I don't think it's a coincidence," Doggett agreed.

She turned back to the computer. "So what are we looking for exactly?"

"I don't know. But I'm hoping I'll know it when I see it."

"Okay, here we go." The file came up, and Meredith read for a moment. "Cause of death was blunt force trauma to the head. She also had liver damage and a ruptured spleen, but the blow to the head killed her. The attending medical examiner ruled it accidental. She was hit by a car."

"Check the toxicology screen."

Meredith did as he asked. "Her BAC was .08, which means she was legally drunk, and there were traces of flunitrazepam in her bloodstream."

"Ruffies," Doggett said grimly. "If someone spiked

her drink and then sent her out to play in traffic, her death might not have been so accidental after all.''

"Yeah, but she might have spiked her own drink," Meredith said. ''Rohypnol is not just the date rape drug anymore. These kids are taking it voluntarily as an alcohol extender and disinhibitory agent. We're seeing ODs come through here like you wouldn't believe."

"Okay," Doggett said. ''That's what I needed to know. You see anything else that stands out?"

Meredith looked up. ''She was a sixteen-year-old runaway who met with a violent death. Unfortunately her autopsy report is depressingly familiar."

WHEN FIONA GOT BACK TO THE office after lunch, Gina Ribisi snagged her again as she got off the elevator.

''This is your week for surprise visitors.'' Her eyes gleamed with something that might have been excitement. ''You'll never guess who's waiting to see you in the conference room."

''Not those two kids who were here yesterday.'' Fiona shifted her briefcase to the other hand as they walked down the hall. She knew Doggett had been trying to track down Nick Grable since their conversation the day before. The kid obviously knew how to make himself scarce.

Gina glanced around, then leaned toward Fiona and lowered her voice. ''It's Sherry Hardison. I thought I'd better warn you before you were ambushed.''

''Sherry Hardison?'' Fiona scowled. ''Why would she want to see me?"

''I haven't a clue,'' Gina said innocently, but she could hardly contain the curiosity in her dark eyes and Fiona suddenly remembered what Milo had said about the office gossip concerning her and Guy Hardison. Obviously Gina had heard the ugly rumors, believed them, and was now certain that Guy's wife had come to confront "the other woman."

Fiona fervently hoped that wasn't the case. An unpleasant scene with a wronged wife was the last thing she needed, particularly considering she wasn't and never would be other woman material. Her sympathies in marital difficulties almost always lay with the wife. "Are you sure she wants to see me? Maybe she's here to see Guy."

But Gina shook her dark head. "She specifically asked to see you. When I told her you were out, she insisted on waiting so I put her in the conference room. I didn't know what else to do." She seemed to be waiting for some sign from Fiona that she'd done the right thing. Or that her suspicions of a torrid love triangle were exactly on target.

Fiona didn't ease her mind on either point. "Where's Guy?" she asked in exasperation. Why wasn't he here dealing with this? She was his wife. He was the one who should have to face her wrath. Fiona was just an innocent bystander, the victim of a malicious smear campaign.

Besides, if Sherry Hardison could have seen her last night with Ray Doggett, she wouldn't be nearly so worried about a possible romantic entanglement between her husband and Fiona.

Thinking about Ray and what they'd almost done brought heat to Fiona's face, making her appear, she was sure, even guiltier in Gina's eyes.

"Guy's been in a meeting all day with Don Hastings," the secretary told her, referring to the current Cook County state's attorney. "I don't know when he'll be back."

Fiona sighed. "Okay. I guess it's up to me to find out what she wants then."

"Good luck," Gina called as Fiona started down the hallway. Fiona didn't look back, but experience told her that Gina was probably even now making a beeline for the watercooler or the coffee machine. The fact that Sherry Hardison was waiting in the conference room to see Fiona was a chunk of gossip too juicy not to share.

Sherry was standing with her back to the window when Fiona entered. Their gazes met and Fiona smiled. "Hello, Sherry."

"Hello, Fiona." There wasn't a drop of warmth in the woman's greeting.

Fiona hesitated for a split second, then she entered the room and closed the door behind her. She'd forgotten what a pretty woman Sherry was, and how impeccably groomed she always managed to be. Everything about her appearance seemed well thought out. Her dark suit had been carefully designed and tailored to flatter a figure that was no longer as slender and firm as it once had been, and her hair had been tinted a shade of blond that was just dark enough to be believable. She wore it pulled back in a French twist, a style that showed off her long, graceful neck, her high cheekbones, and her beautifully arched eyebrows. She'd always reminded Fiona a little of the late Grace Kelly once she'd started to show her age.

"Well," Fiona said as she crossed the room to the conference table. "This is a surprise. It's been awhile, hasn't it? I was trying to remember the last time we saw each other. I think it must have been at your Christmas party year before last." She placed her briefcase on the floor and then pulled out a chair, but when Sherry made no move toward the table, Fiona didn't bother to sit, either.

To hell with niceties, she decided. This was so uncomfortable, she just wanted to get it over with. "What can I do for you, Sherry?"

Sherry walked over then and stood across the table from Fiona. The way she tossed a manila envelope onto the surface was rather like throwing down a gauntlet. "I'm not going to beat around the bush. I'm just going to tell you straight out why I'm here."

Fiona nodded. "That's fine."

"I want to talk to you about the man who was killed last evening. The private detective."

Fiona couldn't have been more surprised. She stared at Sherry for a moment. "You mean Simon Byrd?"

She nodded. "Yes. I knew him."

And the surprises just kept coming. "You knew him professionally?"

"I hired him a few weeks ago to follow you."

Fiona's mouth gaped. "To follow *me?* But…*why?*"

"Because I thought you were having an affair with my husband," Sherry said bluntly. "Oh, don't bother denying it. I know now it's not true. Mr. Byrd told me that your life consists of work and not much else. You come in early, stay late and then go straight home almost every night. You don't have a social life any more than I do. I guess we have that in common," she said a trifle bitterly.

Fiona put a hand to her head. "I don't understand. If you thought Guy was having an affair, why not have *him* followed?"

"Because at the time I thought he might still have a political future." And with that telling revelation, Sherry paused, pressing her fingers to her mouth for a moment as if she needed to quell her emotions. "I didn't want word to get out that his wife had hired a private investigator to prove he was cheating on her. So I gave Mr. Byrd a false name, paid him in cash and asked him to follow you. I was so convinced you were the one, I thought having you tailed would serve the same purpose."

"You actually had me under surveillance." Fiona couldn't believe it. What a terrible invasion of her privacy.

She wasn't certain whether to be outraged or relieved because ever since David Mackenzie had been killed, she'd had paranoid delusions that he was following her. They'd faded in time, but during the past few weeks, the sensation had come back stronger than ever. Fiona had chalked it up to the stress of the DeMarco trial—or the fact that she might be more than a little crazy—but now she realized that she hadn't been delusional at all. Someone *had* been following her.

She thought back to that day in the courthouse stairwell. Had that been Simon Byrd?

"I know what you must think of me." Sherry lifted her chin defensively. "And I'm sorry I dragged you into this, but I had to know for sure if Guy was cheating on me. I had to know if there was any chance for us. And I know now that there's not." She battled again to control her emotions, and Fiona waved her hand toward a chair.

"Why don't we sit?"

When they were settled, Fiona said anxiously, "Are you okay? Do you need a glass of water or anything?"

"I'm fine." But she didn't look fine. Up close, Fiona could see the lines around the woman's mouth, the crepe-like skin around her eyes. She'd aged since Fiona had last seen her, but it wasn't the passage of time that detracted from her beauty. It was the hardness in her eyes, the bitter set of her lips. The defeated slump of her shoulders. She'd faced some unpleasant truths lately, Fiona thought, and it had taken a toll.

Fiona suddenly remembered something else Milo had told her. *"Just...be careful around Hardison, okay? There's a lot more to that guy than he lets on."*

"Like what?"

"Take my word for it. Guy Hardison is not the picture of propriety he wants everyone to believe he is."

Fiona shivered as she studied Sherry Hardison's haggard features.

"He's asked me for a trial separation," she said finally. "Do you know what he said to me? 'Don't take it personally, Sherry. It's not you. It's me.' That's what they always say, isn't it? Then they go out and find themselves a younger, thinner, prettier woman. But we're not supposed to take it personally."

She brushed a hand across her eyes. "He said it was because we'd gotten married so young. We'd both missed out on so much. Lately he was starting to feel as if life was passing him by. He had to do something before it was too late." She closed her eyes briefly. "Twenty-five years of marriage, two children together, and he decides it's over. I don't have any say in it. I'm just supposed to sit by and do nothing while he destroys my life." Her gaze lifted to Fiona's. "Can you even imagine what that's like? Of course, you can't," she said angrily. "You're still young and beautiful. Men still want you. You take it all for granted, don't you? You probably hardly even notice the way they stare at you, but you will someday, when they stop looking."

Fiona had no idea what to say to that. She sat quietly and let Sherry talk.

Sherry spread her hands in supplication, as if pleading for nothing more than understanding. "I couldn't sit by and watch my marriage fall apart and do nothing, could I? I had to know exactly what I was dealing with so that's why I hired Mr. Byrd. When I found out you weren't the one, I decided to level with him."

"He started following Guy?"

She drew a long breath. "All those nights when I thought he was working late..." She trailed off. "The cliché is true, you know. The wife is the last to know."

She took another moment to compose herself. "When Guy leaves here in the evening, he goes to a nightclub on Division Street called Neptune's Palace where he picks up women. A different woman every night, but always someone young. Sometimes as young or younger than our daughters." She almost choked on the words, and glanced away, not wanting Fiona to see her humiliation.

"I'm sorry, Sherry. I am. But...I'm not sure why you're telling me all this," Fiona said helplessly. "I'm not even sure it's appropriate. This is between you and Guy."

"I had to tell someone," Sherry said almost desperately. "Don't you see? I couldn't keep it to myself. Not after Mr. Byrd was murdered."

Fiona's heart gave a funny little bounce against her chest. "What do you mean?"

She pushed the envelope across the table toward Fiona. "These are Mr. Byrd's last surveillance photographs. They were delivered to my house this morning. Go ahead. Open them," she urged when Fiona hesitated.

The shots were all of Guy Hardison coming out of a nightclub. In some of them, he was with women who were obviously not his wife or his daughters. And as she flipped through pictures, it occurred to Fiona that the tables had turned. Now it was she who held Guy Hardison's future in her hands.

Suddenly she froze on a picture, her blood going cold with shock.

Sherry said anxiously, "It's her, isn't it? The Mercer girl? I recognized her from her picture in the paper."

The photograph had been taken with a telephoto lens, and Guy Hardison was obviously the intended subject. But Alicia Mercer had been caught in the background of the shot, coming out of a nightclub, dressed in the clothing she'd been found in later that night.

Sherry looked on the verge of collapse. Her face was the color of chalk. "You see what this means? You see why I couldn't keep this to myself?" She got up and began to pace in agitation. "That girl and Guy were at the same club the night she died. But he never said a word about it to the police."

"It doesn't look as if they were together," Fiona said, her hands trembling in shock. "Maybe he didn't see Alicia that night or recognize her later when she turned up dead." That was plausible, wasn't it?

"Maybe." Sherry paused, her gaze meeting Fiona's. "But what about Simon Byrd?" she asked in a hushed voice. "What if whoever killed him was looking for these pictures?"

Fiona got up, too. "You need to be very careful, Sherry, because someone might construe from what you're saying that you believe your husband had something to do with these murders."

Something dark glittered in Sherry's eyes. Something that made Fiona very nervous because she was having a hard time reading the woman's emotions.

"I don't know what I believe," Sherry said softly. "But I do know that the man in that picture is not the man I married."

"FIONA GALLAGHER."

The moment Doggett heard Fiona's voice, he wanted to kiss her. He wanted a total and accurate reenactment of the night before, except without the interruption. She could even rip off his clothes again—all of them this time—if the urge struck her. Of course, if he hadn't had his dry cleaning in the back of his car last night, he might have had a hell of a time explaining at the crime scene how he'd managed to lose every single button on his shirt. But it would have been worth it.

"It's Doggett," he said.

"Hi." She sounded so breathless that he almost didn't recognize her voice.

Was she thinking about last night, too?

He cleared his throat. "Got a minute? I need to talk to you about something."

She lowered her voice. "I need to talk to you, too, but you go first."

"I ran a background check on Simon Byrd. Turns out he has a record. He was convicted of robbery six years ago. You're not going to believe who his attorney was."

"Not Paul Guest?"

"Close. Lori Guest."

He heard the sharp intake of her breath. "Are you sure about that?"

"Oh, yeah, no mistake."

Fiona was silent for a moment. "Do you think that's how Alicia found out about him? Through Lori?"

"I don't know," he said, "but I think I need to have another chat with both the Guests. In the meantime, what was it you wanted to tell me?"

Her voice lowered again. "Hold on. Let me close the door."

She put him on hold, but was back in a matter of seconds. "I had a surprise visitor this afternoon. Guy Hardison's wife, Sherry."

"And?"

"It seems she had reason to believe that Guy was being unfaithful to her so she hired Simon Byrd to follow him."

"Byrd was a busy guy," Doggett said dryly. "It's a bit of a coincidence that Hardison's wife and Alicia Mercer hooked up with the same P.I. Unless I'm missing a connection somewhere.''

"Oh, there's a connection,'' Fiona told him. ''I'm just not sure what it means. Byrd took pictures of Guy coming out of a nightclub on Division Street called Neptune's Palace on the night Alicia Mercer was killed. She was caught in one of the shots.''

Doggett had already suspected that Alicia had been at the club, but Guy Hardison was a surprise. Then again, maybe he wasn't. Twenty years ago, he'd been the prosecutor assigned to Ruby's case. Doggett had always suspected a connection between Hardison, Tate and Frank Quinlan. Maybe now, two decades later, it was all finally starting to fall into place.

"Ray?''

"Yeah?''

"You don't seem that surprised by all this.''

Her tone sounded suspicious, and Doggett wondered if she still had doubts about him. Well, maybe she should. He hadn't exactly leveled with her, but that wasn't altogether his fault. "I'm just thinking here, trying to put it all together. Were Hardison and Alicia together in the shot?''

"I don't think so, and it's possible their paths never crossed that night, but—''

"Alicia was the kind of girl who'd get noticed in a club.''

"Exactly.''

"And Hardison's the kind of guy that would want to cover his ass, especially if he has political aspirations.''

"That's the part that doesn't make sense,'' Fiona said. "He's extremely ambitious. I know he wants to run for state's attorney. But he had to know he was taking a huge risk by going to a club like that, much less being seen with women who weren't his wife.''

''Maybe that was part of the excitement.'' Doggett paused. ''He's not there with you, is he?''

''No, he's in a meeting. I haven't had a chance to talk to him about any of this.''

''Then don't.'' Doggett was beginning to get a very bad feeling about Hardison. ''Listen to me, Fiona. Don't get yourself caught alone with that guy. Not until I have a chance to check this out. And don't work late tonight. Make sure you leave while there are still plenty of people around. In fact, get one of the security guards to walk you to your door.''

''I hardly think that's necessary—''

''I do. After last night, I don't want you taking any chances.''

There was a long pause, then Fiona said very quietly, ''You sound as if you're worried about me. I think I like that.''

''You like that I'm worried?''

''I like it that you care.''

Doggett didn't quite know what to say to that. It was true, of course. He did care. Probably more than he should, but he had a hard time putting his feelings into words. It was too soon.

When the silence drew out too long, Fiona said, ''I haven't frightened you off, have I?''

''No,'' Doggett said in a low voice. ''In fact, I was just wondering about the possibility of a repeat of last night…''

GINA TRAILED BEHIND FIONA as they both hurried down the hall to Guy's office. His secretary, Helen Davenport, rose when she saw them and came around the desk to meet them.

"I don't know what to do." She bit her lip worriedly. "Mrs. Hardison stopped by my desk a little while ago, wanting to know when Guy would be back. I told her I didn't expect him until later this afternoon, so she said she wanted to leave him a note. She went into the office and closed the door, and when she didn't come back out after several minutes, I knocked and asked if she was all right. She said she wasn't feeling well and needed to lie down. I took her in some water, but she was just standing at the window staring out. I offered to arrange a cab for her, but she said it was just a dizzy spell and would pass." Helen paused to take a breath. "I thought it was a little strange, but there was nothing I could do, so I came back out to my desk and went to work. A little while later, I checked on her again. The door was locked. I knocked, but she didn't answer."

"Are you sure she's still in there?" Fiona asked. "Could she have left when you were away from your desk?"

Helen shook her head. "I haven't been away from my desk more than a couple of minutes at a time. And if she did leave, why would she have locked the door behind her?"

"Force of habit?" Fiona walked over to the office door and knocked softly. "Sherry? Are you okay?" When there was no answer, she knocked a little louder. "Sherry, it's Fiona. We're getting a little worried about you."

Nothing but silence.

Okay, this was not good. Especially considering Sherry's earlier state of mind. A shiver traced up Fiona's spine as she gave Helen an uneasy glance over her shoulder. "Do you have a key for his office?"

"Sure." Helen got it from her key ring and handed it to Fiona.

Fiona turned the lock and opened the door.

And staggered back.

The first thing she saw was the blood. It seemed to be everywhere. All over the floor. All over Guy's desk. All over Sherry Hardison's beautiful clothes.

And the confetti. Where the hell had all the confetti come from?

Then Fiona realized the bits of paper scattered about the office was all that was left of the photographs Sherry had shown her earlier. She'd painstakingly chopped them into tiny pieces, and that done, she'd taken the knife to her wrists.

CHAPTER TWENTY-ONE

IT WAS AFTER EIGHT THAT night when Milo drove Fiona home. They'd been at the hospital for hours, waiting to find out if Sherry Hardison would pull through before they could bring themselves to leave. Finally they'd been told that she was still in critical condition, but the doctors were hopeful she'd make a full recovery, in spite of all the blood she'd lost.

Fiona leaned her head back against the seat and closed her eyes. She was mentally and physically exhausted.

"Some day, huh?"

She opened her eyes to find Milo staring at her intently. "I still can't believe it happened." But she knew the image of Sherry Hardison slumped over her husband's desk, covered in blood, would be with her for a long time. She would be dreaming about it for nights to come. She turned her head to Milo. "Can I ask you something?"

He shrugged. "Sure."

"You saw Guy at that club, didn't you? That's why you warned me about him." On the way to the hospital earlier, Fiona had told Milo a little of what Sherry had said to her.

Milo nodded. "The club I told you about—Blondie's—is only a few doors down from Neptune's Palace. Some friends and I were walking by one night, and I spotted Guy coming out of one of the side doors with a blond young enough to be his daughter. They were...well, let's just say, he wasn't exactly behaving in a fatherly manner toward her. After that, I saw him a few more times, always with a different woman.''

"Did you ever go inside that club?" Fiona asked.

"Once or twice." Milo grimaced. "It's a little too much for me. The decor is supposed to resemble an underwater city with all these marble columns and statues and waitresses decked out in togas. They have these big fish tanks recessed into the walls, like portholes, and black lights make everything glow in the dark. It's kind of like a cheesy James Bond set, and the music is terrible." He leaned toward Fiona slightly. "I can tell you one thing. Guy Hardison isn't the only married man who goes to that club. That place is a meat market for rich, middle-aged men. The girls are young, though. Like I said, young enough to be Guy Hardison's daughters. I think they must pay them."

"You know what I still can't figure out?" Fiona stared out the window. "Why would a man in Guy's position, a man with his ambition, take such chances? He had to know sooner or later he'd get caught. Was it just for the excitement? The thrill of trying to get away with something?"

"That, and maybe a part of him *wanted* to get caught. Maybe he thought that was the only way he'd be able to stop."

"So his picking up younger women was a cry for help?" Fiona asked dryly.

"You never know what drives someone to do the things they do," Milo said softly. Something in his voice caused Fiona to turn and stare at him. He shrugged. "Maybe Sherry's unloading all that stuff on you was also a cry for help."

A cry Fiona hadn't heard.

She'd already thought of that, of course. She'd sat across the conference table from Sherry, witnessed the woman's agony and despair, and still Fiona hadn't suspected that she might be contemplating suicide. She should have known. She should have been able to stop her, but she hadn't.

Just like she hadn't been able to stop David from killing those women.

It's not your fault.

No, of course, it wasn't. Rationally Fiona knew that. But it was the worst kind of irony that she'd looked into another person's eyes and hadn't seen the potential for violence.

She let herself into her apartment a few minutes later and headed straight for the bathroom. For the second night in a row, she climbed in the shower to wash someone else's blood from her skin.

It was strange. She'd been viciously attacked the night before, almost killed, but she was more shaken tonight by what had happened to Sherry.

Fiona supposed it was a control thing. Last night, even under attack, she'd still been capable of taking action, able to fight back. But watching the blood gush from the slashes in Sherry's wrists, Fiona had felt completely helpless. She'd tried to staunch the flow as best she could until the paramedics arrived, but she wasn't sure she'd done much to save her.

Still shivering, she stepped out of the shower and dried off, then wrapped herself in a thick, terry-cloth robe. Curling up on her bed, she closed her eyes, but she knew she wouldn't be able to sleep. Her emotions were still too raw.

Restless and wired, she got up and walked into the living room. When the phone rang, she started to let the machine answer, afraid that it might be a reporter who'd already gotten wind of the story. But then something made her reach out and pick it up.

"Hello?"

"Hey."

A shiver tingled through Fiona at the sound of Doggett's voice. "Hey."

"I heard what happened. I tried to call earlier, but you weren't home."

"I've been at the hospital all evening. Guy was there with their daughters." Her eyes closed briefly. "It was horrible, Ray."

"I know."

A long silence, then Fiona said, very softly, "I could really use a drink."

"It won't help."

"I know." Besides, she'd poured out every drop of alcohol in her apartment. But the liquor store down the street delivered if she really wanted one that bad. Did she?

"Don't do it, Fiona."

She clung to the phone. "I won't."

"Are you sure?"

She drew a trembling breath. "Yes. It's just been an incredibly hard day."

Another silence. "Would it help if I came over?"

Another trembling breath. "How soon can you be here?"

"In less than a minute. I'm parked outside your building."

Fiona carried the cordless phone over to the window and stared down at the street. Doggett leaned against his car, cell phone to his ear. His gaze lifted to her window, and even from a distance, she could feel the potency of his stare. She shivered, as if he had physically touched her, and her heart started to pound in anticipation.

For the longest moment, he made no move toward her building, just stood there with his cell phone to his ear, staring up at her.

They were still connected. Fiona thought she could even hear his breath. She wondered if he was thinking what she was thinking, that this was it. Tonight was the night. If she said the word, he would be at her door in seconds. And there would be no turning back.

She gazed down at him, knowing what he wanted. Because it was what she wanted, too. The heat was already starting to build inside her. She felt breathless, a little out of control as she tightened her grip on the phone. ''So are you coming up or what?''

''I guess I'm coming up.'' He started across the street.

''Ray?''

''Yeah?''

''Hurry, okay?''

He hung up the phone and started to run.

SHE ANSWERED THE DOOR WEARING nothing but a robe. Doggett didn't know how he knew there was nothing on underneath, but somehow he did. And somehow he knew why she'd wanted him to hurry, why she was looking at him now as if she would come apart if he touched her. Or if he didn't.

But he still wavered at the door, wanting to make sure he hadn't misread her signals. Or to give her time to change her mind.

She was in his arms in a flash, dragging his mouth down to hers, kissing him so hard and so deep there was no mistaking her intent.

She caught him completely by surprise, stunned him so totally that he didn't even respond for a brief moment.

Then he grabbed her, kissing her back as he walked her

into the apartment. He kicked the door closed, then spun her around and pressed her up against the wall, his fingers tangling in her hair, holding her face still as his tongue plunged inside her mouth.

He finally broke away, breathing hard. "Are you sure about this?"

She didn't say a word, simply undid the tie at her waist and slid off her robe.

Doggett stepped back and looked at her. He couldn't stop looking at her. She was so hot and gorgeous and... *hot.*

She stared back at him, almost defiantly, her blue eyes blazing with passion. Her hair was loose tonight, and it was everything Doggett had known it would be. The fiery curls spilled over her shoulders and he couldn't resist touching it. He wrapped it around his fist. God, he loved her hair. He loved her body, loved the way she wrapped a leg around him and pressed herself against him. The way she aroused him with so little effort.

"Does that answer your question?"

"Oh, yeah."

She smiled then, knowing full well what she was doing to him, and wound a hand around his neck, drawing him back to her. She worked his tie loose and slid it from around his neck, then shoved his jacket from his shoulders and down his arms. The next thing he knew, she'd jerked his shirt from his pants and slipped her hands inside.

Her hands against his bare skin made him feel as if he were a time bomb ready to explode. He groaned and kissed her again, hard and deep and fast, and then he worked his mouth along her neck, her breasts, sliding his tongue down her stomach, wanting to taste her. Needing to taste her.

She gasped and arched her back. Plowed her fingers into his hair.

He ran his hands up her sleek, sexy legs, cupped her buttocks, pressing her against his mouth. She started to tremble. Her breath came faster as her head fell back against the wall. "Oh, God…not yet…"

He stood then and together they moved down the narrow hallway, struggling with his clothes, still kissing. By the time they got to the bedroom, he was as naked as she.

They fell across the bed, and Doggett moved over, running his hands through her hair, kissing her, making her groan with pleasure when his finger and thumb found her breast. She lifted her hips against him, letting him know right off what she wanted.

"I have to get something," he murmured. But she wouldn't let him go. She lifted herself to one elbow and reached beneath one of the pillows. Ripping open the package, she slid the condom on him and then guided him exactly where she wanted him to be.

He pressed against her. Tried not to be too aggressive. She pulled him to her. "Ray?"

"Yeah?"

"Don't be gentle, okay?"

That was almost his undoing. Her sexy voice telling him not to be gentle. And the way she looked, all heavy-lidded and sultry, lips swollen from their kissing.

He plunged inside her, went so deep he thought he might have hurt her when she stiffened, when she made a sound deep in her throat. She went completely still for one split second, then she seemed to explode around him, her body racked by shudders.

She fell back against the bed, covering her face with her hands. "I'm sorry. That wasn't supposed to happen."

"You don't hear me complaining, do you?" But it was

all Doggett could do not to follow her lead. He held himself perfectly still, not daring to move, not daring to think about where he was and who he was with. If he thought about Fiona, if he moved even one little millimeter, it would all be over.

"It's just been a long time for me," Fiona whispered from behind her hands.

"How long?"

"Since before…you know…"

"David Mackenzie?"

She nodded.

He drew her hands away from her face. "Seven years? Fiona, that's not healthy."

"And that sounds so typically male. People survive all the time without sex."

"Yeah, I know," he said dryly. "But I don't recommend it."

HER LACK OF SELF-CONTROL embarrassed Fiona at first, but then she realized that Doggett really didn't seem to mind. And he was doing everything he could to relax her, to give her time to recover. He was still lying over, in her, but he wasn't moving. He was just kissing her, long, slow, deep kisses that made her feel languid and sated at first. Then, his fingers around her wrists, he lifted her arms above her head, imprisoning her beneath him, and Fiona's heart started to pound all over gain.

He wasn't holding her that tightly. She could have gotten away if she wanted to. But she didn't want to because he was starting to move inside her, and Fiona could feel the pressure building to an excruciating pitch. She wanted her hands free to touch him, to pull him even closer, but the feeling of entrapment heightened the sense of urgency that made her strain against him, that made her call out his name as she moved closer to the brink.

She gasped. "I can't believe how good this is. I don't want you to ever stop…"

HE DIDN'T WANT TO STOP. He tried to make it last. He really did. But he was only human. And considering that he'd felt damn near the edge every time he looked at her, he thought he'd done pretty well.

But enough was enough. She was straining beneath him, moaning softly into his shoulders as she frantically met and matched his thrusts. He'd never felt anything so good in his life.

He let her hands go free, finally, and she wrapped her arms and legs around him, rocking against him as her muscles began to contract.

"Ray, I'm right *there,*" she breathed.

"Then take me with you," he said.

FIONA'S RELEASE TORE through her like a rocket, leaving her gasping for breath. She clung to Doggett and heard him whisper her name as his climax exploded almost violently.

DOGGETT WAS ON HIS BACK, staring at the ceiling, and Fiona lay on her side, curled up against him. She ran her hand over his chest, feeling the still rapid beat of his heart.

"That was—"

She lifted her head. "The best sex ever?"

He gave her that grin. "Had to be." He brushed his fingers through her hair. "You're not anything like I thought you'd be. You know that?"

She rested her chin on his chest. "No? What did you think I'd be like?"

"Reserved. Standoffish. Maybe even a little cold."

She moved away, offended. "Why?"

"Fiona, they call you the Iron Maiden."

She propped herself on her elbow and glared at him. "Undeservedly so, I might add. I'm aggressive in the courtroom, and I like to win. Is there anything wrong with that?"

"No. But I'm glad we're on the same side."

She studied him for a moment. "We are on the same side, aren't we, Ray?"

He turned his head toward her. "What do you mean by that?"

"Sometimes I get the feeling you're still holding out on me. You are telling me everything you know about this case, aren't you?"

Something flashed in his eyes. She hoped it was anger, but it looked a little like guilt to her. "I've worked closer with you on this case than I've ever worked with any prosecutor. I've kept you informed every step of the way."

"I know. You've been great."

"Then why the doubts?"

She hesitated. "I have to wonder if you would have told me anything about your interview with Nick Grable if he hadn't come to see me."

He stiffened. "I explained that."

"Yes, I know. You wanted to check it out first. I understand that. But, Ray, I get the feeling you still haven't completely leveled with me about that."

"I have."

"There's nothing about this investigation you've kept from me?"

He lay back against the pillow and stared at the ceiling. "No."

"Today when I told you about Alicia being at that nightclub, you asked if she and Guy were together. But you didn't seem surprised to find out that she'd been there on the night she died. It was like you already knew."

He ran a hand through his hair. "Are you sure you want to talk about this now?"

"I think I have to talk about this now," she said softly. "I think I have to make sure I haven't had some terrible lapse in judgment."

His features hardened. "By having sex with me, you mean."

She paused. "No. By making love with you."

He shifted himself upon his elbow and gazed at her. "Is that what we did?" He touched her hair, and then leaned over to kiss her. When he pulled away, his expression was serious. "Okay, you're right. There is something I haven't told you about the investigation."

It was she who lay back against the pillows now, staring at the ceiling. "Is this something…that's going to change things between us?"

"I hope not. But you're right, it is something you need to hear." He absently wound a strand of her hair around his finger. "I wasn't surprised about Alicia Mercer having gone to that club because I'd already figured it out. Sarah Bertram was at that same club on the night she died, too. The symbol on their left shoulders, the trident, tipped me off. I remembered seeing it before. It's a stamp used by a club on Division. Neptune's Palace."

She almost gasped. "Why didn't you say anything today when I told you about Guy being at that club?"

"I guess I was still trying to put it all together. Look, Fiona, there's a lot at stake here, okay? If Alicia's murder is somehow tied to her sister's disappearance and to the disappearance of other runaways, we have to be careful. We can't tip our hand too soon."

"Meaning?"

"We don't just want the guys who are taking those girls off the street. We want the big guns."

"We?"

"Me, you, everyone else involved in the investigation."

"Who else knows about this?"

His gaze flickered before he glanced away.

"Does Clare know?"

"I haven't talked to her about specifics," he said evasively. "I've told you a hell of a lot more than I've told her."

And that was supposed to make her feel better? Oddly, enough, it did. "So how did you know about that symbol? Have you been to that club?" He didn't seem the type to go to nightclubs, especially a place called Neptune's Palace.

"The owner of the club is a man named Marcus Tate. He used to be a small-time drug dealer who ran a dive on the bad end of Madison. I've kept track of him over the years because he was the chief suspect in Ruby's murder."

Fiona turned in shock. "He's the one you said Quinlan let get away? Why?"

Doggett's mouth turned grim. "I never knew for sure. I figured Quinlan was either on the take or else Tate had something on him. Over the years, I've started to wonder if it wasn't a little of both. Maybe they had an ongoing business arrangement. Quinlan wasn't just turning a blind eye. He was neck deep in Tate's business."

"You said Clare was part of the investigation, too. Did she know about this?"

"A lot of people had suspicions, but nothing could ever be proven." He drew a long breath. "My past is part of the reason I haven't been completely up-front with you. I was afraid it might seem that my going after Tate is some sort of vendetta. Ruby didn't just work for him, Fiona. She was...involved with him."

"She had an affair with him?" Fiona turned on her side to face him, studying his features, looking for signs of an old hurt.

"She denied it, but Tate has always implied it. And he did have some kind of hold over her. I tried to tell myself it was just the drugs, but honestly, I don't know."

And there it was, Fiona thought. The flicker of pain she'd been searching for. The remnants of a betrayal that, after all these years, still haunted him.

Fiona wondered if a part of Doggett was still in love with Ruby. If a part of him always would be.

"HE'S DEAD, FIONA. My God, you killed him."

She came awake on a gasp, her eyes flying open to frantically search the darkness. Someone was leaning over her, and she thought it was David. She put up her hands to fight him off, but he caught her around the wrists and Doggett's voice—not David's—said very tenderly, "Hey, it's okay. You were having a nightmare."

She was trembling and he put his arms around her, drawing her close. "Want to tell me about it?"

She shook her head, burying her face in his chest.

He smoothed his hand down her hair. "It might help." When she didn't answer, he said, "Must have been some dream. You were muttering something about killing him. You weren't talking about me, I hope," he halfway joked.

Fiona squeezed her eyes closed. Oh, God, what else

had she said? Enough that he'd figured everything out? She started shaking even harder.

"You were dreaming about David Mackenzie, weren't you?"

He *did* know.

"I've read the police report," he said softly.

She jerked herself away from him then. "*Why?* Why would you do that?"

He was surprised by her response. "Is there some reason why I shouldn't have?"

"You might talk to me first," she said angrily, "Before you go poking around in my private life."

"Fiona, the case closed. The police report is a matter of public record. Why are you so upset by this?"

"Because what happened back then has nothing to do with the present."

"I disagree." He gave her a long scrutiny. "You're still having nightmares about it. It still makes you want to drink at four o'clock in the morning. I'd say it has everything to do with now."

She drew the covers up around her. "I don't want to talk about this. I can't talk about it."

"Then let me do the talking."

It was dark in the bedroom, but light from the street spilled in through the window, allowing Fiona to see his eyes. He was staring at her so intently she could hardly bear it. She tried to turn away, but he took her arm, hauling her back to him. She wanted to resist, but she couldn't. Already, he had that much power over her.

"Mackenzie was holding you and Eve Barrett hostage in your father's fishing cabin when Tony found you. Mackenzie fled on foot through a densely wooded area, and Tony hung around to untie you while Eve pursued a suspect considered armed and extremely dangerous. At some point, you and Tony got in a vehicle and tried to head him off. Mackenzie came running out of the woods and was struck head-on by the car Tony was driving. Mackenzie died at the scene.'' He paused. ''Do I have it about right?''

''You read the police report,'' she said bitterly. ''You should know.''

''Yeah, but there's something about the report that's been bothering me,'' Doggett said. ''Yeah, because see, I know Tony Gallagher, and there is no friggin' way in hell he would have allowed Eve Barrett to go running after an armed suspect alone.''

''She's a cop.''

Doggett shook his head. ''I don't care. She's his wife now. He was already involved with her back then. I just don't buy that he would have let her go chasing after that guy alone, cop or no cop.''

''That's a rather male chauvinist attitude,'' Fiona sniffed.

''No, it's a real one.'' His gaze was still on her. ''You know what I think?''

''No.'' Fiona got up, drawing the covers around her as she walked over to the window.

After a moment, Doggett followed her. He didn't touch her, but he stood very close. She could feel his breath hot on her neck, and she shivered.

''You were driving that car, Fiona. You were the one who struck and killed David Mackenzie.''

She closed her eyes.

''You can deny it,'' he said. ''You can tell me I'm full of shit. Tell me you didn't do it, Fiona.''

She shook her head. ''I...can't.''

''So I'm right?'' His voice seemed to harden. ''What happened?''

"It was an accident."

"I'm not doubting that. But why the cover-up? Why not just report it the way it really happened?"

"Because Tony didn't want me to. He was afraid—" She broke off, wiping a hand across her eyes.

"Afraid of what?"

"You've got to understand how it was," she said softly. "When I found out what David had done to those women, how he'd used me to get to Tony, I was...devastated. I can't even begin to describe how I felt. Used. Degraded. Horrified. The whole time he had me in that cabin, there was no doubt in my mind he would kill me, too. I was terrified at first, but when he brought Eve in and threatened to kill her just to get to Tony, something snapped inside me. I've never felt such rage before or since. It consumed me."

She took a breath. "When he fled from the cabin, Eve and Tony both went after him. I don't think I had any conscious effort of trying to track him down myself, but suddenly, I was driving in the car and he was just there, in my headlights. And then he wasn't." She shuddered, remembering the impact. "I told myself over and over there was no way I could have stopped in time. But the truth is, I don't know. And Tony could see the doubt in my face. He was afraid of what would happen if I had to face a jury, so he took the blame."

She turned to face Doggett. "So now you know. And now you hold Tony's career and mine in your hands. Question is, what's a good cop like you going to do about it?"

He stared down at her for the longest moment, then he took her face in his hands and kissed her.

SOMETIME AFTER MIDNIGHT, the sound of the phone awakened Fiona. She rolled over to answer it, but Doggett was already getting up, reaching for his clothes. "It's my cell," he said softly. "I'll take it in the other room. Go back to sleep."

He slipped on his pants and disappeared down the hall. Fiona wasn't quite sure why, but something compelled her to get up and follow him. She paused at the end of the hallway, in shadows, to watch him.

He stood at the window, his back to her, speaking so softly she could barely hear him. She moved a little closer to the doorway.

"I know," he said anxiously, "but we don't have much time."

As he listened, he glanced over his shoulder. Fiona flattened herself against the wall.

He was silent for another moment, then she heard him say, "Tomorrow night. Right. And don't worry. She won't get in the way. I'll see to that."

Stomach churning, Fiona turned and tiptoed back down the hallway. She crawled into bed and pulled the covers up over her shoulders. She didn't turn when she heard Doggett come back into the bedroom, didn't move when she felt him slip into bed. She didn't even respond when he slid a hand under the cover to cup her breast. She kept her eyes closed, pretending to sleep, until minutes later, when she heard the front door close behind him.

CHAPTER TWENTY-TWO

"IF I'M GOING TO PLAY ETHEL to your Lucy," Milo complained the next night. "You could at least fill me in on what we're getting ourselves into."

"If I knew, I'd tell you," Fiona said as they walked through the entrance to Neptune's Palace. In truth, she had no idea why she'd even asked Milo to bring her here tonight except that she was curious about the place, and she had a little niggling suspicion since that phone call last night that Doggett might be here. And if he was, she wanted to find out for herself what he was up to. What he'd meant by, "She won't get in the way."

Don't jump to conclusions, she warned herself. She had no reason to distrust Doggett.

But maybe the real problem was, she had no reason to trust him. How well did she even really know him? She'd let herself get completely swept up in the moment. She'd let down her guard, told him things she'd never told anyone else, things that had the power to ruin—not just her life—but Tony's and Eve's. She'd had no right to do that.

And by Doggett's own admission, he hadn't completely leveled with her about the case. She suspected he was still keeping things from her, and she'd been worrying all day that maybe she'd been a little too quick to spill her guts.

Milo gazed around the crowded club and grimaced. "Holy shit. Do you get the feeling we're trapped in some psychedelic *Poseidon Adventure* here? Honest to God, if

Shelley Winters comes swimming by, it's every man for himself. I'm getting the hell out of here.''

"Oh, come on," Fiona said. "It's not that bad."

But it was, in fact, pretty terrible with all the glow-in-the-dark fish tanks, toga-clad waitresses, and a special effects lighting that made the whole room seem as if it were swaying underwater. Fiona felt a bit seasick as she watched the dancers gyrating on the floor.

Milo had told her the night before that it was a place for wealthy, older men to pick up young women, but Fiona saw a mix of ages tonight, although there did seem to be an uneven ratio of women to men. And the girls, for the most part, were very young and very beautiful.

"I need a drink," Milo muttered beside her. "You want something?"

"Just a Coke."

He hurried off to the bar, and when he returned, he said, "I saw a couple of empty tables on the other side of the room. Plus, there's some interesting action with a mermaid in a fish tank. Actually I think I'm starting to enjoy myself. This place is so tacky it's almost chic."

He led Fiona through the crowd to a table on the other side of the bar, away from the dance floor. The area was dimly illuminated with lights shaped like sea urchins on every table and wall sconces that were giant seashells. Curtained booths lined the walls where couples could have a drink, or whatever, in private.

Against the far wall, a wide set of stairs led up to a second level where a balcony overlooked the dance floor. There was probably a private club up there as well, Fiona decided, because the stairs were guarded by a bouncer.

Milo leaned in close to make himself heard over the music. "Hey. Isn't that Detective Doggett over there?"

Fiona started. A man stood at the bottom of the stairs,

talking to the bouncer. He had his back to Milo and Fiona, but when he turned slightly, she could see his profile. Even in the badly lighted room, she knew it was Doggett. She'd know him anywhere.

He talked to the bouncer for a few more seconds, then the guy nodded and stepped aside. Doggett walked up the stairs and disappeared through a door at the top, as if he knew exactly where he was going.

As if he'd been there a hundred times before.

MARCUS TATE GLANCED UP with a scowl as Doggett was escorted, not gently, through the door of his office. "What the hell—"

"You invited me to drop by sometime, and tonight seemed as good a time as any," Doggett said with a shrug.

Tate gave the bodyguard a brief nod, and the man disappeared through the door.

"So," Tate said. "How'd you get by Billy?"

"I told him we were old friends, and he didn't blink an eye. You know, your security isn't what it should be for a man in your line of work."

Tate lifted a brow. "And you know all about my line of work, do you?"

"I know a lot more about it than you think I do."

"For what that'll get you." Tate smirked. "A promotion? A clap on the back for a job well done? Ten dollars added to your monthly pension when you retire in another ten years? You know," he said, coming around to stand in front of the desk. "I never could figure out what makes a man like you tick."

"What makes me tick is putting guys like you behind bars," Doggett said. "The rush I get from busting your ass will keep me happy for years."

Tate shook his head. "You still don't get it, do you?

It's like I told you the other day. You couldn't touch me back then, and you can't touch me now. But I guess you'll have to learn that the hard way, won't you?'' He punched a button on his desk, and a panel opened up on the wall to reveal several television monitors that displayed various views of the main club below. ''Let me show you something before you leave so you'll know just exactly who you're dealing with.''

They walked over to the monitors, and Tate opened up a control panel from which the surveillance cameras planted throughout the main nightclub could be remotely manipulated. ''I can scan the whole room or I can zero in on one particular individual.'' He demonstrated by bringing a man's features into sharp focus. ''Recognize him? If I'm not mistaken, he's a deputy superintendent with Chicago PD. And this guy?'' He focused in on another face. ''One of the mayor's closest advisors. See what I'm talking about, Doggett? I've got friends in high places, while you—'' He ran a critical eye over Doggett's inexpensive suit. ''You'll always be just a flatfoot, a man without much imagination or ambition, plodding along day in and day out, making your little arrests, celebrating your little victories. But in the end, you'll end up alone. A cop who couldn't be bought, and that'll be your downfall.''

Doggett wasn't paying much attention to what Tate was saying. He was too busy studying the monitors and the controls. ''So this is how you do it,'' he muttered.

''Do what?''

Tate's clients would come up here and watch the girls on the monitors. If they saw something they liked, they'd put in a bid.

Doggett reached over and touched one of the controls. The camera zoomed in on a girl that looked as if she couldn't be much past junior high school age. There was a glazed look in her eyes. She wore a strapless dress, and Doggett could see a trident on her left shoulder. And the significance of the mark suddenly hit him.

"You stamp their shoulders so your clients will know they're available," he said. "That's how it works, isn't it?"

"I was wrong about you, Doggett. You do have quite an imagination." Tate reached over and maneuvered another camera. "There's someone else here tonight I think might interest you."

Doggett sucked in a breath as Fiona's face came into view. What the hell—

As he watched, a man came over and bent to whisper in her ear. She nodded, and as she got up, the man took her elbow, escorting her away from the camera.

Doggett whirled, grabbing Tate by the lapels. "You lay one finger on her, and I swear I'll—"

"You'll what? Arrest me?" Tate laughed in his face. "There's no way in hell you'll ever make any charges against me stick. Face it, Doggett. You lose. And if you ever want to see that sexy redhead again, you'll get the hell out of my club and stay out. Do I make myself clear?"

He walked over to his desk, touched another button, and the bodyguard came back into the room. "Show Detective Doggett to the door, Jimmy."

The man grabbed Doggett's arm, but Doggett shook him off. As he started through the door, Tate called him back. "One last thing, Doggett." He reached in his drawer and brought out a woman's shoe. The red rhinestones glittered in the light as he tossed the high heel toward Doggett.

Doggett caught it and held it for a moment, a rage like

nothing he'd never known before welling inside him. His gaze lifted. "You son of a bitch."

"A little souvenir from Ruby," Tate said, smiling. "And a reminder that you wouldn't want what happened to her to happen to the redhead downstairs, now would you?"

Doggett lunged toward Tate, but the man behind him slammed a gun butt against the back of his head. Doggett went down without a sound.

"WHERE'S DETECTIVE DOGGETT?" Fiona asked, glancing around the nightclub. She'd followed the man around to the other side of the room where he'd said Doggett would be waiting for her. "Hold on," she said sharply. "I'm not going any farther until I see Detective Doggett."

"Doggett's tied up," a voice said behind her. "But I'm here, Counselor. And I think it's time you and I made up for lost time."

She spun at the sound of that voice, and her gaze met Vince DeMarco's. He stared down at her, grinning like an idiot, his eyes gleaming in the dim light.

His eyes...

Oh, my God, Fiona thought. She'd seen those eyes before. In her nightmares. On the witness stand. And glinting through slits in a ski mask...

She tried to brush by him. When he didn't move, she said, "Get the hell out of my way."

He caught her arm. "Come on," he breathed against her ear. "Let's dance." He hauled her against him, and before Fiona could fight him off, she felt a sharp prick in her upper arm. She glanced down as DeMarco withdrew the needle, and before she could scream, the room started to spin.

DOGGETT AWOKE SOMETIME later to the ringing of his telephone. He tried to lift himself onto his elbows to answer, but the mother of all headaches flattened him again.

He reached out to blindly grope for the telephone, just to shut it up. "Doggett."

"Ray? Where the hell have you been? I've been trying to reach you for hours."

He pushed himself up against the headboard, rubbing his eyes, trying to clear the cobwebs from his brain. His hand moved around to the back of his head where he gingerly probed a bump the size of an egg. What the hell—

"Ray, are you there?"

"What do you want, Clare?"

"What do I want? You were supposed to report back to me hours ago. What happened with Tate?"

Tate? What was she talking about? Doggett squinted his eyes, trying to remember.

"Ray, did you go to that club or not?"

"Yeah, I think I did."

"You think?"

"I think somebody must have clipped me pretty good. My short-term memory is shot to hell."

"Well, you'd better get it back and fast because we've got big problems."

"What are you talking about?"

"I'm talking about Fiona Gallagher. She went to that club tonight and now she's gone missing. Some prissy ASA is screaming his ass off at headquarters that she's been kidnapped—"

Doggett was instantly alert. "I'm going back to the club. They can't have taken her far." He'd tear that place from top to bottom if he had to.

"I'll call for backup," Clare said. "We'll meet you there—"

But he didn't wait to hear the rest.

It wasn't until Doggett reached for his gun—and found it missing—that he wondered how in the hell he'd ended up back in his apartment.

Unlocking a safe in his closet, he pulled out another weapon and checked the clip, then stuck the gun in the waist of his pants. By the time he was going out the door, the cell phone in his jacket pocket was ringing.

THE CLUB WAS ALL BUT deserted by the time Doggett got there. He'd been out for hours. Lost all that time when Fiona had needed him.

But he wouldn't think about that now. He'd find her. One way or another, he'd find her.

He went in the back way. The door to the alley was open, which could mean one of two things. Someone had gotten careless, or he was walking into a trap. And Doggett didn't think Marcus Tate or the men who worked for him were the careless types. But since no other choice presented itself to him at the moment, he proceeded through the darkened club, making his way up the back stairs to Tate's office.

No one accosted him. No one followed him. But Doggett knew his arrival had not gone unnoticed.

Weapon drawn, he pushed open the door to Tate's office with his foot, glanced around the shadowy interior, then stepped inside. Taking out his flashlight, he played the beam over the room.

Tate was slumped over his desk, the back of his head a bloody mess where a bullet had ripped through his skull. Doggett went over and felt for a pulse anyway.

"He's dead," Clare said from the doorway.

Doggett turned and caught her in the glare of his flashlight.

"Put that down, will you?" she said impatiently.

He flicked off the flashlight. "What happened?"

"You tell me."

He shrugged. "He was dead when I got here."

"That's strange," Clare said, "because ballistics will show that he was shot with your gun, Ray."

She walked slowly into the room, making her way to the desk. Doggett turned with her. "What are you talking about?"

"I'm talking about the vendetta you've carried against Tate all these years. He killed your wife, but you never could prove it. Then when you found out he was selling young girls on the black market, something just snapped inside you, Ray. You killed him. And then you ate your own muzzle."

"Yeah?" Doggett tried to keep himself calm, tried not to give away how wired he really was. "How do you figure that's going to happen? It's just you and me, Clare, and I'm the one holding the gun."

He'd turned as she walked around the desk, and now Doggett realized his mistake. Someone else was standing in the doorway. "Drop the gun, Doggett," DeMarco ordered.

When Doggett hesitated, Clare said, "If you want to save Fiona Gallagher's life, you'll do as he says."

"How do I know she's even still alive?" Doggett demanded, his heart racing inside him. This could go down bad, if he wasn't careful.

"I guess you'll just have to trust me on that one, Ray."

"Trust you? That's pretty funny, considering the circumstances." But he placed his gun on the floor and kicked it toward Clare. She bent and picked it up. "It was you all along, wasn't it, Clare? All these years I thought Frank Quinlan was the one in bed with Tate, but it was you."

"A girl's got to make a living," she said with a shrug. "I like nice things, and you don't get nice things on a cop's salary."

His gaze slid to Tate. "So why kill the golden goose?"

"You know why," she said almost angrily. "I'm going to be the first female superintendent in Chicago PD history. That'll mean book deals, movie deals. Hell, I'll probably even be on *Oprah*. But a guy like Tate." She all but spat his name. "He would always be there, Ray. Always turning the screws. What I had to do was get rid of him. And when you came to me asking for that transfer, I knew you'd be the perfect patsy."

"And I played right into your hands, didn't I?"

"You know what your problem is, Ray? You always have to be the hero. It's a classic symptom of an adult child of an alcoholic. You have to be the protector. That's why you worked the ghettos all those years. That's why it was so easy for me to get you over here tonight. You wanted to be Fiona Gallagher's hero." She didn't bother disguising the bitterness in her voice.

"Where is she, Clare?"

"She's alive. For now." She nodded toward DeMarco. "You got the needle?"

When Doggett moved suddenly, Clare leveled the gun on him. "Don't make me do this the hard way, Ray. It'll go easier on Fiona if you don't."

He paused, trying to stay in control. "Just tell me one thing, Clare. Why kill Alicia Mercer?"

"Because she was asking too damned many questions, that's why. Her and that P.I. she hired."

"So you got Psycho Vinnie here to help you out, is that it?"

DeMarco lifted his gun and clipped Doggett on the back of the head. He went down, his skull exploding in pain. DeMarco kicked him in the back, and Doggett groaned.

"That's enough, Vince," Clare said. "We don't want to rough him up too much. It's got to look like a suicide." She started toward Doggett. "Go take care of the others. I can finish up in here."

DeMarco aimed another kick at Doggett's kidneys before he turned and left the room.

When he was finally able to catch his breath, Doggett said, "You're never going to get away with this. Faking a suicide is damn near impossible, and you know it."

She stood over him. "You're forgetting something, aren't you? I'm deputy chief of detectives. I'll handle the investigation myself if I have to." She knelt beside him.

"Before you do it," Doggett said. "I have something to tell you."

"A deathbed confession, Ray? How touching. I can hardly wait to hear it."

"You have the right to remain silent—"

She laughed in his face. "Good one, Ray. You really had me going."

He drew a long breath, fighting the pain. "There's something you don't know about me, Clare."

"Yeah, Ray? What's that?"

"I'm wearing a wire. Everything you just said has been recorded. And this place is surrounded."

She started to laugh, but then all hell broke loose behind her. A SWAT team stormed into the room, and within seconds, half a dozen weapons were aimed directly at her.

She rose, not missing a beat. "I'm Deputy Chief of Detectives Clare Fox," she said urgently. "This man has committed murder and conspiracy to kidnap—"

"This man," a deep voice boomed from the doorway, "is working for me. You're under arrest, Deputy Chief Fox. I suggest you surrender your weapon immediately."

Clare hesitated, still clinging to Doggett's gun as Superintendent Booker walked into the room. Then glancing around, she shrugged and threw the weapon to the floor.

Her gaze met Doggett's one last time. "Good one, Ray."

FIONA CAME TO WITH A START as cold water splashed into her face. For a moment she thought she was drowning, and she struggled for breath. Then she realized she was lying on a stone floor, and a man was standing over her. He threw water in her face again, and Fiona gasped.

DeMarco knelt and slapped her cheeks. "Come on, that's it. Open your eyes. I want you to be awake for this. You're going to enjoy every minute of it, Counselor. Just like Kimbra did."

Still in a daze, Fiona tried to shrink away from him, but then realized one of her arms was shackled to the wall.

Shackled to the wall.

Oh, God. Oh, dear God, where was she?

The room was so dark, she could barely make out DeMarco kneeling beside her. But from across the room, she heard something that sounded like a whimper, and for a moment, she held out a glimmer of hope that whoever was in the room with them would help her.

But that hope faded quickly when DeMarco moved over her. With one vicious jerk, he ripped open her top. She tried to fight him with her one free hand, but the drugs had stolen her strength. She could hardly do more than whimper herself when he reached out and put his hand on her breasts.

"Don't," she whispered. "Please…"

And then suddenly someone grabbed him from behind and dragged him off her. Doggett's voice growled from the darkness, "You're a dead man, you son of a bitch."

There were other voices in the dark now, men who came to pull Doggett away from DeMarco. They led him away while Doggett knelt beside her. He had a key and he freed her from the shackles.

"Are you all right?" he whispered raggedly.

"I think so." She still couldn't quite comprehend everything that had happened. "He tore my blouse, Ray."

"Goddamn him," Doggett said, and then pulled her in his arms as she began to cry.

WHEN FIONA CAME TO AGAIN, there were faces all around her bed, staring down at her. "Are you awake, honey?" her mother asked.

"You're going to be okay," her father assured her.

Her brothers were all there, too, and her grandmother. They were all gazing down at her with anxious expressions. "What are you all doing here?" she asked in confusion.

"Where else would we be?" her mother demanded. "You needed us, darling."

Fiona's throat clogged with tears. "I'm glad to see you," she whispered. "All of you."

"We're happy to see you, too, honey," her dad said gruffly. "And you might like to know that the other girl is going to be fine, too."

"Other girl?"

"You don't remember anything, do you?" her mother said. She patted Fiona's hand. "It's the drugs they gave you. The doctor said you might experience some memory loss. Maybe it's for the best.''

What was her mother talking about? Fiona knew she was in the hospital, but she couldn't for the life of her remember why.

After her family left, Doggett came in a few moments later. He seemed ill at ease, as if he didn't quite know what he was doing there. Finally he cleared his throat and said, "Lexi is going to be okay."

Fiona felt a wave of relief rush over her. "She was in the tunnel with me, wasn't she? She must have been there the whole time. When I came to, I think I knew she was there, but I couldn't do anything to help her." Tears welled in Fiona's eyes, and she turned away.

Doggett said softly, "Hey, it's okay. She'll be fine."

"After what she's been through?" Fiona turned to stare up at him. "She's not going to be fine, Ray. Not for a long time."

"At least she has her mother with her."

"Lori's here at the hospital?"

Doggett nodded. "I spent some time with her after I found out…after I knew you were going to be okay."

"How's she holding up?"

"She's stronger than she looks," he said with a hint of admiration. "She's determined to help Lexi get through this no matter what."

"And Paul?"

"He's gone back to Houston."

Fiona lifted her brows in surprise. "When?"

Doggett shrugged. "I don't know. I guess Lori sent him back. She says she's filing for divorce as soon as things settle down and she knows Lexi's going to be all right."

Fiona put a hand to her mouth. "Oh, my God. Was he…then he really was involved in all this?"

"No, we were wrong about that. He didn't have any-thing to do with Alicia's murder or Lexi's disappearance. I think his and Lori's problems go back for years. She's suspected for a long time he's been leading a double life here in Chicago so she hired Simon Byrd to follow him. Apparently Alicia went with her to meet with Byrd. That's how she knew about him."

Fiona frowned. "What kind of double life are you talk-ing about?"

Doggett shrugged again. "She didn't say and I didn't ask. Some things are best left private between a husband and wife. But I don't think it would be that hard to guess. Not with a man like Guest."

Fiona shook her head sadly. "On the surface, he and Guy Hardison couldn't seem more different, and yet they both ended up hurting the people who loved them the most. Why do men do that, Ray?"

"Hey," he said with a frown. "Don't lump us all into the same category. Besides, Guy Hardison's paying a pretty big price for his mistakes. Whether he helped Quin-lan get Tate off for Ruby's murder or not, his career is over."

"What about Quinlan?"

"I have a feeling he's history, too. He's been dirty for years. Booker's determined to clean up the department, and it looks like a lot of cops may do some time over this, Quinlan and Vince DeMarco included."

"And Clare?" Fiona asked softly.

"She was behind it all, Fiona. She had that girl killed just to cover her tracks, and I didn't see one bit of remorse in her eyes last night. To think—"

He dropped his head, and Fiona took his hand. "Hey. You're not responsible for what she did. You know that, right?"

"Yeah, but for the first time, I think I understand what you've been going through all these years."

A look passed between them, and Fiona squeezed his hand. "You're an honorable man, Ray. You saved my life last night. I don't know how I can ever thank you."

His gaze deepened. "It's over now. You and Lexi are safe, and that's all that matters."

"I know, but—" She broke off, trying to get her emotions under control. "I'm sorry I ever doubted you. I'm sorry I didn't trust you."

"I didn't give you a lot of reason to. I wanted to level with you about working for Booker, but I couldn't. We suspected Quinlan was dirty, but we had no idea how deep the corruption went."

"And I have three brothers on the police force. You couldn't risk me talking to them."

"That's right."

"So how long have you been working for Booker?"

"Since my transfer to Area Three. It was his idea. I thought we were after Quinlan, but I think Booker suspected Clare all along."

Fiona paused, thinking about everything he'd said. "There's something I have to ask you."

"Anything."

"What I told you last night...about David. I know you're a good cop, Ray. I know what I told you has put you in a difficult position. But...it's not just about me. We're talking about my brother, too. That's why I have to ask you. What are you going to do with the information I gave you?"

His gaze held hers for the longest moment, then he smiled, and in so doing, took her breath away. "I don't know what you're talking about. If we had a conversation about you and your brother, I don't remember it."

She closed her eyes. "Are you sure you can live with that?"

He bent down and kissed her. He kissed her gently, but for a very long time. When he finally lifted his head, he said, "Does that answer your question?"

She nodded and pulled him back to her. As their kiss deepened, Fiona felt the ghosts of their pasts finally drift away.

COLLEEN GALLAGHER PEEPED around the door and nodded in satisfaction. From the moment she'd first set eyes on Ray Doggett, she'd known he was the perfect man for her granddaughter. Now it looked as if Fiona was finally getting that message, too, and it was none too soon as far as Colleen was concerned. Men like Ray were hard to come by these days.

She put her coupled hands to her heart and smiled secretively as she watched the couple embrace. God willing, the first of her redheaded grandchildren could be here by this time next year. After all, Fiona wasn't getting any younger so there was no time to waste.

Luckily, Ray Doggett didn't appear to be a man who believed in wasting time...

Corruption, power and commitment...

TAKING THE HEAT

A gritty story in which single mom and prison guard Gabrielle Hadley becomes involved with prison inmate Randall Tucker. When Randall escapes, she follows him— and soon the guard becomes the prisoner's captive... and more.

"Talented, versatile Brenda Novak dishes up a new treat with every page!"

—*USA TODAY*
bestselling author
Merline Lovelace

brenda novak

Available wherever books are sold in February 2003.

HARLEQUIN®
Makes any time special ®

Two women in jeopardy...
Two shattering secrets...
Two dramatic stories...

VEILS OF DECEIT

USA TODAY bestselling author

JASMINE CRESSWELL

B.J. DANIELS

A riveting volume of scandalous secrets, political intrigue and
unforgettable passion that you will not want to miss!

*Look for VEILS OF DECEIT in April 2003
at your favorite retail outlet.*

HARLEQUIN®
INTRIGUE®

Cupid has his bow loaded with double-barreled romantic suspense that will make your heart pound. So look for these **special Valentine selections** from Harlequin Intrigue to make your holiday breathless!

McQUEEN'S HEAT
BY HARPER ALLEN

SENTENCED TO WED
BY ADRIANNE LEE

CONFESSIONS OF THE HEART
BY AMANDA STEVENS

Available throughout January and February 2003 wherever Harlequin books are sold.

HARLEQUIN®
Makes any time special ®

HIVAL